God's Betrayal: The Credo

God's Betrayal: The Credo

Ben Leiter

DISCLAIMER

This book is a work of fiction. All plots, themes, dates, events, locations, organizations, persons, and characters contained in this material are completely fictional. Any resemblance to any locations, organizations, persons or characters, real or fictional, living or deceased, is entirely coincidental and unintentional. All characters and character descriptions are products of the author's imagination or are used fictitiously.

AUTHOR:
Copyright 2017 Daniel G. Hobbs
writing as Ben Letter
All rights reserved.

ISBN: 1537396714
ISBN 13: 9781537396712

Dedication

I dedicate this book to my late, beloved son, Daniel Richard Hobbs, who was making his own spiritual journey.

A religious person follows the teachings of his church; the spiritual person follows the guidance of his soul.

Table of Contents

Rome: 1981
It Begins

The Year 3793, Hebrew Calendar

Rome: 1982

Author Note

Algerian writer, Tahar Djaout, murdered by the Armed Islamic Group during Algeria's civil war of the 1990s: "If you speak, you die. If you do not speak, you die. So, speak and die."

Today
Washington, D.C., Northeast

CHAPTER 1

Just A Word

COLOR ME DAMNED? I'M NOT sure, yet. Here's my story.

My name is Father Gabriel Alphonso Esquivel Garza. I am a Roman Catholic priest, faith-challenged in the extreme. Seems like I spent most of my life questioning why I stayed with this sinful institution. I need to find out if I am damned—or a prophetic voice for my church.

Ordained in the Holy Ghost Order, they immediately loaned me to the Archdiocese of Washington, D.C. in 1972 because of their exploding Hispanic congregation.

Bilingual, I was raised in a time when speaking Spanish was frowned upon, but not in *my* household, not with *my* parents.

We're all connected, you know. That's how it is. No magic. You may have even suspected it. That's the practicality of it, the physics of it, and the spirituality. Everything goes back to the initial singularity of this reality. Every proton owns a relationship with every other proton in the universe.

The spirituality of the one-ness is the spirit *BECOMING* within our four- dimensional world. As biological, five-sensed vertebrates with an analog-digital brain, we are currently the finest observers of the universe with the best antennae of consciousness—for now—on this blue organic rock hurtling through violent space-time.

However, I have to point out that my peeps, homo sapiens, holds the record among all organisms for driving the most plant and animal species to their extinctions. We hold the dubious distinction of being the deadliest species in the annals of biology.

So, I'm thinking, if we keep screwing up . . . well, maybe the porpoises will take over from us? They always have a smile on their faces and seem to take care of one another.

CHAPTER 2

Phone Call

"And he entered the temple, and began to cast out those who were selling and buying in the temple; and he overturned the tables of the money-changers and the seats of those who sold the doves . . . And the chief priests and the Scribes heard it, and they sought a way to destroy him. . ."
Gospel of Mark

The phone call surprised me. *After all these years?*

"Gabriel?" Whistling and static sounds behind the voice on the phone.

"Yes?" I said. Only my mother and one other person had ever called me "Gabriel." I was always "Gabe." In grade school, it was "G-man" or "Garza." Then later, "Father," "Father Garza"— or at The Poker Club—"Padre" from Murph. Sometimes the mail read "Reverend."

The phone voice said, "No names. Do not say my name, eh?"

"Eh," with the merest Italian accent was the give-away. *I know who it is.*

"I am in terrible rush and must abandon Rome. Also, short call is harder to trace. Remember how I conducted our tours? Do that from now on. Imitate me like you practice your imitation of Christ, eh? Trust no one."

He gave a wry chuckle, stripped of humor. "Quien tiene una hora de espacio, no muere ahorcado." Always the little quips in Italian, I thought: He who has an hour's start will not be hanged.

I flashed on his past tours of Vatican City with me in tow, his eyes moving all the time with the slightest of head moves, checking our surroundings.

This 49th Begat, Paolo Nasrani, my Vatican Master's thesis coordinator from decades ago, then said, "What I sent your mother, destroy all. Now. Do not hesitate, eh? Also, your Master's thesis. I checked the offices of Vatican Intelligence and your original thesis copy is missing from the file."

"What file? What offices? What?" I said.

"The secret file, opened on you in 1982. Do not ask how I know over the phone, eh?"

In my mind's eye, I could see him rubbing the vertical line on his right earlobe.

I had retrieved the Nasrani files when I returned to Santa Fe for my mother's funeral a decade ago. The files now rested with my Master's Thesis, *On A Unified Christianity*, interred in its original worn cardboard box in my rectory office.

"I understand," I said.

I did understand. There were files on famous Americans who supported Hitler; the Church assisting ex-Nazi war criminals; the Kennedy assassinations; Nixon's treason; Vatican/Mafia financing; CIA atrocities; a poisoned pope; massive clerical pedophilia. The damned list just went on.

"Gabriel, I have the bad feelings about this. I do not think this is about files. Most of those secrets from the Nazis to the child pedophilia scandals have come out. I think it is about your thesis."

"Are you in danger now?" I asked.

"At great risk. My SDRs show that I am being followed. I judge thirty minutes before the Vatican Police ETA." *Estimated Time of Arrival? He didn't used to talk like that. SDRs? I know that means surveillance detection routes, but forget how they work.*

"I received warning. I go to Israel. Gabriel, I have good news, then I must ring off, eh? There is a 50th Begat."

"P . . . p . . . " I had almost said "Paolo." Caught myself just in time. I recovered, "Congratulations. That's wonderful. Preserve the bloodline."

"Thank you, Gabriel. Surely what our God would want, eh?"

"Our God" . . . just like the old days back in Rome.

Click.

Then empty static.

The black Suburban down the street squatted like a large preying beetle, facing away from the rectory. A swarthy, windbreaker-clad man with a two-day growth on his face, finishing his twelve-hour shift, scrunched behind the steering wheel. He peered back at the rectory through the tilted rear-view mirror.

Washington, D.C. : 1980

CHAPTER 3

Follow The Rules!

Because the pastoral need was so great, the Holy Ghost Fathers accelerated his ordination by a year and assigned Father Gabriel Alphonso Esquivel Garza to the Archbishop of Washington, D.C., where the growing Hispanic flock needed shepherding by one of their own. Let rough D.C. neighborhoods train Garza for the missions in Africa and South America.

As a thank-you, the rich Washington diocese would provide a sizable annual stipend to the Holy Ghost Order to cover ten seminarian scholarships for low-income students.

In convening Vatican II, Pope John XXIII had said, "It is time to open the windows of the Church to let in some fresh air." Instead, the current Washington, D.C hierarchy nailed the windows shut, drew the curtains closed and turned off the downstairs lights like they were afraid of trick-or-treaters on Halloween. The Archbishop, Patrick J. Doolin, had a way of focusing his eyes on you as if you were lying, when you said "hi."

"Father Garza, what *am* I going to do with you now? I am responsible for one of the most important dioceses in the country, trying to keep the flock together, and then I have to deal with your foolishness."

Gabe tried to keep his face as blank as an unaddressed envelope. He stared at the marble floor as if there might be answers in the grout. Doolin caught the priest looking down at his feet.

Peering down at Father Garza's worn sandals, he said, "By the way, we're not Franciscans here. You *can* wear shoes." The Archbishop was not smiling.

He's saying he wants me to wear shoes? Is that what this is all about? The smart move is to say nothing. Keep my mouth shut. But . . .

"Archbishop, you know that I have taken a vow of poverty. All the priests in the Holy Ghost Order do. The sandals save on socks. Besides, I have seriously sweaty feet." *He's wincing. Either I've ticked him off or it's TMI, too much information.*

Archbishop Doolin winced, "I've got reports you're out there setting your own agenda, doing God knows what. What are you up to now with . . . shall we pick a topic? Civil rights? Liberation theology? Birth control? Or, how about your favorite, social justice? I brought you here to help me out, not to create more problems. Understand?"

Garza understands. Do you? "Your Excellency, I'm at your service. The Order assigned me here in the nation's capital to help you with your challenges. If I'm not doing that, then . . . "

Garza's throat had constricted on "Your Excellency." *Phony medieval titles; wearing silly robes; this isn't the Middle Ages. Holy Ghost Fathers get the job done with jeans and boots in the missions. Okay, we wear the liturgical robes on Christmas and Easter. Rest of the time, just a stole. Pageantry can stand in the way of the "Good News." That's probably something Father Kaine said back in the seminary.*

Heated exchanges in other conversations occurred when His Excellency would make references in the same sentence to immortal souls, mortal sin, and eternal damnation.

If he was feeling bold that day, Father Garza might speculate out loud about Catholics who ate meat on Friday before 1965. Did they go to hell? The Church changed the rules in the 1960s. Were rules eternal, especially if they carried that awful penalty of eternal damnation? *Or only good until expiration?*

"Again, just wondering—since the message of Jesus of Nazareth says God loves his creations—why put such strong yearnings in them and then damn them for a tortuous eternity when his creatures embraced their desires? A life-game rigged by the Divinity?"

Doolin's official answer: "It's a mystery."

Father Garza would joke about the possible cancellation of Limbo. "Maybe we'll bury it one of these days and all those souls can go to heaven. Changes are coming."

Doolin gave a studied glare through the Garza questions and the quips and said, "Christ gave Peter the keys to the kingdom. You know that. Don't play-act with me." His glare was not merely the look that kills. This look would kill and then smoke-cure the carcass and eat it.

Archbishop Doolin was of the Irish persuasion, Father Garza was Spanish, which meant Latin. Ethnic origins drove their theology.

The English-Irish version of law was an Anglo-Saxon interpretation, a literal one. Whatever the law said must be obeyed, to the letter.

The Hispanic-Latin view of the world, and therefore of religion, was more relaxed. Commandments were like goals. Father Gabe knew that the word "sin" was derived from original meanings that translated "to miss the mark." We strive to follow The Commandments. We are human. We fail. We confess. We try again.

Archbishop Doolin sought salvation for himself and his diocese by religiously following the rules. That's why the rules were there. Why else would you have rules?

Father Garza preached the message of the Nazarene. Do your best for God and your neighbor. Then try to do a little more.

Father Garza walked back to St. Anthony's, a modest street hike from the Archbishop's residence. *How in the hell did I end up arguing with this Archbishop all the time? Because his patron saint is St. Status Quo? Only guy I know with clenched hair. Put a flower in his hand and it'll wilt immediately. I should have gone to the overseas missions.*

Garza knew. It was the Men-In-Black who started it all for him.

<late 1960s, ANN ARBOR, MICHIGAN>

CHAPTER 4

Men In Black

THESE MEN IN BLACK WERE salesmen for souls.

"Good morning." Everything black: pants, shirt, coat, shoes, even the glasses on his jowly face. The voice, though, was warm and soothing, like a favorite uncle.

"Thank you for inviting me. I'm Father John Coffey. I'm from the Holy Ghost Fathers, a missionary order started in France in 1703. We serve two foreign missions, Africa and South America. We go where others won't. We call ourselves 'the pope's Marines.'

"Who did Jesus reach out to in his lifetime? It wasn't the rich and powerful. Our Jesuit colleagues specialize in educating the children of the rich and powerful—their strategy to influence society with the Gospel. Our approach is different, no in-between. We go directly to the hopeless souls needing the good news."

A clerical pied piper, Coffey spun a spell of religious challenge that captivated idealistic young men in the eighth-grade classrooms of Catholic schools.

"Come on up to Ann Arbor for a weekend and see our place," he offered.

"Eighty-three acres in the beautiful Michigan countryside. We'll challenge you with a life of adventure to share the liberating Gospel message. You'll enjoy our seminary; lots of sports, excellent education and religious companionship."

"A missionary overseas?" someone always asked. "Can I do those things? Would I have to live in a shack?"

Coffey's sunshine smile relieved youthful anxieties about daily hardships in foreign lands with amusing stories starring Africa and South America. "You'll have clothing and food and running water," he said. Then he chuckled. "Maybe not electricity all the time."

Coffey had done his homework with the parochial school principal beforehand and directed his gaze at Garza several times during the presentation. He asked Garza to meet with him after the class. Father Coffey sold Garza on trading the warmth of New Mexico for frigid Michigan.

Gabriel Alphonso Esquivel Garza stood 5'6' and weighed a pudgy 185 pounds. His straight black hair framed his smooth round face with thoughtful brown eyes. He was bilingual in English and Spanish and a straight-A student at St. Bernard's elementary school in Santa Fe. His father's roots traced back as an Indian native of New Mexico; his mother a descendant of Spanish conquistadores who settled in New Mexico in the 1500s.

Gabe inherited his mother's pleasant disposition with just a touch of the arrogance that comes with the DNA of rumored Spanish royalty. He was also heir to her desire for a priestly vocation in the family. "My Gabriel," she said, "there is nothing greater than helping your fellow travelers on this journey we call life."

From Dad, Gabe received his last name, Indian complexion, and suppressed anger at the grievances of being an Indian-Hispanic in an imperialistic White American culture, a culture late to the hemisphere, following after the Bering Strait crossers, the Indians, the Aztecs and then the Spanish Conquistadores.

Since his father worked for the rail maintenance section in Santa Fe, the company provided free housing. The family no longer noticed the trains, even when their house next to the railroad tracks shook. If they were at dinner, they would stop talking until the train passed.

Gabe's mother—God bless her—full of that special love that Hispanic women show for their families, put curtains in the windows and baked the daily smell of homemade tortillas. Her home came with frequent hugs and squeezes.

The change from warm, Hispanic New Mexico to frigid Anglo Michigan stabbed Gabe with culture shock. Gabe saw no sunshine from November to March in that part of eastern Michigan because of the lake effect, always overcast. Snow remained for the season and turned from white to grimy black. No one spoke Spanish.

The quiet of the seminary's country setting unnerved Gabe at first. The modern beige brick buildings of the seminary complex resembled a junior college with dorms, instead of a high school. Only, this campus had a chapel at its center. The eighty-four seminarians' daily uniform consisted of black pants, a white tee shirt, a black sports coat, and plain black shoes.

Gabe roomed for two years with Owen Friel, from Hamilton, Ohio. Gabe and Owen came of age in the seminary as the Church began to change. At least it talked about changing. Maybe, sometime in the future . . . perhaps.

Their religion class reflected the radical changes of Vatican II. The teacher, Father Larry Kaine, a former missionary and a rumored ex-Marine in a previous life (it was the Marine part that most impressed the boys), talked about the sins of the Church towards the Jews.

Kaine still projected youthfulness at the senile age of forty-seven; that is, he still had his hair and teeth and could hit a baseball with the varsity team. On the field, he was Coach Kaine.

In class, he often chronicled the massacres, burnings, inquisitions, and pogroms aimed at the Jews for centuries. The priest's message: the Church has much to atone for.

The details of the historical blood lettings evaporated with time, but Kaine's joke stayed with Garza: "One Jew says to another, 'Why do we suffer so much as a people?' His Jewish compatriot responds,

'We are the Chosen People of God. Those whom he loves, he makes suffer.' The first Jew says, 'Please tell God to not love us so much.'"

Father Kaine had spent five years in the missions of South America and he had seen things, bad things.

His shorthand description: "No one gets up in the morning and says, 'Let's see the evil I can do today, or, how I can fuck up everything. People do what they do for a reason. You need to know *why* they do what they do to be effective as a priest. You will make your personal judgements—you can't resist that—but understand human nature first, render judgements later."

Kaine paused for several seconds to keep their attention. "And, always put the welfare of the people you serve ahead of everything else."

"Everything?" Garza asked in the class.

"Everything," Kaine replied.

"Even ahead of the Church?" Garza asked.

"Do what Jesus would do."

Gabriel Garza remembered the Kaine insights because he had used the 'F' word. You didn't use that word in the seminary. It wasn't a sin, at least not a serious one. Marines used the "F" word a lot, he figured.

Father Kaine proclaimed optimism over the reforms of Vatican II. "There's no going back. We're done with medieval silliness. We will apologize to the Jews, and to the native peoples for our colonialism, and slavery, and burning witches, and burning books. It's a new day, a new Church. We move forward with the Gospel."

He waved his arm, sweeping to the horizons he saw beyond the classroom wall.

"Mark my words. There will be married priests and women priests. Forget the medieval costumes. Soon, the Roman Church will form a new structure with the Episcopal Church, the Greek Orthodox Church, and the Lutheran Church. It'll take a few more years to come together with the Presbyterians, Methodists, Baptists and other Christian sects. But we are guaranteed to get there. Reform has taken hold."

Gabe and his fellow students looked at each other. They had never heard such things. Kaine's eyes shone. He saw the New Christian Church in his soul.

"And we will come to practice our Christian religion as a generous way of life based in compassion, not a set of rigid doctrines."

The only problem—it was spring now after a long, frigid winter, and the lecture melted away with the warm afternoon sunshine and the promise of baseball practice.

So much for atrocities and the New Church.

The strict seminary routine irritated Gabe at first, coming from his carefree home. However, the ritualized schedule evolved its own sense of comfort. No one wasted a moment. A spiritual boot camp, even weekends had study halls. Occasionally, there was a film in the gym on Saturday night, like *The Ten Commandments*, starring Charlton Heston.

Gabe and his roommate both grew accustomed to the wooded country setting on forty acres, ten miles from Ann Arbor, Michigan. So quiet. There were times you could reach out and touch God, or at least hear Him in the spring breezes bursting with smells and new life.

Everyone had assigned duties: laundry, bathrooms, and kitchen cleaning; grounds maintenance; and special assignments such as picking apples in the orchard. Gabe heard that some seniors would collect apples, make cider, and then load the collection up with aspirin. It would make the cider ferment, creating an alcoholic effect. This was not an approved drink at the seminary.

Gabe wondered, *If they don't want to follow the rules, why are they in the seminary? Rules are there for a reason. Why don't they leave?*

Many did. Their reasons? Bridling at the strict regimen; girls; wanting freedom as a teen in the rock and roll era; and some deciding they did not have a vocation, the calling to be a Roman Catholic priest for the rest of their lives.

Owen Friel, Gabe's roommate, left after two years to chase those young people with the long legs in short skirts, full chests, and winsome smiles. They smelled nice too, like flowers. Some had voices like wind chimes.

Gabe Garza stayed and froze in the Michigan winters.

He missed the sunshine Spanish rhythms of his old neighborhood. But Gabe believed he had a calling. There was no stirring to chase girls. He now appreciated the all-male, structured, quiet lifestyle and the free, quality education.

Since his railroad maintenance father couldn't afford his seminary education, Gabe was on a full scholarship. The Holy Ghost Fathers had successfully sold several generous benefactors on the everlasting merits of underwriting seminary scholarships.

While Gabe felt attraction to one or two of his fellow students, it didn't matter because he would be taking a vow of chastity. He reined in any wrong impulses. He knew the whispered refrain, *God made man and woman, Adam and Eve—not Adam and Steve.*

Gabe questioned, to himself, the Church's fierce stand against homosexuals. God created them too, and he didn't think God cared if two of his creatures were of the same sex and loved one another. Isn't that what his Son said, "Love one another?" Did God make mistakes? It seemed to be a big universe—from his science classes. But, it was one of those things you didn't ask about, for a lot of reasons.

The sales pitch of the Holy Ghost Fathers to young men enjoyed success because it was down-to-earth. There was no fire and brimstone; no Church regulatory paraphernalia; no threats of excommunication. But there was the anti-homosexuality interdiction.

The Order presented itself in modern fashion, without the black cassocks or other medieval apparel. Their daily uniform in the missions consisted of jeans, denim shirts, and work boots. The priestly vocation challenge appealed to idealistic minds. They committed to the Lord and to saving souls for eternity.

The Holy Ghost Fathers preached a gospel of saving bodies too, which was unusual. They established schools in their overseas missions and health services— the social gospel. They had a sense of humor about it, able to laugh at themselves and at their shortcomings, but never at their mission.

The Order was still recovering its perspective and sense of faith after the January 1, 1962, slaying of twenty colleagues in the Belgian Congo, the result of the nationalistic uprisings sweeping the continent. All of the teaching priests at the Ann Arbor seminary had friends numbered among the dead at Kongolo, a small town in Northern Katanga. The murdered missionaries had surrendered their opportunity to escape. They cast their lot with the congregations they served. They were taking care of their people, as Father Kaine had taught. The seminary still offered one Mass each week in their memory.

Gabe remembered these things.

Even though they were roommates for only two years, Owen Friel and Gabe Garza exchanged letters over the following years. These included congratulatory cards when Owen graduated from the University of Dayton, and Gabe graduated from the seminary in Connecticut and was ordained.

Compatible roommates, but so different. Owen Friel had the mid-western blond look. Gabe Garza was the olive-skinned Indian from New Mexico.

Owen left the seminary to chase skirts. He wouldn't say it that way, but that's what it was. Just nature kicking in, nothing to be ashamed of, although Owen was ashamed of it.

Gabe stayed. It was where he belonged for all the right reasons, and one he didn't talk about. He preferred being around them . . . the high testosterone, the pushing and shoving, the verbal repartee, the way they smelled . . . most of the time.

So, Gabe did something unusual. To deal with the unwelcome tensions, he took up weight-lifting. What triggered it was Owen's leaving, and a comment he had made.

Owen Friel had told him how his dad bought him a set of weights the previous Christmas, encouraging him to use them as a way to work off the tensions and frustrations of being a teen. Gabe decided to try it. Since he looked like an Hispanic version of the Pillsbury Doughboy, what could he lose?

On summer break from the seminary, Gabe went to the Goodwill store in Santa Fe and bought someone's discarded barbell, two dumbbells, and free weights. He sanded off the rust and sprayed them black with Rustoleum paint. Lifting progressively heavier weights, he started to see results within weeks.

Since he was traveling by bus back to Michigan in September, he carefully selected which weights to take. He settled on a dumbbell and two ten-pound weights. Not much weight, but he'd perform daily reps in the hundreds.

After the summer break, he found the seminary had already furnished a side room off the basketball gym with a near-professional set of weights.

Gabe practiced his new sport with passion. His daily routine consisted of one set of ten reps—repetitions—at first, for his biceps and triceps. Then, he began to add more sets and an extra ten pounds a week to the barbell. After six months, Gabe was up to one hundred pounds with five sets of ten reps twice a day.

Over the years, Gabe changed his profile from a Pillsbury Doughboy ad—Hispanic version— to that of a mobile muscle, built like a fireplug and rock hard.

Preparing himself for tough overseas missions or gang-infested hoods in big cities, it couldn't hurt to be in shape. Felt good too. Confrontations can come in many forms: gangsters, archbishops, theological disputes, and poker clubs. Be prepared. Gabe suspected that Jesus was in pretty good shape, being the son of a carpenter and all.

The results of the workouts also helped with the unspoken issue—his orientation. Extreme physical fitness said "he don't take no shit." *There are situations where you need that, just to open the door for better communication.*

<LAUREL, MARYLAND> 1980

CHAPTER 5

Poker Club—A Full House

"We are each dealt a hand of cards to play in the game of life."
ROBERT MURPHY CRAIG

THEY HAD BEEN ROOMMATES IN the frozen wasteland of Ann Arbor, Michigan ten years ago, but stayed in touch.

"Gabe, it's Owen. How you doin'?

"Owen! If I was doing any better, they'd have to change my meds."

"Yeah, I hope you're not still smoking those funny little cigarettes."

"Once in a while. Howzitgoing?"

"Great news! They just hired me as the Assistant City Manager in Rockville, Maryland, down the street from you in D.C.—well, a city away."

"Last time we talked you said you were looking at other jobs. I'm glad you landed close. Rockville's changing fast. Used to be real redneck." Gabe chuckled.

"What's funny?"

"Oh, the term 'redneck.' Different meanings. I could look in the mirror, you know, and I'd see lots of red."

"Yeah, but the Rockville rednecks are real pale. I'm starting right away—the first week in April. Also, I got back in touch with a couple of guys I went to the University of Dayton with and they play poker on the first Friday of the month. It's over in Laurel, towards Baltimore, not too far from you. How about joining us? Try it out. Be good to see you."

"Thanks. Need a break. Feel like I'm trying to save God's children and dodge bullets at the same time. Kids in my neighborhood do their math at school by adding and subtracting shell casings."

"That's what signing on with the Holy Ghost Fathers was all about, right Gabe?"

"Well . . . here, if I don't wear my Roman collar out in the parish, I run into trouble. But, I'm getting better known in the neighborhood. They call me 'brother hermano.' Cute, huh."

"Gladys Knight I hear in the background?"

"Yeah, she's singing about the best thing that ever happened to her."

"I thought you just listened to Gregorian chant? What happened?"

"R and B plays better in my parish."

"I'll call with more info about the poker after I move over. I think you'll enjoy these guys. One's pretty funny, another's got an ego problem, but we usually handle that. We've got a serious guy, served in 'Nam. Bring your best game, or these guys will do you out of $50. They're not going to care about your vow of poverty. Stay safe buddy. Good talkin' to you."

"Same here. "

At Easter time, Father Gabriel Garza joined The Poker Club.

For some, poker is just a game. To others, it is a social glue. For a few people, poker can be an obsession. For poets and writers, it is an allegory for life.

For The Poker Club, in Laurel, Maryland, on the first Friday of the month, it was all of the above.

Fifty-two cards; that's what it took.

For thirty years.

Over the decades, there were seven regular players.

These were the Nights of the Round Table.

The game lasted into the first decade of the new century. Over the life of this Poker Club, there were murders, betrayals, a suicide, a disappearance, affairs and . . . life—always uncertain. It became an anchor for this poker varsity which played through job changes, marriages, children, and divorces.

Sometimes they died before their time because it was Washington and things happened; not to others like in novels or movies—but to people we know, people we play cards with.

The decades held their hostages and claimed their casualties.

These laminated, lamented pieces of cardboard, two and three-eighths inches by three and three-eighths inches, brought together the City of Rockville, the CIA, an information technology expert, the Treasury Department, a high-powered downtown law firm, the Roman Catholic Church, and the Laurel Deli where Murph worked. He arrived at his deli at 6:00 a.m. every day and started making the best sandwiches northeast of Washington, D.C.

They say that if you are exceptional at what you do, you end up in either New York or Washington, sometime during your career.

The monthly poker games took place at Murph's bachelor apartment in Laurel, Maryland twenty-one miles northeast of Washington, off the I-95.

Pitted like the surface of the moon, Murph's fatigued-wood poker table, which he acquired from God-knows-where, could squeeze seven players into six chip wells. The fungus-green felt testified to longevity with cigarette burns and old rips covered with gray duct tape. During the week, the table wore a thin plywood top where Murph stored unopened mail and old Playboys. The fold-up chairs were from Sears.

The players arrived from around the Washington metro area. Except for Murph and Gabe, they'd all graduated from the University of Dayton, in Ohio, known as UD. It was part of "fly-over" country between the two coasts and provided the lack of color in "white-bread."

The Poker Club rules solidified, like Church doctrines over the millennia, as the group morphed from ad hoc poker to routine monthly Friday night card pilgrimages. Murph blessed the monthly fraternity with bylaws:

The first six players to commit reserved a seat. The seventh could stand-by or squeeze in, no problem. Often someone was busy, had family obligations or was visiting a girlfriend. Murph kept a list of substitutes who represented fresh meat—new money—and could be called at the last minute.

Murph shuffled the cards for the first deal at 8 p.m. Be there.

The house bought the beer, chips, and pretzels. Everyone had to kick in $10, $20 if you called ahead for the culinary ecstasy known as a Murph sandwich.

Murph set the limits: a one dollar ante per hand, fifty cents a bet; no limit on the number of raises; "sandbagging," that is, checking and then raising, was permitted—even encouraged. Cheap David Molinsky didn't like that, but Murph pointed out it raised the pot and the tension level.

A normal pot was twenty dollars; a good pot sixty dollars.

Someone had to tell an interesting story from work at each game. Over time, a challenge of one-ups-manship developed. And information hit the table that shouldn't have and that sharing caused trouble. Eventually . . . big trouble. Jackson Bass, for example, listened hard for any secret not meant for public ears. He had reports to write.

The Players:

Gabe Garza: ordained priest in the Holy Ghost Fathers religious order; assigned to St. Anthony's parish in NE Washington.

Committed to the Social Gospel, Father Garza found himself at odds with his traditionalist boss, Archbishop Doolin.

Bill Peters: University of Dayton graduate; V.P. of an information technology company. He resembled the gene mix of an adult looking Howdy Doody and a watered down Robert Redford. Haunted by lost loves. "You love being in love," accused Jackson Bass, at least once a year. "Guilty as charged," admitted Bill. Divorced.

Owen Friel: former high school seminarian in the Order of the Holy Ghost Fathers; roommate of Gabriel Garza; University of Dayton graduate; City Manager for Rockville, Maryland; later, Assistant Manager of the Fiscal Services Division, the Central Intelligence Agency. Owen came to resemble an aging Owen Wilson, with a full head of dirty blond hair. Divorced.

Jackson Bass: University of Dayton; Georgetown Law School; junior staffer for Senate Watergate Committee. Member of a powerful downtown law firm. Cultivated his natural resemblance to Jimmy Stewart. Collected 'frienemies' and secrets.

Robert Murphy "the Murph" Craig: W.C. Fields imitator. Attended Prince George's Community College. Manager of the Laurel Deli, best sandwiches in town, daily five-finger discount on a six-pack, if your last name is Craig. Secret writer.

Clark DeGuire: University of Dayton graduate; Vietnam War Veteran; Ph.D. in Economics. Economist at U.S. Treasury Department; tall, Ron-Howard-prematurely-balding-blond look-alike; married college sweetheart; one child. Rumored candidate for Budget Director, had Gore won the election.

Clark would correct his poker colleagues, whose historical recall was weak, that Gore did win the election. The Republican-appointed majority Supreme Court stole the election.

David Molinsky: University of Dayton graduate; M.A. Princeton University; U.S. State Department; served in Peru and Bolivia. Groucho Marx without the mustache. Compelled to remove his heavy black framed glasses and to remind colleagues that Mr. Marx possessed Hollywood-handsome looks in his prime. Eventual life hostage and casualty.

Gabe savored the timeout from being God's-go-to-guy. The mixed smell of smoke, sweat, and testosterone offered a change from burning candles and incense.

On the job, Gabe wore a black beret, a roman collar with a black shirt and a black sports coat and black shoes. Lots of black.

Off the job, Gabe wore Washington Redskins sweatshirts with worn blue jeans, before tattered was "the look." He owned six of the sweatshirts, in various color combinations, but most were gray with the red Indian logo. It all harmonized with his sandals or scuffed Dan Post cowboy boots in the winter. He produced the informal look as often as possible because it wearied him to see people walking on eggshells when they found out he was a priest. *Everybody needs and deserves a little time to just be themselves, don't they?*

At The Poker Club, Murph welcomed Gabe, "Been dipping into that poor box again, Padre? We'll still take your money. So . . . what do I call you? Father? I've already got one of those, or did have—he died three years ago."

Murph gave the blue-jeans-and-sandals-wearing cleric a pretend-puzzled look. "Gabe? Reverend Garza? El Jefe? Your Holiness?"

"Murph you don't have to call me anything. It's that old Motown song—just call me and I'll be here."

"Hey, do you think it's a sin to play poker on Sunday?" Murph asked the priest.

"The guys told me, the way you play poker, it's a sin any day of the week."

Murph wouldn't let him have the last word: "Sorry, Father. I don't trust men who wear robes, whether they're priests or oil-rich Arabs. They both fuck us over."

Gabe tried to take it down a notch: "Did you go to college with these guys?"

"No, Amigo, I didn't go to school with these yahoos. I run the Laurel Deli down the street. I went to the local community college for a year. You know why I love poker?"

"Why?"

"Because . . . no big ideas involved. Just cards and money. Bet, raise, check, bluff. Every once in a while try to deal yourself an ace from the bottom of the deck. All that education leads to trouble. You end up with wars and religious fights. Somebody wants to impose their big idea on someone else."

Gabe wondered what was coming next.

"Here's one example, Jefe. You've got your basic Jews fighting the same camel-jockeys today they fought three thousand years ago. Your Egyptians didn't get the memo that Moses and his folks were serious about leaving and setting up their own shop. Real bad neighborhood over there."

Gabe reached for someone's cigarettes and lighter on the table and shook one loose from the pack. Murphy watched.

"Hey Mr. Padre, I'm a Pall Mall guy. The authentic smokers suck away on Pall Malls. The dilettantes ask for Pell Mells. Which are you? Pall Mall? Or Pell Mell?"

The priest just looked at him.

Murph went on, "The Christian-Muslim fight goes back to the 700s when your basic Muslims spread their god-vision with fire and the sword. That's the Christian view, as if your Christians never used the sword and the burning stake."

Gabe lit up and blew some O's. Pall Mall smoke.

"I think the world would be a better place if we all played poker instead, Compadre. You see, si?"

"Murph," Jack interrupted, "if you're going to major in philosophy maybe you should take some courses first."

"Hey, slick," responded Murph. ". . . and the horse you came riding in on," accompanied with a raised middle finger.

"I should name this group the 'over' club."

"Why?" asked Gabe, not familiar with the Murph setup routine, yet.

"Because everyone here is *over*-educated, *over*-ambitious, and *over*-here. Just kidding about that last one. I need them over here because I love their monthly contributions to my beer and sandwich fund."

After dealing the hand, Murph said, "Let's play some cards. Hold them up so I can see where I marked them."

"Bet five," said Gabe, earning a half-smile from Murph.

"Raise three," said Owen.

"Okay," said Jack.

"Re-raise you ten big ones," said Bill.

"I'm in," said Murph.

"See you and raise you another ten," added Owen.

Pause.

Everyone could hear the whir of the ceiling fan.

"I'm out. Don't believe in miracles," said Jack.

Two more rounds of bets.

Gabe stayed in and called.

"Pot right?" said Murph. "$225. Not bad." Murph leaned back in his chair, a show of confidence.

"Allriightt! I've got three of a kind," said Murph, moving back to the table and turning the winning cards face up.

"Three well-dressed 'Ladies' for you ladies. Anybody beat that?" Murph reached for the chips, backed up by Queen-triplets.

"I've got two pair," said Gabe, his cards face down on the table.

Murph halted his mid-air sweep. "Two pair?" throwing Gabe a dark look. "Christ-on-a-crutch, Garza! I thought you knew how to play this game! If you don't, then don't waste our time, okay? Three of a kind always beats two pair. Do you com-fucking-prende, padre?"

"Well, Murph, I've got two pairs of sevens."

Murph looked at Garza without blinking. His lips flat-lined. He tugged his Cincinnati Reds ball cap, got up from the table, and went to the fridge for a cold can of Pabst Blue Ribbon.

Next month, experiencing a losing streak, Gabe stepped outside for a break and a smoke.

"You can smoke in here," said Murph. "It keeps the cockroaches down."

"Thanks, Murph. I need a little fresh air."

"I'll come with you," said Owen. Since there were seven players for the six seats that night, it wouldn't slow the play.

Gabe and Owen stood on the back porch, taking in the dry musk of fall foliage in the cool night air.

"That's a funny smelling cigarette, Gabe."

Gabe laughed. "What are they going to do, arrest a priest? I'd rather do this than drink. The bottle kept my dad down for years. He tried to drown his anger.

"What was he angry about?" Owen thinking he knew.

"Life. No education. Being invisible, an Indian in cowboy country. Unable to give mom everything she deserved. He felt blessed with her—and he was. He didn't have money, but he was rich because of her. He knew it. But things still got to him. I think he felt he'd been dealt marked cards and resented having to play the game. It was tough paying the bills."

Gabe took a deep inhale, offered it to Owen. Owen shook his head no. His employers frowned on that kind of smoking.

"I'm a priest today, because of her. I'm a *good* priest because he taught me to watch out for bullshit. It comes at you from everywhere, all the time. He thought I was a fool for wanting to be a priest. 'Biggest rigged game in town,' he used to call it. He used to point to the pictures of Jesus with the Sacred Heart, saying, 'Who's that hombre with the blue eyes? Son, Jesus looked like you, not some blond Anglo. He smelled too. Ever wonder why they were always washing their feet?'"

A torn moon peered through the clouds for a second before they dragged it back inside.

"I know," said Owen. "I get crapola for my work, too. Because I work for government, I'm considered 'on the public dole.' I guess we're both institutional men."

"You mean we should be institutionalized?"

"Probably."

"Here's the latest. I'm supposed to read a letter from the Archbishop for the Sunday Mass at the Shrine. You know, at the Shrine of the Immaculate Conception, our national Catholic Cathedral."

"Gabe, just because I left the seminary doesn't mean I don't remember that stuff, although why the hell they call it 'The Shrine,' I never could figure out. Weird design too, if you ask me."

"Okay, so this letter states the official church doctrine against contraception. Here's the kicker. Because my dinosaur-boss knows there's strong opposition to the party line, he's requiring every priest to read the letter without comment. He needs me as his token Hispanic, especially since the 11 a.m. Mass is pretty mixed. I don't want to read that stupid letter, but what can I do?"

Gabe took another hit, a deep one. Held it.

"Let me frame the issue in a way you can take it to the Archbishop," said Owen. "You say, 'Arch,'—'Arch' will get his attention." Owen's smile grew. *This is fun.*

"Here's the deal. We've got the White middle-class vote pretty much locked down. I mean, Arch, they're all in the pews on Sunday praying and nodding yes—most of the time. It's the other folks we need to get on board. So, what we do, Arch, we launch a PR campaign that says:

> 'Meet Jesus of Nazareth: He was a foreign-born, dark-skinned, non-English speaking Jewish man who healed the sick and fed the poor, defended women from being slut-shamed, opposed tax collectors, spoke out against the death penalty, supported peace and opposed war, never forced anyone to go along with what he wanted, and opposed the religious and political nonsense of his day. For us, **HE'S THE MAN!**'"

Gabe didn't blink. He looked down at the ember of his cigarette as if it contained hallucinogens. He made his mouth move. "Sometimes you surprise the hell out of me. I can't tell if you're serious or not, but . . . can you write that down for me right now, so I get it word for word? I think you've given me an idea."

"What are you going to do?" Owen wanted to add *I was just kidding around.* But the look on Father Garza's face told him the Sunday Mass had come early to the Friday night Poker Club.

CHAPTER 6

Just Read The Damned Letter

AFTER READING THE GOSPEL, STANDING in the ornate, raised pulpit of The Basilica of the National Shrine of the Immaculate Conception, Father Garza remained . . . quiet.

He sometimes walked down to the main floor of the Church in front of the congregation with a portable microphone to give his sermon and to do a Q and A session. Once or twice a year, he would break into joyful song, to good-natured groaning of the congregants.

When he strode up and down the aisle, the parishioners could see his frayed blue jeans peaking below the vestments, topping his scuffed sandals. Frayed blue jeans might be haute couture in the future. Garza was early with the worn jeans look.

Except, this day, he stayed in the pulpit.

Father Garza announced, "The Archbishop has directed all priests in his Washington Archdiocese to read the following letter from him at every Mass without comment. I will proceed to do that unless I get a show of hands from those who want me to sing today instead."

Father Garza looked out at the congregation. People glanced at each other puzzled or stared straight ahead.

"Come on. Let me see a show of hands. Touch some sky!"

Several hands went up.

"Well, I guess I'll have to do the letter. Just as well. That way I won't get into trouble."

The Archbishop's letter opened with "My fellow Catholics." The letter damned the selfish evils of contraception which violated God's mandate to 'increase and multiply.' Catholics were forbidden to use any form of contraception or engage in sexual activity which would frustrate the purpose of the act of procreation.

Gabe believed there was a better way to look at it. *God had shared the powers of co-creation with man. If you were a thinking being, you planned. That was being fully human.*

The pastoral letter finished with the traditional Catholic references to mortal sin and eternal hell-fire. Father Garza stood in the pulpit, silently looking at the congregation, no expression. *Sure is fun being a Catholic these days.*

A puzzled buzz vibrated among the Sunday faithful. Father Garza stared ahead, not moving.

Murmuring: "Why isn't he saying anything?"

Loud whispers: "Is Father Garza okay?"

The Right Reverend Father Gabriel Alphonso Esquivel Garza crumpled the letter into a paper ball, threw it from the pulpit onto the pristine marble floor below, and walked back to the altar.

Silence.

Throat clearing.

A cough.

More silence.

Someone clapped; then someone else. The heavens opened up, thunderous applause broke out—a standing ovation and cheering. Gabe tried to stop, but the smile grew on his face.

CHAPTER 7

Jesus Calls

Question: Was Jesus in the Carpenter's Union?

Father Gabriel Garza tossed and turned. He preferred to bury his face in the pillow. Sleeping face down made it stay dark, longer.

Finally, sleep came.

The phone rang by his bed.

It felt like mere moments. *Oh, Lord, will I be able to get back to sleep?*

Fumbling, he picked up the receiver.

"Hello?"

"Gabe," said the warm, inviting voice. "Gabe."

He looked at the clock. 2:47 a.m. "Jesus Christ! Do you know what time it is! Who's calling?"

"Yes, Gabe. You're right."

"Right! Right about what?"

"About who."

"What about who?"

"It's me."

"Who?"

"Jesus Christ."

"What?"

"Not What, Who. Jesus of Nazareth, the one they crucified because I spoke the truth."

Gabe didn't know what was going on but felt that glow, that state of grace that came with his religion when it was early morning quiet in the church, he was saying Mass, and it was time to change the bread and wine into something else.

"Wha . . . whas . . . what's this all about? I have an important meeting tomorrow, early."

"Hey, man, I just wanted to let you know I think you're doing a helluva job."

"You do?"

"Yeah. You keep it real."

"You're talking funny for someone who lived 2,000 years ago."

"I'm just playing with you, Mi Hermano. Seriously, you know we are all one and should look out for one another. We all walk this vale of tears. It's a grueling reality, but after the transition, it *is* beautiful."

Am I awake? What's going on here?

The Voice continued, "I've had serious conversations with the Father about the painful nature of this reality. It's because when he proclaimed 'create,' every possible existence that could be, was. You guys got stuck with this one."

"Sorry for taking your name in vain earlier, Lord."

""Hakuna Matata. No worries."

"What?"

"No, he's on second base. I've used your name too, a lot. The Archangel Gabriel tries to pull rank with the others because he split my mother's egg without a sperm."

"Huh?"

"Gabriel started saying *he* was my father. Dad had to sit him down and straighten him out. He told my father he was just joking around. And, Gabriel's always competing with Michael about whose trumpet is bigger. He's a prima donna. He reminds me of your Archbishop."

Gabe felt warm energy.

"Gabe, you keep preaching the good news to my brethren and tell them to keep faith. I'll see you when I see you. Illegitimi non carborundum. Goodnight."

Gabe's eyes closed.

When the alarm clock woke him at 6:00 a.m., he recalled the dream in stereophonic clarity. A smile danced on his face. *That was one of the better dreams. Good one, Jesus riffing on that old Abbott and Costello baseball routine and using Latin for a joke. Haven't heard that one in years, "Don't let the bastards wear you down."*

Looking over at the bedside table, he saw that the phone had fallen off its hook during the night.

CHAPTER 8

Exile

On Monday at 7 a.m., Father Garza prepared to meet with His Eminence. He traded his favorite sweatshirt and jeans for a black shirt and black slacks. He put on his old pair of plain black shoes from the back of the closet. He added heavy splashes of Old Spice. Dad had worn Old Spice. Putting on the uniform of black girded him to face the forces of *tradition*. He made sure to arrive five minutes early for this mandated 8:30 a.m. conversation. He was often late, but not today.

The Archbishop kept Father Garza waiting for forty-five minutes. His Excellency's smooth cherubic face was redder than usual. Today it wasn't due to his wrestling with the bottle, a match he lost most nights.

"Father Garza, I heard about the stunt you pulled yesterday at the eleven o'clock Mass. That's why I had my assistant here, Monsignor Ryan, call you last night. No, don't sit down. We're not going to be meeting that long."

I don't even get a "hello" or a "good morning." Well, it means I don't have to kiss the big ring today. I'll just stand in front of the desk.

"Garza, I was so damned mad, if I had the authority, I would have de-frocked you on the spot."

"Yes, sir." *This sure isn't the time for my usual theological debate with him.*

"Then I got to thinking about it. I know there's disagreement with my position on birth control—correction—the Church's position on birth control. At least you had the obedience to do what you were told but unfortunately, the bad judgement to show how you felt. I should give you back to the Holy Ghost Fathers and let them ship you overseas."

"Yes, Your Eminence, I understand."

"I am too tolerant of your foolishness but I admire your poor background, similar to my immigrant upbringing. We were both blessed with saintly mothers dedicated to God's message, through His Holy Church."

We. He said "we," the brotherly collective pronoun. If I interrupt, he may start all over again. That could be unpleasant for both of us.

"I know the warmth you have for people, how they receive you. I'm envious of that. You'll be a priest until the day you die, not like some fly-by-nighters, who set their vows aside because they think the times have changed and a pretty skirt catches their eye."

"Yes, Your Excellency," Father Graza said, staring at the floor as if there might be answers in the tile grout, and trying to maintain radio silence.

"'Preach every day, and if you have to, speak.' I didn't get it at first. Then my secretary explained your motto to me, Garza. Your sermon is 'how you live day to day'. Good for you. That is what the Our Lord wants."

The Archbishop stood up and went behind the expensive high-backed leather chair, resting his hands on top.

"When I was your age, I too was impatient at how slow things were. But, it's that way for a reason. The Church's message is eternal. A few years in our time makes no difference. What Holy Mother Church asks of us can be difficult, but we must bear it. We need rules to keep us together. Otherwise, we'll be like Protestants, not knowing what we believe and fragmented into a thousand pieces."

I should keep my mouth shut. But ...

"Archbishop, with respect, I wonder if perhaps there is room for interpretation on the issues of procreation and birth control? The Church's message about the sacredness of life must not be compromised. The Church says we are called to be co-creators with

God. Since we are co-creators, and I think the Church uses that term, shouldn't we plan our creations, as thinking beings?"

No lightning bolts, but no promise of fair weather, either. Should I stop? Using his gentle counseling voice, under the threat of a verbal storm, Father Garza persisted. "I work with families, people trying to do the right thing. They can't be having children all the time. Abstinence, as an alternative, is a practice that only old celibate men in Rome would mandate, if you'll pardon my frankness."

"'Old celibate men in Rome?' A bit rude, don't you think? Especially since I'll never see my 70s again. I just happen to not be in Rome."

They say when the Archbishop twists that big expensive ring on the third finger of his right hand—look out. Is he twisting the ring?

He's not twisting it. "Excuse me, Your Grace. Do we have to pay so much attention to this issue? Look what's going on. You know the list. Cities burning with racial hatred; nuclear standoff with the Russians; we've just finished massive slaughter in Vietnam; revolution is still sweeping Africa and South America."

Gonna keep going but keep the passion out of my voice or he'll take it as a challenge. "Our Church has a healing message. The world hungers to hear our good news. Yet, we spend all our time talking about the rhythm method. Where's the perspective, sir?"

"Garza, you think you're right, youth always does. But those kids running around with the long hair out there say you can't be trusted because you're thirty-one. You're going to discover the importance of everyone following the rules. If you don't have rules, you have chaos, nothing. If we aren't vigilant, we'll end up with a menu for a religion. The faithful will pick and choose which doctrines they want to follow and which they don't. Then, where would we be?"

Maybe we'd focus back on the original Gospel message? Jesus didn't say much about the rhythm method, Father Garza wanted to say. *I've gone far enough and I'll be lucky if he doesn't make an example out of me.*

"Yes, Your Excellency, I apologize for embarrassing you. I was caught up in the moment."

"All right," said Doolin, "we've had our talk. Let me figure out what I'm going to do with you."

It sounded to Father Garza as if the Archbishop might already have a plan.

The U.S. constituted one of the Catholic Church's growing, affluent populations. The Washington Archbishop carried gravitas in Rome.

Archbishop Doolin suspected the time was passing for his kind. *I've fought the good fight for Holy Mother Church. The rules will be changing, if they keep* any *rules. Meat on Friday, Mass in English, ecumenism—as if all Churches are equal—what next? I don't want responsibility for God's children if we can't rely on clear, firm rules. The rules tell you what to do. It has worked for two thousand years.*

At the Conference of Catholic Bishops last year, they urged us to adopt a more empathetic pastoral style. Touchy-feely isn't going to get us through what I've seen: a murdered Catholic president; his successor Catholic brother shot down; cities on fire; war protests; women running around improperly dressed, and it's not just the short skirts but the lack of appropriate undergarments. Mother would have had a coronary, God Bless Elizabeth, she was a saint.

The Archdiocese will need different leadership in the future. Good luck to them without rules.

At the lunch he hosted in his dining room the next day, Archbishop Doolin tested his plan.

"Mario, I have an excellent candidate for your new Vatican Fellowship Program. Is it still proposed to be two years, with a Master's in Theology? I know that normally only Ph.D. candidates go to Rome."

"Yes. A sought after program for those with Church potential. Who do you have in mind?" said Mario Guglielmo, the Vatican's Ambassador to the United States.

"An exceptional young priest, Hispanic, serving as Assistant Pastor in one of our most challenging parishes. He's a member of the Holy Ghost Fathers on loan to me. He advocates changes in the Church. A stint in Rome would give him more seasoning."

"If he is a Holy Ghost Father, then there's no question. It's almost as good as being a Jesuit," the Jesuit Nuncio quipped. "What do you see for him in the future, and why Rome?"

The Archbishop elaborated. "I may not appreciate the so-called reforms taking place, but I have projected Church growth in America. The government tilted the previous U.S. immigration law to White Western Europeans, based on their current percentages of population in America. The new Immigration Reform Act that Congress passed in 1965 will change the face of America. Few understand that. The Church must pay attention to the coming immigrant explosion. These new Americans will come from the Philippines, Mexico, and Central America—all Catholic."

Guglielmo studied Doolin, eyes showing interest.

Doolin added, "The Church must establish leadership that these immigrants can identify with. When he acquires more gray hair, Father Garza may have bishop potential. His order specializes in Central and South American missions. Irish-American clergy will become dinosaurs."

Doolin removed his glasses and cleaned them with his white linen handkerchief. *I don't want the Nuncio to see how badly I want this transfer. Maybe the Holy Spirit inspires Garza but I doubt it. The Lord Himself knows my days are growing short.*

"In some quarters they do refer to you as the 'Grand Dinosaur.'" Mario's smile took some of the bite out of the quip. "Would your request have anything to do with conflict on the birth control doctrines, Your Eminence?"

"Your Vatican intelligence is right up to date," the Archbishop said, leaning in, putting his glasses back on. "Do you maintain liaison with our CIA, too?" He twisted the purple-stoned ring on the third finger of his right hand.

"Patrick . . . Patrick. A prophet is without honor, only in his own country. I know you have heard that a thousand times. We all have because there is truth there. It was true for Our Lord and the Jewish prophets before him. You do not receive deserved credit as a loyal son of the Church. If this priest is causing you trouble, send him back where he came from. Maybe he could serve God better in the South American missions?"

"I've considered that, but I've got a growing Hispanic population and they love him. And the Whites, too. If I send him back, it looks bad for me, for him, for everybody. I must do the corporate thing and promote him out of my hair, what's left of it."

"Okay, Patrick. Let me see your population growth projections. The American Church is a mainstay for us financially. Your Catholics are strong in their faith. We must protect both."

"Mario, I fear the floodgates of heresy will open with these Vatican II changes and challenge the flock in ways we can't see. We could breed a generation of Catholics who pick and choose what they want to believe in."

The wrinkles in the Archbishop's face said *I'm worried about this.* He added, "These coming immigrants could restore the American true faith in the Church. We Irish and Italians did. Third-world Catholics know how to genuflect."

Guglielmo nodded. "Right now, we find ourselves preoccupied with the world-wide communist challenge and these internal pressures for change in the Church. Some changes are long overdue; others will perform the devil's work for him. I look forward to your report on America's demographics. I will look into Father Garza's candidacy for the new Vatican Fellowship and see if we can help you."

Archbishop Doolin knew a simple personnel request at these rarified levels guaranteed an automatic outcome. He thanked the Papal Nuncio for his time and walked him down the hall to the elaborate, leaded glass front door.

Decades later, if historians had known about the meeting, they would have concluded that the lunch had been an expensive meal for the Holy Roman Catholic Church. There had been no lunch on October 31, 1517, in Wittenberg, Saxony, when theses had been attached to a church door.

CHAPTER 9

The Black Box

SATURDAY, 3 P.M., AND FATHER Garza sat in the confessional at St. Anthony's Church. From 3 p.m. to 5 p.m., he listened to the sad litany of failings.

Most parishioners at St. Anthony's preferred going to confession with him. He always concluded with "Go in peace and remember Jesus came to save the sinners, and if it wasn't for us, Jesus would be out of business. So, I thank you and Jesus thanks you for stopping by and now say an Our Father for me and a Hail Mary for the sins of the Catholic Church."

Father Garza valued the forgiveness part of the "Good News". He remembered the Bible story where many questioned the Nazarene's authority to forgive sins in his so-called Father's name. The Jewish religious leadership wondered what would happen to their 'eye-for-an-eye' formula—a reasonable principle for exacting what you were owed—if this wandering carpenter's preachings were adopted?

He worked on his own theology of sin, different from the Church in Rome's pronouncements. *Garza don't play that "sin game." The Church says masturbation, adultery, and murder are all mortal sins. Guess that also includes the genocides committed by those Christian Germans. So much for sin categories. My New Testament talks about sin in general and the need for a penitent heart. Momma always said it's the heart that matters.*

Father Garza believed there was an original sin, but not as described in the Baltimore catechism, the little Q and A booklet everyone learned in Catholic grade school. Man's failings derived from an inherited animal nature, not some fictional Adam and Eve who couldn't keep their hands off each other and sinned by eating that one special apple. Parts of the human brain were reptilian in their origins. Human embryos, in an early stage of their formation, resembled reptiles.

We don't come into this world on a level playing field for right and wrong. The deck is stacked against us with the genes and the environment. Jesus knew what his brothers and sisters faced. He called on us to do better, to be better. In itself, that's a powerful message.

That's why I signed on with him.

Weekly black box duty bestowed the chance to peer into men's souls, sometimes to hear muted shrieks and screams. Many penitents sought a kind word or a moment of recognition from someone who would give witness to their daily struggles.

Her hoarse voice whispered, "My adult son is disabled and I am the only one to care for him. His father left years ago, actually a good man but couldn't take it anymore. Left saying, 'I just want a little bit of life. Sorry.' No one knows what this is like. My hours at work help me keep my sanity while a caregiver is watching over him. But even then I worry. My confession, Father, is that I have days when I wish my only son would die. Aren't I entitled to a life, too? I just hope my son and I die within three minutes of each other."

Father Garza could hear the tears running down her cheeks. *How do you hear tears?*

After she left, it was quiet with no confessional lines. He used his rosary to meditate and settle down after the previous confession. One of the guys in The Poker Club, Bill Peters, said he used the trendy Transcendental Meditation by the Maharishi Mahesh Yogi, to Gabe's amusement. Gabe achieved his bliss the old fashioned way, with an unbroken mantra of Hail Marys.

From the clicking clatter of high heels on marble and the perfume, Gabe could tell a woman had entered the confessional booth. The still, stale air now wafted a floral scent.

"Bless me, Father, for I have sinned. It's been two months since my last confession."

"Go ahead, my sister."

"Father Garza, I don't know what to do. My husband and I have five children. He wants to use birth control because we can't afford a larger family. He thinks having more children would be unfair to the children we already have. The Church says birth control is wrong. What should I do?"

"Do you love your husband?"

"Yes, Father Garza, very much. He's the center of my life."

"Does he love you?"

"Yes. We love being married, and . . . we . . . uh . . . that is . . . we like showing our love to each other."

"Well, my dear, the Church teaches that the ultimate guide for each person is their conscience. However, the conscience must be a well-informed one; that is, one that takes into account the message of Jesus and the pronouncements of his Church. In the end, you have to decide. The Church has wisely taken a for-life stand in support of the family."

He chuckled. "We could make the case that you and your husband have already met the obligation to increase and multiply."

"But, Father, aren't there encyclicals and Papal Bulls defining this? Aren't we obligated to follow the pope and the bishops, as God's representatives on earth? There are rules."

My parishioners don't talk this way and they don't argue with me when I'm trying to give them room to live their lives? What's going on? An echo . . . there are rules . . . hmmm.

The fragrance of lilacs in the confessional, stronger now, tripped the mental alarm. *That flower smell belongs to the secretary who stands guard at her desk in the bishop's outer office. That exact smell.*

"My dear, I would suggest you read the Gospels of Matthew, Mark, Luke and John and meditate on the message of Jesus. Then, ask yourself, 'what would Jesus say'?"

"I understand, Father Garza. Thank you."

"You're welcome. Tell the Archbishop I said hello."

Maybe it's time to look into options.

Rome: 1981
It Begins

"Omnes viae Roman ducunt." *All roads lead to Rome.*

CHAPTER 10

Rome

Father Garza's last conversation with the Archbishop sealed the deal.

"Father Garza, have you ever been to Rome?" said the Archbishop, without preamble or chit-chat. His lips flat-lined automatically now when he talked to Garza.

"Your Eminence, it's always been on my 'to do' list." *What's he up to?*

"Well, Garza, it's time you moved it to the top of the list."

Father Gabriel Garza accepted the two-year Vatican fellowship and a working assignment that went with it. *A two-year all-expenses paid program in Rome? I can live with that. St. Anthony's will still be here when I return.*

I'll tell Owen that the December poker club meeting will be my last one for a while. I'm sure somebody can sub for me until I come back—if Doolin lets me come back.

At the December meeting of The Poker Club, they gave me a Christmas present in a big box, wrapped with gold paper and an oversized bright red ribbon. Only me. They said it was from all of them, but I suspected Owen.

Brand new cowboy boots, size 10, medium width. Owen remembered me complaining last winter about my boots leaking when I trudged through the alley shortcuts in the neighborhood. These were the expensive waterproofed Dan Post Men's Albuquerque Western boots. I'd have them for at least ten years if I took care of them.

Man, that brown leather was smooth! Smelled good too. I couldn't wait to start breaking them in. So I put them on right there.

Folks think cowboy boots are uncomfortable, and they are, at first. If you know how to break them in, they will wear like Italian loafers with strong arch supports. When you pull on the cowboy boots you should hear a soft "pop" when your foot drops into the boot.

Pop! There it was. I was in heaven.

You have to wear them around for short periods of time with two pairs of heavy socks while the new boots rub your heels and pinch your toes. They will form to the shape of your feet.

Because wet leather is so pliable, you can change their shape and size by wetting the interior of the boot. It will not ruin the boots. Wear the wet boots around the house, or your rectory. It works.

Use saddle soap on the exterior with its softening ingredients. It also contains beeswax that helps protect the leather. It is used at the horse track to help soften the saddles for the jockeys. Thus, the name "saddle soap."

When you are not wearing your boots, pack them with damp newspapers before storing them. Let the boots dry overnight and then repeat the process. After about a week, the boots should conform to your feet.

Murph handed me a brown paper grocery bag from the Laurel Deli to put my old boots in. Giving up a pair of Dan Post boots is saying goodbye to a special friend. I'd have to decide on burial or cremation.

I shook everybody's hand and gave Owen a shoulder punch. If we were alone, I would've given him a head noogie.

To go with the new boots, I now had three different berets. They all colored coordinated with my Washington Redskins sweatshirts. The black one was for official meetings, those with the Archbishop, or special functions down the street at Catholic U.

The gray beret was for working in the community and most other occasions. The deep maroon accompanied me to The Poker Club.

I would hear occasional background noise, whispers about the political correctness of using the name "Redskin" with the Indian silhouette on my favorite sweatshirts.

I had always admired the strong, respectful Washington Redskin profile in contrast to that goofy-smiling, native American who advertised the Cleveland Indians baseball team. Cleveland never had much of a team.

I'd hate to give up my Redskins sweatshirts. I came up in a time when the only Indian profiles in the American culture were the dead Indians gunned down by John Wayne. Those silly savages rode around the circled wagon trains, yelling, targeting their profiles until the White settlers shot them off their horses.

My grandfather told me the real Indians used a surprise Mongol sweeping attack on horseback combined with the speed of a Nazi offensive. Despite operating as the mini-blitzkriegs of the plains, there were just a whole lot more White people with better guns.

And, there was Tonto, who grunted with a vocabulary of twenty-nine words, none more than two syllables. His job description required him to make the White Kemosabe with the black mask look good.

Modern day linguists note that "Tonto," in Spanish, means "stupid" or "crazy." "Kemosabe" sounds similar to the Spanish phrase "quien no sabe," "he who doesn't understand." A below-the-surface dynamic between the two characters? Is the Lone Ranger a racist who calls his partner an idiot? Is Tonto a subversive when he addresses his White companion as an ignoramus?

Works for me.

At a young age, I tilted to the heroic Zorro for obvious reasons.

Back to fashion-concerns. I didn't have to worry about my bluejeans. The Marxists had not yet won the workers' hearts and minds in their revolution but were succeeding in a blue jeans proletarian look for the new world order. They were becoming a fashion uniform with different brands.

I couldn't take credit for the fashion statement. I just wore Levis.

Thirty days later, Father Gabriel Garza left for Rome to start his advanced coursework in theology and Church history. When he completes his studies, Garza will have a Master's Degree in Church Theology, an excellent credential in ecclesiastical circles; otherwise, not too useful.

Gabe arrived at the stucco building ten blocks from Vatican City. Once white, it was now a grimy beige. The apartment entrance opened off of the cobbled stone alley. *Looks medieval, but probably dates back a mere three hundred years.*

There were forty-eight steps up three flights to Gabe's top floor apartment. He counted the steps because he knew he'd be up and down a lot. *It's a built-in exercise and penitence program together. Good.*

Each floor had its own color character, ranging from dark brown to dark green. Every landing shone a low-watt, uncovered light bulb. He smelled a mix of old wood, fresh paint, and garlic. *If it weren't for the paint, this place would be the anus mundi.*

After he worked the key back and forth, Gabe stepped into the apartment and flicked the light switch. Two large-watt bulbs at both ends of the room came on. He could see pieces of off-white paint peeling from the ceiling. *But unless you ate them, a few thousand paint chips never hurt anyone.* The visual damage report also showed brown ceiling stains from a leaky roof, a small stove, an old refrigerator. *Wonder if the stove does double-duty as a heater in the winter?*

One melancholy window in the kitchen area probably wept when it rained and it stared at a decrepit red brick building thirty feet across the alley he had just left.

There was a well-worn, dark wooden floor. No carpet. *That's for the best. Can't imagine what would be lurking in there.*

The apartment reeked resignation but it was clean and almost dry . . . and in Rome. *Not as comfortable as the rectory at St. Anthony's, but compared to the missions, this is good living. If I were in Manhattan, this square footage would qualify as a loft apartment. So, I could pretend I'm in New York's little Italy . . . in Rome? Too complicated and I can't complain. Where's the john and the shower?*

Gabe went out into the hallway. The "water closet"—European for "toilet"— was at the end of the hallway. *I don't think I even want to see it yet. Need a minute to adjust. I'll be okay. Where's the shower? On another floor? Boy, are we spoiled in the U.S.*

The one room apartment came with a prehistoric wooden table and two chairs, several cooking pans, and mixed dishware next to the sink. At the opposite end of the room, there was a wooden bed frame with slats and a thin mattress, two sheets and one blanket.

My first order of business is the food market down the street and then getting a real mattress. I don't trust that thing. Bet it goes back to when Mick Jagger was a virgin. Those are some ugly stains.

Gabe's daily routine soon consisted of completing his daily breviary and getting to bed by 11 p.m.

Rise and shine at 6:30 to say Mass at 7:30 in one of the chapels at St. Anne's Church, just inside St. Anne's Gate at the Vatican. Quick breakfast at a nearby cafe outside the Vatican wall.

Then off to classes and more Vatican research.

CHAPTER 11

Credo And Crusades

So, I SHOW UP FOR my work assignment. We are a multi-disciplinary team charged with updating the English wording of the Nicene Creed used at Mass, the statement of basic Catholic beliefs. Our first meeting is in the morning. The other meetings will be afternoons.

Our assigned Vatican team leader, a linguist named Paolo Nasrani, wakes us up in class even though it's 8:45 a.m.—that's too early for the Italian representatives—by announcing:

"In 300 A.D. you could be killed *for being* a Christian.

"In 400 A.D. you could be killed *for not being* a Christian.

"How and why that happened has much to do with the credo that we have in the Holy Roman Catholic Church. As you know, 'credo' is Latin for 'I believe.' Re-examining the language of credo, which compels so much in our system of beliefs, could be profound in its consequence. Eh?"

With generational roots in Palestine, Nasrani owns fluency in Hebrew, Latin, Italian, and English. He also possesses a working knowledge of Aramaic and Greek.

He says, "This 1600-year-old proclamation recites the core Christian beliefs in a series of brief statements, starting with 'I believe in One God, the Father Almighty' and ending with 'the resurrection of the body and life everlasting.'"

I place this Nasrani guy in his early forties, intelligent with a restless edge that comes across as feral when he lets his guard down. I watch him closely.

Our black-cassock group of twelve listens intently. I am number thirteen, for good luck, I guess. I wear my usual blue jeans, new Dan Post boots, and a clean Washington Redskins sweatshirt. I brought three with me. I keep a pair of black pants and a black sports coat in my apartment for special occasions—*if the pope drops by to say hi.*

Joke.

Nasrani's eyes crawl up and down my casual ensemble, his face complaining *you Americans.*

But I'm thinking so many people around here dress in black that Vatican City seems like a place of perpetual grief with its somber cloth.

Nasrani lectures. "Despite this 'credo,' this 'I believe,' bitter division wracked Christianity from the beginning as it tried to meet the challenges of various 'isms' over the centuries. These 'isms' have raised their ugly heads for two thousand years: paganism, Judaism, pantheism, Gnosticism, Arianism, atheism, Islam, nationalism; colonialism, capitalism, modernism, fascism, socialism, marxism, communism; consumerism; and Islam—again. Eh?"

Our task force functions as a fluid group coming in and going out as their other work assignments and studies are completed. *Typical Italian organization.* And then I think *that's unkind.* And then, *yeah, unkind but true.*

There is a core group of five of us who do most of the work and research.

With my official Church assignment credentials, I possess direct access to the restricted Vatican archives. One of the oldest libraries in the world, the Vatican library holds 75,000 manuscripts and 1.1 million printed books. Maybe there will be things there no one has seen for centuries?

I find out about the Secret Archives of the Vatican. They were separated in the 17th century, under the orders of Pope Paul V. They contain another 150,000 items. There are fifty-two miles of shelving and 35,000 select volumes indexed.

Since my closet-sized apartment overlooking the alley is only a fifteen-minute walk from the archives, I plan to spend as much research time there as I can. It's not like I'll be back in Rome any time soon after I finish my degree.

I decide to complete my Master's Thesis on the origins of the Nicene Creed, tying in with my teamwork assignment. My thinking—rather than divide my time and energy on two totally different activities—focus everything on one research mission to go as deep as I can.

There's no way I am going back to Washington in an ABT status, "All But Thesis." I know about ABT, a condition for many graduate students who become distracted after finishing their coursework. If I don't wrap everything up before I leave Rome, I won't complete the thesis. I'll be too busy with daily parish duties and run, run, run.

Archbishop Doolin read me right as a loyal son of the Church, despite our disagreements on silly Church externalities. Doolin knows I love the message of the Church and its guiding stability.

Access to one of the world's most clandestine archives will satisfy my historical curiosities. If what I find doesn't directly impact my thesis on the credo, I can attach the research findings as appendices to demonstrate the thoroughness in my Master's dissertation. That will add "gravitas" to my thesis. After all, that's how they play the academic research game, isn't it? Weigh the thesis?

In the fourth week of our work-study program, after my morning classes but before the afternoon work group, I meet Paolo Nasrani for an espresso at Ciampini's near the Pantheon.

Nasrani had given me the historical thumbnail sketch. A former Roman temple, the Pantheon was built on the site of an earlier temple commissioned by Marcus Agrippa during the reign of Augustus (27 BC – 14 AD). The present building was completed by Emperor Hadrian. Almost two thousand years after it was built, the Pantheon's dome is still the world's largest unreinforced concrete dome. Another one of those many Roman tourist attractions.

It's my first espresso of the day. It's Nasrani's fourth. *When in Rome, you do espresso, strong and burning hot.*

After ordering, amidst the fresh aromas of cookies, chocolate bars, and cakes, I share my concern. "Paolo, I know you've been on Vatican thesis assignments for over ten years and have more perspective than I do. But, I'm beginning to uncover Church history that I never heard of before."

"What history?" says Nasrani, sitting in the center of two thousand years of non-stop, world-shaping events. I don't know if his "what history" is a joke or an attempt at avoidance.

I keep going. "I knew about some of these issues in general, but not the details: the persecutions of Arian Christians under Constantine; the bloodletting of the Crusades in Jesus' name; and of course, the Nazi Holocaust. How could this 20th-century crime be committed by a Catholic and Lutheran nation against Jesus's own people?"

"Hm," Paolo says and adds a shrug for *maybe*.

Paolo is short, olive complexioned with black hair and a thin face. *Sometimes I feel the bore of his gaze; those eyes seem to study me, with predatory interest. What is that look?*

I reach into the side pocket of my black sports coat, worn over the sweatshirt—it was chilly that day—and pull out two wrinkled sheets.

"I wrote some notes from my research in the secret Vatican archives."

"Eh?"

I smooth out the sheets of paper on the small cafe table.

"First, this issue of Christianity as the state religion. This is glossed over in our history and religion texts as the conversion of Europe from barbarism to Christianity. This Church/State partnership led to bloody enterprises. For example, Charles Martel, the Frankish savior of Christian Europe from the invading Muslims at the battle of Tours in 732, expanded his empire by compelling adjoining territories, after he conquered them, to convert to Christianity or be executed."

"Go on," says Paolo, as the expert in church history sips his espresso.

"Then some details on the Crusades I didn't know," again smoothing my sheets. "The First Crusade was begun in 1095, proclaimed by Pope Urban II. The battle cry was 'Deus Vult', God Wills It, with the mandate to destroy infidels in the Holy Land. But, here's what I didn't know. The Crusade destroyed thousands along the march to the Holy Land. In the Rhine Valley, Jews by the thousands were dragged from their homes or hiding places and hacked to death or burned alive. In school, they made it sound like Christian boys merely engaged in mischief."

Paolo continues to sip his espresso, expressionless.

"Paolo, they've got detailed records of what happened. It's unbelievable. When they got to Jerusalem, they killed nearly every inhabitant. Here's a direct quote: 'In the temple of Solomon, one rode in blood up to the knees and even to the horses' bridles, by the just and marvelous judgment of God.' This was an eyewitness account of what happened."

"I may have ancestors who were victims," says Palestinian Paolo. "To the Crusaders, the Christians in the Holy Lands wore robes like Muslims and were therefore treated as infidels."

"Really?" I say. "Then, get this. Saint Bernard of Clairvaux declared in launching the Second Crusade, 'The Christian glories in the death of a pagan because thereby Christ himself is glorified.' Are these the same saints my mother told me about as a youngster? I attended St. Bernard's elementary school back in New Mexico; that same St. Bernard?"

He still wasn't reacting.

"Paolo, in the Third Crusade, after Richard the Lion-Hearted conquered Acre in 1191, he ordered 3,000 captives, mostly women and children, taken outside the city and slaughtered. Many were disemboweled in a search for swallowed gems. Bishops intoned blessings while this was going on."

"Wasn't he the king in your American Robin Hood movies?" asks Paolo.

"No, that was the evil King John who took over the English throne from Richard. And then Robin Hood came on the scene."

"It appears to me that King John needed a better public relations manager. Compared to Richard, he was not that awful, eh?"

I try to ignore the flip remark, even though my face is coloring. *He hears me, but is this guy listening?*

"All right, let me read this roll call of crime for what was supposed to be a post-Enlightenment period." I look at Paolo, hard.

"Pope Paul IV, from 1555-1559. Months after ascending to the papacy, he follows the example of the city of Venice and expels the Jews of Rome to a bad quarter on the bank of the Tiber. The same pope burns in Ancona twenty-four Marranos who had fled Portugal. These were Jews who had officially converted to Christianity but saw themselves as Jews and practiced Judaism in secret. In addition, the pope banned the Talmud and all its interpretations."

Nasrani says, "I know well who the Marranos were."

I go on. "Pius V, from 1566 to 1572. He had been the Grand Inquisitor under Paul IV. He issued an anti-Jewish bull *Hebronus gens sola* which in practice meant the expulsion of even long-established Jewish communities.

"This next guy was a real peach, Pope Gregory XIII, from 1572-1585. In his first year, he celebrated a *Te Deum*, a special hymn of prayer and praise, in gratitude for the mass-murder of 3,000 Protestant Huguenots on St. Bartholomew's Eve in Paris. "

Nasrani interrupts, "Again, we know this history. They justified the violence as a preemptive strike, protecting the Catholic crown from a Protestant revolt. Tensions had been building for over a decade."

"Listen," I say, "that same pope planned for the invasion of England and the murder of Queen Elizabeth. He extended the rights of the Inquisition against the Jews and commanded compulsory sermons for Jews in Rome. In 1578 he had seven Marranos executed before the Latin Gate."

"Marranos again," says Nasrani.

Tired, my voice has more sadness than anger now. "Paolo, that's just an outline. It goes on and on. These guys were leaders of the Catholic Church."

I stop and take a needed sip of my now-cold espresso. *Murders and live burnings tend to upset me, especially when my Church performs them. It makes me want to drink a little more of the altar wine when I say Mass.*

Paolo thinks I don't notice how he looks at me in an appraising way. His eyes were speaking, but I don't yet have the means to translate yet.

Do I need to be more careful about what I say to this guy?

CHAPTER 12

Kill Them All!

"Do not think that I have come to bring peace on earth. I have not come to bring peace, but the sword."
GOSPEL OF MATTHEW

NASRANI AND I MEET ONE week later, this time at Caffe San Pietro, down the street from the Piazza San Pietro, which means that every tourist bus passes by on the way to the Vatican. I later understand this stratagem for hiding in plain sight.

"Caffe San Pietro opened its doors in 1775, coinciding with the beginning of the American Revolution." Paolo shares this historical nugget as we take a small table against the cafe wall outside on the street.

I open up with more research findings. "Here's one from where we left off the other day. In 1209, Pope Innocent III launched an armed crusade against Albigensian Christians in southern France. According to the Cistercian writer Caesar of Heisterbach, Arnaud-Amaury, when asked by a crusader how to distinguish the heretical Cathars from the true Catholics, the papal legate answered: 'Caedite eos! Novit enim Dominus qui sunt eius. – Kill them all! Surely the Lord discerns which are his.' Nearly 20,000 were slaughtered—many first blinded, mutilated, dragged behind horses, or used for target practice. 20,000 people!"

"Hmm," said Paulo, as he raises his right eyebrow.

Turning my notated sheet over, I add, "Also during the 1200's, the hunt for Albigensian heretics led to the establishment of the

Inquisition, which spread over Europe. Pope Innocent IV authorized torture. Under interrogation by Dominican priests, screaming victims were stretched, burned, pierced, and broken on pain machines to make them confess to disbelief and to identify fellow transgressors."

Paolo says nothing, looking at me with what seem to be thousand-year-old eyes.

"I'm getting this directly from the Vatican archives. They kept the official Inquisition records, including actual transcripts! The worst part of the transcripts is how the inquisitors justify what they are doing to save the eternal souls of the victims they are torturing."

Paolo leans forward over the black wrought iron cafe table between us. I notice how he oh-so-casually looks around before he closes the space between us and whispers, "My friend, do you think this is news? Why do you disinter that which should remain buried in our history books? Eh? Do we not need to move on? Why revisit this here in the Eternal City, which has seen so much?"

I respond. "Well, my Catholic elementary school history books did briefly mentioned these crimes but glossed over them."

Paolo smiles, a little, "Well, mistakes happen. You must put these actions in the context of the times. My Middle Eastern roots trace back to the time of Jesus and my ancestors witnessed the inexcusable.

Shaking my head, *How do you put these crimes in any context?*

I study my notes while Paolo studies me.

I look up. "I remember reading generally about the Inquisition but listen to what else I pulled from the records. In the 1400s, the Inquisition shifted its focus to witchcraft. Priests tortured untold thousands of women into confessing they were witches who flew through the sky and engaged in sex with the devil. Then they were burned or hanged for their confessions. Estimates of the number executed varied from one hundred thousand to two million over a period of three centuries."

"With respect, Father Garza, there is significant disparity between those two numbers, the difference between venial sin and mortal sin, eh? Always the fixation on sex. Did you know that worms are of both sexes and that any worm can love any other worm?"

"What?" I say. *Another avoidance attempt?*

Paolo displays a half-smile. "What I recall about witchcraft is that Jacobus Sprenger, a pre-Reformation Dominican, wrote a rambling, famous work, *Hammer of Witches*, while at the same time promoting the Marian devotion of the rosary. Twisted irony there."

"How do you know this?"

"Oh, from one of the thesis groups I coordinated, years ago. Maybe only forty or fifty thousand people died in Europe and colonial North America on witchcraft charges between 1400 and 1800."

He adds, "What stayed in my memory from the group's discussion was that the common stereotype of the witch as a gnarled old woman did not reflect that reality in England. In England, they were usually prosperous or important figures in their communities, but not the most likable, eh? There was also a lack of male protection when their husbands died."

"Huh?" I say. *What else are you going to say to this?*

With an unblinking glare, I respond five heartbeats later. "I'm looking at this male dominated church institution differently. The Christian message liberated women from their chattel state in pagan cultures, but we seem to have a ways to go."

One of the seminary arguments against the ordination of women was that Jesus was a male . . . okay, did that mean Catholic priests had to be Jewish and carpenters too? Hmm.

I don't mention to Paolo what I have uncovered in The Gospel of Mary, a gospel of Mary Magdalene not included in the approved texts of The New Testament. It contained a different message with Jesus as the Savior because he teaches people to accept and celebrate their humanity. There is no proclamation of Jesus coming to save, or to forgive, or to make people holy. The focus is on being real human beings.

I think I now recognize a message so different from the guilt-laden writings of later theologians, Augustine and Martin Luther. Guilt is barely present in the early gospels which focus on the message of love above all.

There are four missing pages in the middle of this document. Mary has announced that Jesus gave her special teachings and the disciples ask her to tell them. She starts and that's right where the document breaks off.

A surviving portion of the document reveals how Peter set the tone for the next 2,000 years, giving Mary Magdalene a hard time.

> **Peter responded and spoke concerning these same things. He questioned them about the Savior, "Did he speak with a woman without our knowing about it? Are we to turn around and all listen to her? Did he choose her over us?"**
>
> **Then Mary wept and said to Peter, "My brother, Peter, what are you thinking? Do you think I have thought this up myself in my heart, or that I am telling lies about the Savior?"**
>
> **Levi responded and said to Peter, "Peter, you have always been an angry person. Now I see you contending against the woman like the adversaries. But if the Savior made her worthy, who are you, then, to reject her? Surely the Savior's knowledge of her is trustworthy. That is why he loved her more than us."**

I wonder. *Was this Gospel not included in the New Testament because it was not in keeping with the male-dominated culture of the time? Interesting expression "of the time." Turned out to be all of the time, for the last 2,000 years. Peculiar. Everything else about the Good News is so radical, offering equality in God's eyes for slaves and women?*

I'm going to keep this research about Mary's manuscript to myself, for now. Don't know where it might lead. I'm having too much trouble with what I've already uncovered. And, I don't know how Paolo reacts to all of this.

What if someone is doing reports on me back to my Archbishop?

And then there was the other Mary, the one who was the mother of this wandering, preaching teacher who seemed to be able to reach into men's hearts.

She kept these thoughts to herself. *I agreed with the angel to be the handmaiden. I was always faithful to my YHWH. I agreed to be the unwed mother of who I was told would be the Messiah of the Jewish people. I was twelve!*

I loved my son so dearly. He was everything to me. Those penetrating eyes. The way his tiny baby fist held onto to my finger. The warm intimacy of his sucking the milk from my breast. His grace. His thoughtfulness. And then this god that asked me to bear his son takes him from me, like THAT! Crucified by the accursed Romans between two thieves! I stood there. Three hours. What if it had been three days? Crucifixions can last as long as seven days! This god! He treated me like a stupid young whore. Made me take his child. And then he wrenches him from me in such a fashion!

I can say none of these things to my son's disciples. They would not understand. It would interfere with the message my son wished them to share with everyone. The fulfillment of the Jewish law is proclaimed and there is a new law that there is no law except love for one another.

But, I tell you, God, or Jehovah, or YHWH, or whatever your name is, or whoever you are, I would trade the salvation of the entire Jewish people for one more moment with my beloved Yeshua. He was everything to me. Why did you not ask this of someone else? A daughter of the high priest? Instead, you asked me, a twelve-year-old girl who carried jars of water every day for her mother from the village well, donkey dust between her toes, and who dreamt at night of the newly born lambs in the family's flock—not of men, or sons, or redeemers.

GIVE ME MY YESHUA BACK!

This Mary remained unknown to Father Gabriel Garza.

CHAPTER 13

Troublesome Issues

"Lord," he said to him, "at your side I am prepared to face imprisonment and death itself."
THE GOSPEL OF LUKE

THE WEEKLY TASK FORCE MEETINGS ramped up to three times a week. I shared other troublesome issues. Documented sludge oozed to the surface from the archives.

Paolo suggested we defer these unpleasant findings. "I understand your inquiries, Father Garza. But our assigned responsibility is The Credo. We will meet at separate times on these other matters. I will review your papers. I will take them and make notes on them, eh? Then, I will return your papers to you after I sort your work out."

I nodded okay. *But I feel hesitant giving him my research. He's paying attention, but now he seems too interested and tries to not show it. Or, is he humoring me to shut me up?*

"Paolo. I'll do a verbal summary for you and give you my written findings. You can edit and provide whatever you think is appropriate to the team." *But I'm making a copy of everything I give you.*

After the next task force meeting, Paolo and I remained in the Vatican meeting room. I smoothed my typed sheets out on the aged wood of the conference table. The sheets were the product of my old blue portable Brother typewriter which I brought with me to Rome. Loved the name of that typewriter; spent a lot of hours with it over the years. It was my piano and I aspired to be the Mozart of Vatican research.

"First, Paolo, a theological problem. I made a comparison of the Gospel of John with the Gospel of Thomas. Hardly anyone has heard of Thomas, written about the same time. Thomas proclaims that God's light shines in all of us potentially, not just Jesus. Very different from John who presents Jesus as God incarnate. The gospels of Mark, Matthew and Luke proclaim a view of Jesus as a human being divinely chosen as God's messiah."

Somehow, Nasrani knew about this too. He said, "Many have called this one of the Gnostic writings. It may be more complicated than that. The whole concept of 'gnostic' is up for re-examination. This Gospel of Thomas is unlike any other gospel text and has been an enigma ever since its discovery in the Nag Hammadi library in 1945. Do you wish me to continue?"

"Yes," I said. *Of course.*

"Fine. There is another problem with characterizing the Gospel of Thomas as 'Gnostic.' Based on its textual features, many scholars date it as early as the Gospel of Mark. The Gospel of Thomas shares many sayings with New Testament gospels, but with less elaboration and no narrative framework."

Paolo surprised me with more information .

"A footnote to your findings. Some scholars say that Mark and the other evangelists used titles that Christians today believe indicated Christ's divinity; titles such as 'son of God' and 'messiah,' when those titles actually designate *human* roles. Fifteen hundred years later, when translated into English, these titles were capitalized since they showed that Jesus was uniquely related to God. The capitalization was a linguistic convention that does not occur in Greek. This may have misled contemporary interpretations. Please continue. Linguistics is my specialty and I could not help the interruption. My apologies."

I gave him a slight head nod. *Maybe this guy knows his stuff? Or, just talks a good game?*

I looked down at my list. I went on. "Then there are disturbing historical issues. Colonialism: I have felt the personal touch of this 'ism.' I know the chronicles of the Spanish missions and the New World colonization from my grandfather, whose great-grandfather was an indentured servant, read that as 'slave,' under the Spanish in New Mexico. The cross, following the flag, produced oppression and the eradication of native cultures." I paused, as if the slaughters had momentarily taken my breath away . . . which they had.

"The Jewish Holocaust. I think my Church has a serious apology to make. I've heard all the excuses. My God! Hitler, Goebbels, Himmler, Heydrich and many German Generals were Roman Catholics! Where was the pope when the Third Reich annihilated Jesus's people? The Jews carried the Christ's bloodline. No one else did."

Interpreter Nasrani, apparently also an expert in historical research, responded with a mini-lecture: The Vatican and many in Germany believed they faced two distasteful choices after the civil turbulence and inflation following World War I: communism or fascism.

Communism was godless. The priest who eventually had become Pope Pius XII was appointed Papal Nuncio in Bavaria until 1929. He knew Germany. The Papacy viewed Germany as the only bulwark against godless hordes from the East. The Third Reich's excesses, especially against the Jews, were unfortunate. The Reich would moderate after they established the new European Order.

When he had been Rome's chief envoy in Germany, the future Pope Pius XII, Eugenio Pacelli, had negotiated a concordat with Hitler which promised to preserve freedom for the Catholic Church in the new 'Third Reich,' putative successor to the Holy Roman

Empire. The Fuhrer exacted the dissolution of the Zentrum and Catholic trade unions and a ban on any political activity on the part of the Church's clergy. Governments come and go. The Church remains; that was how to survive for another day.

Nasrani continued his historical command. Many promulgated a vision of European civilization saved by pan-Germanism. They detested Bolshevism and painted the communist East as the anti-Christ. Anti-Semites added the identification of Jews with international communism. The irony: while Marx was Jewish and Lenin was partially Jewish, both had converted to Christianity at some point in their lives.

Because it might complicate a simplistic portrayal of demonic Nazism, postwar history glossed over the European nationals who voluntarily joined the German army with their own military divisions from Belgium, Holland, France, Norway, Denmark, and others. Many were anti-Semites, but some were idealists committed to fighting godless Bolshevism and unifying Europe.

This Nasrani knows his history. I didn't know these things. This guy is only a linguist? Why is he acting like an apologist for these crimes?

Paolo concluded his ad hoc discourse, joking, "Tell me. Why did the Nazis always get to wear the cool uniforms, eh?"

I said, "Hey! Inappropriate given what they did, don't you think?"

"No hay peor burla que la verdadera. There is no worse joke than a true one. The uniform appeals to my Italian fashion-sense, yes?"

That was the first joke I ever heard from the ever-so-serious, flat-spoken Nasrani.

I rejoined, "Maybe the American uniforms weren't as snazzy but there were more of them and they won the war, didn't they?"

He rejoined, "Well, some say the Germans abused Europe's two great drugs: alcohol and Christianity. Eh?"

Was that second joke a non-sequitor or a lead-in to something?

My papers went on and on, revealing a thousand years of inbred anti-Semitism in the Christian cultures of Europe. I started to list the persecutions and pogroms—too many. I said I'd have to find a way to summarize and Paolo agreed.

We discussed Pope Pius XII some more. Our debate started to run hot. I was getting tired. I almost yelled, "If these popes were always invoking the bloody examples of martyrs, why didn't Pope Pius XII die a martyr? Put some skin in the game, you know?" *I don't know if this guy knows what that means. Anyhow . . .*

I said, "His martyrdom would have sent seismic shock waves through Christendom. Maybe it would have slowed down the Fascist advance?"

Someone must have heard me. An elderly nun poked her head in the room, concern on her face. Paolo waved at her, a hello-goodbye, like that British Queen Elizabeth revolving wave on the news.

I took it down to a controlled whisper. "As Bishop of Rome, he had the ability to influence 400 million Catholics! This was when Catholics listened to the pope."

"But Father Garza," Paolo replied with no expression, "the Papacy was on record condemning atrocities by both communists and fascists. Eh? A pope is only human. Do you expect miracles?"

He added with a direct gaze, "Remember, Nazi Germany became a completely totalitarian state. People today forget that the camps also contained German dissenters. The Nazi regime sent entire families to the camps according to the German law of Sippenhaft."

"Zip what?" I said.

"The law of Sippenhaft," he said, adjusting the starched shirt cuffs on each wrist. "It is the principle of families sharing the responsibility for a crime committed by one of its members. It is derived from Germanic law in the middle ages. For example, Count Stauffenberg's wife was sent to the Ravensbrück concentration camp because he tried to blow up Hitler. Stauffenberg was strangled with piano wire. His children were sent to orphanages under new names. They were named 'Meister.'"

Paolo could see my facial reaction. I did not know this.

"Another example, Father. After surrendering Konigsberg to the Soviets in 1945, the family of the German commander General Otto Lasch was arrested with heavy publicity—not for any attempted coup, just for failure and surrender.

"The Nazi penalty for sheltering Jews was death or exile to a concentration camp. It was one thing to throw yourself in front of the Fascist machine, but your entire family? Would you risk the death of your entire family to help a Jew, eh?"

I shook my head. "This is . . . all a lot to take in at once . . . " I trailed off.

He said, "These slaughters and enslavements of the Jews—merely part of their history. Egypt, Babylon, the Roman genocide and Temple destruction, continual medieval persecutions . . . "

Paolo removed a yellowed sheet of paper from his black suit coat pocket. "I have been saving this. You mean no evil intent. You naively believe that the New World is better than the corrupt Old World. Read this."

I did.

It said: **Special Field Order 120:**

> **To army corps commanders alone is entrusted the power to destroy mills, houses, cotton-gins, etc. and for them this general principle is laid down: In districts and neighborhoods where the army is unmolested, no destruction of such property should be permitted; but should guerrillas or bushwhackers molest our march, or should the inhabitants burn bridges, obstruct roads, or otherwise manifest local hostility, then army commanders should order and enforce a devastation more or less relentless according to the measure of such hostility.**

It was dated November 9, 1864, and signed by Union General William Tecumseh Sherman, directing his "March to the Sea" in the American Civil War.

Paolo didn't smirk. He looked like someone too familiar with the night side of human nature. He pointed out there were defenders of Pope Pius XII, such as Pinchas Lapide, a Jewish historian and diplomat. Lapide said the action of the pope and the Vatican saved 897,000 Jews during the war.

I said, "Saving thousands of Jewish lives could not excuse the millions put into death chambers. And, to think these victims carried the same group DNA as Jesus of Nazareth! Where was the Church's witness, except in heroic, isolated cases?"

Paolo said, "Have you heard conspiracy theories presented by former high-ranking KGB officers about a Soviet plot to discredit Pope Pius XII in order to divide post-war Jews and Christians? Or, maybe Pope Pius XII knew the terrifying price that would be paid by his flock if he confronted Hitler outright. The Nazis were fighting the godless Bolsheviks, whose atrocities equaled those of the Germans. If the Bolsheviks won, they would sweep Europe and eradicate Christianity. The communists had already done their best to stamp out Christianity since the Russian Revolution of 1917. The gulags were full of good Christians."

The cords in my neck bulged with tension as I said, "When a people were being slaughtered by the millions, why would a pope not make it clear where he stood? Why should members of our Church, a mere thirty-five years later, even have to debate the issue? This was at a time for personal witnessing by the pope. And the Papacy wants to call itself infallible on matters of faith and morals?"

Paolo said, "I give you one more example of the times. The Archbishop of Utrecht was warned by the Nazis not to protest the deportation of Dutch Jews. He spoke out anyway. In retaliation, the Catholic Jews of Holland were sent to their death. One of them was the Carmelite philosopher, Edith Stein."

I looked down, tired. My espresso, brought in at the beginning of our meeting had grown cold, years earlier, and I said, "Paolo, the

Church of St. Peter has sinned gravely. Do you hear the irony in the words 'the church of St. Peter?' This was the same Peter who denied Jesus three times, to save his own skin. How many times has this Church betrayed the Rabbi?"

"Hmmmmm," said Paolo, eyebrow raised, when I used the word "rabbi." *Paolo's thinking something.* Exasperated, and not appropriate since it could never happen, I said, "What's next? A pope who served in the German Army?"

Paolo Nasrani pulled out fresh papers. "What would you do with something like this for your thesis?"

He handed me a summary of an obscure lecture on "Casualties of Christianity," prepared by Arab scholars in response to Western criticisms of their culture.

The casualty highlights were:

+ **The Crusades: as they slaughtered Jews and both Christian and Muslim Arabs, they said, "Kill them all. God will know his own."**

+ **The European Reformation and Counter-reformation era: The Thirty Years' War alone may have cost Germany 40 percent of its population.**

+ **The African slave trade claimed the lives of ten million.**

+ **The Colonial Conquests: estimated that the native Indians slaughtered in North, Central and South Americas ran as high as twenty million over three generations.**

+ **20th-century warfare: estimated that Christians were responsible for 200 million of the 250 million killed (primarily World War I and II) in the century.**

I looked at him. I wanted to answer that Jesus said, "by their fruits shall you know them." *What do you do with this information?*

He said, "Ver, oir y callar. See, hear, and hold your tongue."

With that, he handed me another file and he watched while I read. It shattered any pro-German argument that he made earlier.

Lebensraum, an ideological element of Nazism, advocated Germany's territorial expansion into Eastern Europe. The Nazi policy Generalplan Ost (Master Plan East) was to kill, deport, or enslave the Polish, Ukrainian, Russian and other Slavic populations and other peoples living there considered racially inferior to the Germans and to repopulate Eastern Europe with Germanic peoples. The populations of cities were to be exterminated by starvation, thus creating an agricultural surplus that would feed Germany. Lebensraum explicitly assumed the racial superiority of Germans as an Aryan master race which possessed the right to displace any people they deemed to be Untermenschen (subhumans).

This wasn't just about expanding borders and getting rids of the Jews. They were going to wipe out additional tens of millions of people! I remained mute. *This wasn't World War II Allied propaganda, was it?* I looked at the file folder again, blank on the outside. On the inside of the folder someone had blackened out most of the words, but one peeked through: "INTELLIGENZA."

Watching my eyes, Nasrani added, "Since we speak of atrocities and ironies, Joseph Stalin was the greatest mass murderer in history. Did you know his mother wanted him to be a priest and he attended a seminary?"

Why did Paolo give me these papers and an expectant look?
Jesus would weep over what we had discussed.
He surely would.

CHAPTER 14

Whither Goest Thou?

More morning espresso meetings before the afternoon group work sessions.

We sat at a little sidewalk cafe, looking at the Trevi fountain one block away. I knew the famous legend that if you throw a coin into the Trevi Fountain you will ensure a return trip to the Eternal City. But Nasrani advised that not everyone knew how to do it the right way. You have to toss a coin with your right hand over your left shoulder, with your back to the fountain.

They collected the coins daily to help feed the poor in Rome. I had become sufficiently Roman now in my thinking that I wondered what percentage was taken off the top?

It was a bubbly Baroque fountain with a sculptured collection featuring a center statue as the Ocean, pulled through waves and reefs in a shell-shaped coach drawn by two sea-horses and led by Tritons—demigods that are half human form, half fish.

Famous scenes at the fountain showed up in *La Dolce Vita*—where Anita Ekberg wades through the pool, a sexual she-wolf challenging Marcello Mastroianni.

While we watched tourists throw their money away, Paolo Nasrani asked, "Where are you going with your archival research, eh? Are you preparing for another Reformation?"

No smile. A joke gone flat. He sounded almost serious.

He said, "I do not have degrees. I was never able to afford them or to secure an academic sponsor, eh? Over the years I absorbed much church history from working with study groups. While my job is to handle their logistics, I have also sat in on their deliberations. I paid attention. That is why God gave me two ears, two eyes, and only one mouth. If I may suggest ... ?"

Nasrani's inquiring look requested an answer.

"Of course, please do."

"You must be better organized. You jump around from one historical period to another; from one blood-soaked atrocity to another. I have seen this in Master's candidates before. They become distracted, immersed and overwhelmed by the millions of records, especially the secret ones which are intoxicating."

He put an expensive vellum sheet on the table.

"As you do your research, here is a short list of things to keep in mind. It will help you especially with your credo analysis, I believe." He gave a self-deprecating smile to accompany the pun.

"Okay," I said as he handed me the fancy sheet with the golden crossed keys of the Vatican at the top of the page. It said:

A SUGGESTED VATICAN RESEARCH METHODOLOGY

* **Group the research findings by similar historical periods or geography. Create structure for the inquiry.**
* **What are original statements vs. what statements have been added at a later historical time?**
* **What was the mode of thinking at that time?**
* **How does what is said compare with the science, and the knowledge of history, at the time of scriptures versus what we know today?**
* **What language is used and are there different meanings for critical passages, with different translations?"**
* **What is the source of the document?**
* **Is the author verifiable?**
* **What was the motivation of the author in composing his writing?**

"These are suggestions," he said. "They may facilitate progress, wherever you want to go with this. Keep me informed, eh?"

I said, "What I'm trying to do is reconcile the contradiction between what was proclaimed by Jesus and what was practiced. My research says Jesus did not create an infallible Church; others did, in his name, to spread his message. And we need a separate conversation about what that message is. When I'm down in the archives, I feel I'm standing ankle deep in blood."

I took a sip from my espresso. I was now hooked on the stuff. If I didn't have three cups a day, I'd get a headache.

"Here's the irony for me. I can easily serve a *human* Church to declare the gospel. Then I am not so put off by the blood on everyone's hands. I feel I can do more within my own tradition if it recognizes its own terrible sinfulness. After all, the Catholic Church is the mother of all churches ... I mean, big! Massive organizational structure. Besides, you know what?"

"What?" he said, sipping his espresso.

"Where would I go?" I heard the whine in my voice which I didn't like. "I am doomed if I have to believe the Church is divine. All could be lost for me. I would be beyond a heretic.

That was a footnote to the whine.

Paolo replied, "It is not my belief but perhaps you could tolerate theologian Hans Kung's thesis that when the Church behaves according to the Gospel, the divine is in the Church. When the Church does not behave according to the Gospel message, the Spirit is not there. An honorable compromise?"

Leaning towards me on the table, "Is it fair to judge the past by the standards of today? Burning witches and heretics, enslaving non-whites, the Jewish Holocaust—these things are impossible to justify today. Examine what happened in the context of the culture back then. Is it reasonable to use a 20th-century measuring stick on 14th-century issues? Perhaps that is one way to look at this history."

"Paolo, the Holocaust wasn't the 14th century. Besides, Jews object to the word 'Holocaust' which carries the sense of a Jewish sacrifice. Their preferred term is 'Shoah,' which means 'catastrophe.' *How can he not get it? I've heard about Middle Eastern cynicism, but . . . something crossed his face when I said this, the shadow of a smile . . . or a grimace?*

Nasrani replied, "A footnote for you, eh? Jewish persecutions are part of European medieval history. Jews had to wear identification on their clothing which made clear they were Jews. Do you know who required it?

"Who?" I said, not feeling good about the coming answer.

"The Catholic Church."

I heard my father's DNA screaming, "When are you going to get tired of the Church's bullshit, son?"

I knew for sure that the Jesus message of love has no cultural conditioning that could ever, in any way, permit persecution, slaughter, enslavement, and extermination. Early Christians witnessed the message of Jesus with their martyrdom. The test for all ages is the message of Jesus. *St. Peter's Church has betrayed its itinerant, preaching Rabbi.*

I know Paolo needs to be careful. His Vatican job as linguist, researcher and tour guide supports his mother and two sisters in their cramped Vatican City apartment. Sometimes, though, he seems too comfortable with the night side of human nature. But I do enjoy talking with him. He's so well versed in history and linguistics. Glad he's on my side. Is he on my side? I'm beginning to wonder if that smell in the Vatican archives is more than old documents? What does betrayal smell like?

We rose from the patio table, full of espresso and tired of atrocity talk.

Paolo walked ahead of me from the cafe out onto the ancient gray cobblestones. He turned and said, "Aqua torbida non lava. Dirty water does not wash clean."

Nasrani mused, walking away. *Ah, this Garza. He is a knight in foolish armor bent on rescuing the damsel tied to the tree without any clothes on, but her long, long hair is strategically placed. She smiles at him and shows little sharp predatory teeth.*

The Whore of Babylon.

<THE CITY OF ACRE (79 miles from Jerusalem): AUGUST 20, 1191 in the Year of our Lord>

CHAPTER 15
Acre

"I give you a new commandment: Love one another."
GOSPEL OF JOHN

DOWN IN THE SUB-BASEMENT OF the Vatican archives, where Father Garza performed his research . . . three shelves over, on the bottom gray metal shelf, misfiled for two hundred and thirty-one years, yellowed parchment documents remained silent in an aged leather satchel, with a sheen of greenish mildew on the outside.

Father Garza stirred a fine ancient dust which made him sneeze so hard that he dropped the notebook he was holding. As he knelt down to recover it, batting spider webs away from his eyes, he detected the old worn bag. He glimpsed a two-headed black eagle displayed on a gold shield stamped into the cracked brown leather. He undid the flap, looked inside and examined the pages.

The last time the satchel was opened, someone had performed a translation of the author's original Latin which was a separate document in the deteriorating valise. The old English was difficult to read. But the writing took him back to 1191.

THE ACRE CHRONICLE: ***Prepared for His Holiness Pope Celestine III by Father Johannes Emmerich, of Dulmen, Westphalia of the German lands.***

. . . Hasanah, Muslim infidel, aged eighteen, mother of four children, three deceased. Husband killed.

. . . Nalkah, Muslim infidel, aged twenty-three, mother of six. Three children with her; three deceased. Husband missing.

. . . Halima, Muslim infidel, aged twenty-nine, widow, two children deceased. . .

These are the two thousand seven hundred names I pen in my journal of the glorious Third Crusade in the year of Our Lord 1191 on August 20, the Friday next after the Feast of the Assumption, at Acre, in the Holy Lands. King Richard has assigned two scribes to assist me. It is most rare to find one skilled in writing, especially among soldiers.

I bear holy witness before Jesus and his Mother Mary that what I, Father Johannes Emmerich, compose is true and further swear that I bear witness with my very eyes to these events.

As one of a dozen clerics, I pilgrimaged to these lands with the army of Frederick Barbarossa of Germany. My red-bearded king died on the way to the Holy Lands, much to the great distress of his army.

When we reached Acre, they appointed me Papal Chronicler, charged with committing to parchment all the happenings of this holy movement to recapture sacred lands for Christendom from the infidels. I took an oath to perform my duties without being bound by advisements, inducements, or threats from any person of whatever rank or privilege.

Pope Celestine III himself will read my reports and archive them in Rome for the future honor and glory of the Holy Roman Catholic Church.

One may question why I write all the names. Those of us from the German lands believe in good record keeping. To us, *order* is a manifestation of the divine will.

In the valleys of the Rhine, the record-keeping helps all remember who owns what properties and who owes whom how much. This, in turn, reduces the opportunity for disputes which can turn deadly. We Germans can be a fearsome people.

In the matter of the debts, we must always have a check on the Jews, who are the only ones permitted to engage in the money-lending. For Christians, this activity is usury, a mortal sin.

Thus, as in the case of property and debt records, I am obligated to transcribe with accuracy the details of these events in the Holy Land. At least they were holy at one time. What they are now, I cannot say. I know Our Lord will glory in our Christian occupation, but would he approve of what is taking place in His Holy Name?

The Muslims are being expelled from the city of Acre which now belongs to the Christians. King Richard prepares to leave the city and advance with his army toward additional conquests.

The Muslims are sickly, barely able to walk. They have had no food for a week and there has been no water for two days in this land of blistering sun. The single column hobbling out of the city comprises only women, children, and old men. Men of fighting age have already been killed in battle or taken away.

Rumors say the men taken will work the fields or mines for one year and be released, according to the July 12 surrender terms.

I overhear the following exchange:

Fatimah, twelve years old, asks her mother, "Is it true that they are taking us to their camp for water and food? Why not bring it to us in the city?"

"The Christians won the battle and want all infidels out of the city," says Fatimah's mother.

"Why do they call us 'infidels?' We worship The One God, as they do. And, what will we do in the desert? Why does that man keep making crosses in the air at us?"

"Fatimah, silence! You ask too many questions. I am too tired. We are at their mercy. They tell us we will receive food and water and be exchanged for Christian prisoners outside the city at a place called Ayyadieh. They order us to bring anything of value since we will not return and we may need to bargain for food. Allah will provide. Allahu Akbar! Enough!"

"Will my father be there? Perhaps Allah the Compassionate has spared him," Fatimah said.

This brings tears to the mother, such as she has left. "No, my daughter, I fear he has been killed in the battles."

"Mother, I have prayed every night to Allah for my father's return. Only when I have been too hungry to pray, have I stopped."

The armored Crusaders form a wall on either side of the starved Muslim inhabitants, urging the file forward as it snakes from the city.

A few crusaders still wear the white tunic with a red cross on it, although by this time the material is filthy and tattered.

There are crusaders as young as fourteen, little older than Fatimah.

It is inappropriate to meet their gaze, but Fatimah peeks upwards with her head down, wrapped in the thin white cotton veil. *Their faces show curiosity, hatred, and a strange light hungering for something, but I do not have a word for this. It frightens me.*

Once outside the sun-bleached stone walls of the city, Fatimah spies the long single column of her people stretching to the distant oasis. Thirsty and hungry, many with swollen tongues, the pace quickens, as they approach the oasis.

"My mother, who are the ones with the yellow star sewn onto their robes?"

"They are Jewish women captured by the Crusaders during their long march. Some are from these lands. The Jewish men and uncomely women were slain, as were the children."

"But mother, are not the Jews the people of Jesus whom the Christians worship? Are they not of the same blood?"

"We do not understand these Christians. Their religion proclaims love, but they slaughter. Praise Allah we are being released, and hush."

The mother observes Jewish women ahead searching those in the line and selectively taking young women to soldiers on the other side of the oasis. *Allah, have mercy! All those they are taking away are young, pleasing girls. The soldiers taking them are laughing, pointing. I do not know the language, but I sense what they mean.*

"Daughter, put your arm tightly around my waist as if you are helping me to walk. And, pull your veil up further on your face."

"But mother, I want to see what is happening."

"Listen to me! Do what I say, or you will not live to see the sun set on this day."

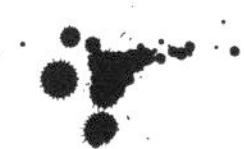

As instructed, his royal tents are set up on the small sandy hill at Ayyadieh, on the other side of the oasis. The King, Richard Coeur de Lion, prepares for a difficult day. Beloved by his English subjects back home, he is a large, golden-haired, handsome man, wearing a royal red cloak over his silver armor. *My soldiers must see me here for this unseemly business. I must steel them.*

"Your highness, the Papal Chronicler is here, as requested," says the armored aide.

"Present him."

Entering the tent and falling to one knee with a bowed head, "My Lord, I am Father Emmerich. I am honored that you wish to see me. How may I be of service to Your Royal Highness?"

"You speak many tongues, priest, including mine. I know you are the official transcriber of today's events. I also know your reports will be dispatched to Rome. I want to guarantee a proper understanding of what I must do today . . . for what *we* must do today in the name of God, who glories in the death of the infidel.

"You see what is taking place. It will continue into the night until we have finished God's work. These executions are swift and less cruel for the non-believers than slow starvation in the desert."

The screams and cries of those being cut open can be heard up the hill, in the king's tent. The cries and moans of the young, still-pretty girls being ravished were muffled, for those were not sanctioned activities—but the king knows.

The king advises, "My soldiers need sport to keep up their morale. After all, these are not Christian women, like some of those in our long march to Acre."

They seize Fatima's cloak, and rip her dirty-white loose tunic from her body, spinning her around. Her pale skin, which has never seen the sun, and which has never been seen by man, rivals in pallor that of the Europeans. The paleness contrasts with her brown face, and brown hands and feet.

The thickset, armor-less Crusader, smelling of old sweat and horses, grasps Fatima by the shoulders, looking her up and down in her delightful, vulnerable nakedness.

"Now, this is a prize. I would have her myself. I hate being in command when I could be taking my pleasure."

Blinded by the brilliant white heat of the remorseless sun, and helpless with fear, Fatimah falls into a crouch with arms crossed to hide her nakedness.

The Crusader yanks Fatimah to her feet by her hair and pushes her toward Little John, standing nearby, the largest fighter in the company and a loyal comrade.

"Have your way, Little John, but be quick. There are so many and we are charged with finishing today. After you have satisfied yourself, you know what you must do. We can only take a few to meet our needs."

"Yes, sir," says Little John, his face growing a smile of cruel anticipation. The Crusaders know the young Muslim women are virgin because of their strict religious code. That means no danger of catching the French pox, a fearsome disease which has infected so many soldiers, leaving them blind, maimed and sterile.

Fatimah shrieks her terror to Allah, flailing her arms and trying to break away. Little John grasps her with his sweat-sheened arms. He drives his fist into her stomach to quiet her and then throws her onto his cloak on the hard sand. He wraps her, a bundle of sticks, lifts her and retires behind a large date palm where there is a sliver of shade.

Other soldiers occupy palm-shaded areas with young female captives and their screams. The soldiers spread open the legs of their captives and take their reward. They will cut them open later for hidden jewels. The lucky ones will be dead beforehand.

It has been forever since Little John has lain with a girl who was not diseased or who did not stink of weeks-old sweat and dried feces.

Fatimah prays, eyes wide with horror, but no breath for further screams: *Allah the Merciful, forgive my nakedness. This is forced upon me. I cannot resist. He is too strong. There is nowhere to go. Perhaps I will be spared if I do not resist? Where is my mother, Allah, please!*

"Chronicler, I tell you why this must take place," says King Richard confiding in me with his royal timbre.

"I know the power of the written word. I want future generations to fully understand this enterprise that I must carry out.

"I do not engage in the unnecessary slaughter of women and children, even when they are non-believers. That is not why I own the heart of a fighting lion. But Salah al-Din Yusuf, the feared Muslim leader, has tested my patience over and over. This Saladin, as he is known, has not met my terms. We agreed on 200,000 gold pieces. He cares naught for these people."

The king swung his royal robe around him, as if to ward off frustration.

"Saladin has stalled our negotiations. He buys time to build forces. He has already sent most of the Christian hostages back, as a sign of good faith. Unbelievable, they did not molest even one of the women. These Muslims are a strange people. But the infidel leader tries to deceive me. Thus, I must declare the lives of the Muslim defenders and their families forfeit. He should have paid what I demanded."

The great English king paces under the royal tent.

"I do not understand him. This is the same leader who, when he took Jerusalem four years ago, forbade his troops to kill civilians or to pillage the city. Why will he not save his own people?"

Standing still for a moment and gazing at me, as if I could answer his question, or maybe absolve him … ?

"August 20 was my deadline. It is now August 20. A king must be strong and seen as such, by both his enemies and his subjects. I leave Acre to expand our conquests. I cannot allow three thousand infidels to remain in this city when we can defend it with only the forces I leave behind.

"Besides, I have insufficient food and water for these Muslims. Saladin's forces limit my resupply by land. All my supplies cannot come in by sea. There are not enough ships.

"I have asked the priests to offer baptism to the infidels as they approach the hill."

He did not tell me then, but I found out later that those few women converting would become camp followers. The others would be stripped and led away to the pit by the Jewish whores, a fitting task for those who rejected their own savior.

Then, by King Richard's decree, they would all be opened up. He has heard that many have swallowed pearls and small jewels. What has been hidden, must be found. He has given this terrible task to the Templars, promising them a portion of all that they find. They are his most loyal troops and he must reward them.

The Lion Hearted One recalls, *Ahhh, but there is one pearl among all the infidel women, my Jew-girl Rebekah. I am glad I promised her mother in the Rhineland to take care of her daughter before the mother was raped and strangled by the Templars. True-believers that they are, Templars have no tolerance for Jews.*

Rebecca knows not what happened to her mother. She was only eleven at the time. She is willing to do anything for my pleasure. She is the best of my women.

After I have made my appearance for an hour, I will retire to my tent and receive Rebeka's special attentions for my pleasure, to the sounds of the screams and cries.

I will clear the tent, saying I wish my repast and for Rebeka to stay with me.

Why do the cries excite me so? She must prolong my fulfillment with her mouth and tongue, for the slaughter will continue the entire day.

Father Garza, having aged centuries in one day, broke off the horrific vision of the past. He gathered his notebook and left the archive sub-basement. Shoulders slumped, he walked past the Vatican City walls and returned to his apartment facing the alley.

A man, working too hard at being a tourist, followed him.

<ROME>

CHAPTER 16
Nasrani

"L'Shana Haba'ah B'Yerushalayim" - *Next Year in Jerusalem.*
OLD SAYING.

MY JOB DESCRIPTION AS A priest requires that I be accepting of God's children—*all* my brothers and sisters. But I didn't like Paolo Nasrani.

At 5'6", with dark furtive looks and a lisp, his effeminate gestures put me off. He's not my type, even with his long Johnny Mathis eyelashes. Paolo was a Mediterranean complexioned Peter Sellers, with Peter Lorre hangdog eyes—eyes that said they may have seen too much. Those eyes . . . you could store loose change in the pockets under his eyes.

He struck me as a man to be seen through with a glance.

He rarely smiled. When he did, with his good teeth, he displayed their whites like a dental hygiene commercial—or like someone ready to bite. Maybe I was jealous. My dad couldn't afford braces for me. Of course, neither could Paolo's—he'd gotten his bright whites from his mother—Mother Nature.

Maybe his Acqua Di Parma cologne irritated me. It misted the handkerchiefs of Italian men with its fresh smell of Mediterranean citrus. Its claim to fame was that both Audrey Hepburn and Cary Grant wore it in their day.

How did I know this?

I confess.

Not having the best shower and laundry facilities, or the time, I needed olfactory camouflage. Every couple of weeks, I'd visit the perfumeries of department stores to request small samples.

The stores reserved their expensive samples for visibly affluent customers. On the occasions of my shopping, I'd wear my one pair of black pants and my black shirt, with the Roman collar, and make sure I had clipped my Vatican I.D. badge on the outside.

Forgive me, but my sweatshirts could get funky without help.

This Paolo Nasrani, a linguist and Vatican City employee, had been assigned to our work group which now met every Monday, Wednesday and Thursday. There could be no Friday meetings because that might interfere with the tradition of a long Roman weekend.

Our credo task force now met in the afternoons at 2:30 p.m. This left the mornings open for those of us who had classes or research to do and also enough time for lunch which could be a drawn out affair.

Occasionally, we met in one of the high-ceilinged conferences rooms of the Vatican library reserved for formal research teams. The Renaissance pictures in the room were priceless, but routine for the Vatican.

This day we met next to the Stanza della Signatura of the Vatican Palace, one of the Raphael rooms. Raphael's paintings were amazing with bright colors and an understanding of light and shade on the human form. He is considered among the greatest painters ever. Raphael had planned every last detail on all four walls and the ceiling. "The School of Athens" was his most famous work.

In this anteroom scheduled by Nasrani, we had to lock our doors, because the tourists next door would barge in. As it was, someone was always rattling the door handle.

Since we were on the Italian clock, it meant we started a little after 2:30 p.m. We would review, discuss and debate until we got too hungry to go on. Our meetings went for two hours, sometimes three.

I confessed my misgivings about Nasrani to a fellow task force member. "Have you noticed how Paola rarely answers a question directly? If it triggers a difficult theological nuance, he has a tendency to change the subject."

I began to wonder about Nasrani's role.

After a month, we should have had twelve Task Force meetings, if you did the math. We had only scheduled seven. Attribute the shortfall to busy people and did I mention we were in Italy?

Nasrani opened a door that could never close again. This was on a Monday.

"Father Garza, I offer you espresso tomorrow at Regoli's after your morning classes. They have wonderful mille feuilles and torts con creme e pinoli. It is near Cipriani's. We can talk more at our leisure. My treat."

I wasn't sure exactly what those foodstuffs were, but the words rolled off his tongue so sweetly, my mouth started to water. But, the piercing look of his dark brown eyes made me wonder if this was some kind of come-on. He kept his eyes on me a beat too long. He may have read my pre-disposition, which I rarely acted on, "Glory to God," as we say.

Nasrani had told me that in Rome and the surrounding area, there are 8,500 bars and cafes and 5,000 restaurants. We could go to a different place for each of our meetings for years and never repeat.

Nasrani changed our planned espresso meeting location at the last minute. He had wanted to sit on the outdoor patio, but rain poured down like it was from God's own personal water closet.

Instead, we met inside at the cafe on Via della Seggiola which specialized in Italian gelato and pastries. Gelato is a form of ice cream and dates back to frozen desserts in Sicily. Ancient Rome made them from snow and ice brought down from mountaintops and preserved below ground.

Never meeting or eating at the same place was an excellent touring technique for busy people who also wanted to sight-see.

I thought that at the time.

Paolo asked me how my courses were coming along and had I learned anything interesting?

I told him my Master's studies required that I re-read the Gospels with a new eye. My professor in New Testament Studies, Dr. Sturzer from Tübingen University in Germany, put forth a radical new theory. *Why always the Germans with the theological breakthroughs?*

Sturzer said, "We know Jesus didn't write anything himself. And the earliest gospel we have is from Mark around the year 70 A.D. This is forty years after the death of Jesus. The experts calculated the Gospels of Matthew and Luke between 80 A.D. and 90 A.D."

Here was the surprise in the latest theories, Sturzer had elaborated. None of these gospels was written by a direct disciple of Jesus. He had disciples with those names, but they weren't the authors. The Gospels were written in Greek, not Aramaic which was Jesus's tongue; or Hebrew which he was likely to have been well versed in.

When I shared this with Paolo, we both agreed that forty to fifty years was a long time to wait . . . and get it right. We noted how people's memories fade and differ just minutes after a traffic accident before they give a report to the police.

But fifty years!

The professor went further and made my head spin. He said that the Gospels were a mix of teachings and reports. "Some were true, some made up. There were things in the New Testament that Jesus had said and done, and things he hadn't. Generally, you could tell them apart. It was separating diamonds from dung."

An example of dung was at the end of Mark's Gospel: "Whoever believes and is baptized will be saved, but whoever doesn't believe will be damned."

That was at odds with everything Jesus had said and in total contradiction with his good news. Along the route of written history, someone had added that to scare someone else."

A diamond was Jesus saying that the kingdom of God was inside everyone.

Instead of proclaiming God's absolute love and forgiveness, many who came after him centuries later preached a doctrine which would condemn people to hell and would only save those who believed that Jesus was the Son of God.

Then, that too, "Son of God," merited its own debate. According to Sturzer, to identify Jesus as the Son of God is to acknowledge his genealogical connection to Israel, his right to the throne of David, and his unparalleled nearness to God.

So, Dr. Sturzer summarized this radical diamond/dung viewpoint. He was careful to label it a "radical-to-be-questioned-and debated-theory;" easier to explain it that way to Vatican authorities, should that ever be necessary, in case they monitored the course, or someone complained about his deviations from approved orthodoxy.

Before the course was over, he went on record to offer traditional theological arguments to undercut the radical diamond/dung proposition. These counter-arguments weren't convincing, mere straw-man constructs. He knew it and we in the class knew it.

When I glanced at Paolo, after explaining Sturzer's lectures, I couldn't tell if he was surprised or just trying on the look. Anyhow, it was time to go. I reached into my pants pocket to check for my keyring. I was hoping I hadn't left it at the apartment or I'd have trouble getting back in since the apartment door was self-locking.

There—got it and I pulled it out. It had my apartment key on it and my car key and the rectory key—*why I didn't leave the car key and rectory key back in Washington, I'll never know, but we are creatures of habit.*

"What's that small silver cylinder on your key chain?" Nasrani asked, with an unexpected interest in his voice. I mean, we were talking about one cheap key chain.

"Something my mother sent me before I came over for the Roman sabbatical. She says she can trace her family back to Spain and that it was handed down from many generations as a religious symbol. Her grandmother always wore it around her neck along with a small crucifix."

I handed him the key chain with its keys and the silver bauble. He inspected the small two-inch by one-inch cylinder.

"Do you know what this is? Did your mother tell you?"

"It's a 'mazu' . . . something. You would theoretically put biblical texts in it. "

"Yes, that is exactly what you would do. Texts from the Tanakh, the Old Testament."

He gave me an appraising look, unusual for Mr. No-Expression. Then his eyes narrowed as he re-examined my key chain and the silver trinket … and then my face.

I reached for the keychain.

"Okay, Paolo. I'll get the espressos next time. Got lots to do. See you."

"Goodbye, Father Garza."

Paolo Nasrani, Vatican employee, watched the American priest leave their table by the window with its outside view, exit the door and walk down the street. The interpreter pinched his right earlobe while he thoughtfully stroked it with his index finger.

This Father Garza—a most interesting man. I suspect he has conversos genes from his mother's Spanish ancestry. It may be why her ancestors left Spain. You could succeed if you kept your Judaism secret. But in Spain, they were always suspicious of conversos, those Jews who converted to

Christianity. As always, the old Spanish Christian natives were covetous, wanting an excuse to take over Jewish lands and wealth.

Like the Jews, this Garza believes in a religion of deed, not creed. "Creed don't feed," Garza had said.

He sounds skeptical of ritualized religion, yet he is a priest. He has seen too many people punch in with their rituals, feeling they are right with God, and then executing nasty deeds. His people wear stoles and robes and miters from over a thousand years ago. Mine wear yarmulkes, black clothes, and long sidelocks . . . well, an exaggeration of course. Even a goy, with saykhel—common sense—knows it to be a stereotype. But this thing, oy vey, always with the clothes . . . ? We should both keep our medieval refineries for special, once-a-year religious theater.

Also like Jews, he seems to be comfortable arguing with God? He questions. Jews encourage their people to explore their own personal relationship with God. This man may be a "God-wrestler."

CHAPTER 17

To Trust Garza?

"Why does evil exist? To thicken the plot."
INDIAN SAINT RAMAKRISHNA

AFTER EXTENSIVE VATICAN RESEARCH AND my meetings with thesis adviser Paolo Nasrani, I was prepared for anything—except what happened.

This was at 11:35 a.m., after the waiter served us espressos with a gelato and pastry at our outside table on the red bricked patio. Nasrani had requested the table with the two chairs by the gray, cobble-stoned street. I had finished the summary of my course-work with Sturzer.

The rattling of motor scooters on the ancient stone streets, pigeons cooing, and passing tourist conversations required us to lean into each other to converse. The sky was steel wool gray and the air thick with humidity. Rain was expected. He had still wanted the table outside.

"Father Garza, whatever your personal preferences . . . and I am not judging here . . . I am not gay. I exaggerate certain gestures to blend into this Vatican culture, this colony of celibates. I am more easily dismissed that way. They see me as 'sacristan de amen'—an amen clerk. I threaten no one and it helps me to hide the anger."

Paolo's lisp had evaporated with the steam of our arrived espressos.

"Anger?" I said. I had colored up at his reference to my sexual preference which I kept hidden and in check. I noticed that his Italian accent was disappearing too. I heard more of the King's English now.

"The same anger I sense in you, the outsider who views the hypocrisy everywhere, from your country to your church. You are a Red man in the world of the White man, eh? You expect them to accept you as an equal, but they never do, do they? Always that slight hesitation, the look-away, the qualification in speech? Or the patronizing attitude when they do help you—'after all, he *is* one of *them*.'"

I did not even blink. Paolo saw the "yes" in my eyes before I looked down. He was hitting close to home.

"You, Father Garza, are the newer generation. *You* can handle these things better. But what can you tell me about your parents? Was their life harder than it should have been because of their heritage? Did your mother age beyond her years, as did my mother?" said with a wintry smile.

"Do you know my mother cannot move her fingers because they are so full of arthritis from decades of cleaning and performing laundry services for Vatican City? The old saying is that no one is a foreigner in Vatican City. Not true. The Italians think they own the Papacy."

Color was rising in Paolo's olive-complected face. His voice now owned a baritone I had never heard before; no more simpering hesitation.

"The wealth they own, their financial dealings with the Mafia—and they refuse to pay a living wage to their employees? Hypocrites."

He touched his right thumb and index finger to his earlobe and rubbed it.

"Can I trust you, Gabriel? I want to trust you."

I looked up from my espresso at two brown liquid pools, pleading. I'm always a sucker when somebody needs help. Of course, the "mother" comments registered on my internal Richter scale. I knew what my mother had suffered. Jesus was close to his mother too, wasn't he? Except for that wise-crack at Cana about the water-wine;

probably taken out of context or a translation issue, if it happened at all. I remembered the Sturzer diamonds-dung thesis.

He persuaded me with the mother-move. "Paolo, if it's important and you worry about trust, then you could tell me under the seal of confession. That's one thing priests are more faithful to than even to their vows."

"Yes. Consider everything I tell you under the seal of confession, eh. I want you to someday use what I tell you, but you may *never* reveal the source. If you do, I am a dead man and my family will disappear."

Sounds rather theatrical. But then, this whole country is a Hollywood set and they have a flair for the dramatic and the waving arms. I remembered the old news reels of Mussolini standing on his balcony, arms folded across his chest, conducting theatrics with his jutting jaw. That was the movie in my mind.

I did not dismiss what he had just said because that was the first time he ever called me "Gabriel." It had been "Father Garza," religiously. Introducing the words "dead" and "disappear" in the same sentence always captured my attention. All the "God Wills It" proclamations in the Vatican archives told me what Holy Mother Church was capable of.

"You have an open heart. Your American sense of fair play and the idea that good always wins appeals to me. But, you are in Europe now with its brutal history and you are in the layered land of Machiavelli. Things are not what they seem."

Paolo's eyes locked onto my face, looking for a reaction. I was trying on one of my inscrutable expressions I had practiced with the Laurel poker club back in Washington, centuries earlier.

"We both suffer the stigma of 'different' because of our ethnicity. It becomes our own personal stigmata, eh?"

Nasrani enjoyed the play on religious words.

" You, because you are Indian in a White man's country. Me, I am disrespected by these arrogant Romans because I do not have money, or titles, or important political connections. Yet, I have bloodlines in Palestine which go back to the time of Jesus. We have a tradition in our family called *The Poem of the Begats*. Each male child must memorize our lineage all the way back to the time of Jesus. I had ancestors who saw Jesus."

His eyes blazed, "Yet, they concede my family no more respect than this cafe chair." The anger flowed off him. I was being presented with a new Paolo. This one was now a stop-or-sprint man, no middle gear.

"Why do I tell you this? Because people I work for believe you will uncover secrets in time with your typical American curiosity. Then you will feel you must do something about it. They do not want that, eh. You must be careful."

There was chill in the late morning, with the Vatican dome just visible over the roof of the apartment building across the street. The espresso wasn't keeping me warm. I felt a shiver. It wasn't the gelato making me feel a frost in my bones.

"If I must, I will tell them everything I have told you, to protect myself and my family. I will say you *insisted* on knowing and I shared information with you to put the Vatican in the best light."

The resolute face looking at me revealed a hint of fear. Paolo's eyes scanned the area around us, using a nonchalant gaze. *That* made me sit up in my chair, with a nervous ramrod for a spine.

There was a whispery intensity to his newly revealed baritone. "I am no St. Peter where I will proclaim my willingness to die with you before I deny you three times. My job and the welfare of my mother and sisters are at stake, perhaps our personal safety."

I looked around. Were there familiar faces, cloaked in different attire from previous weekly meetings?

"If there is the slightest leak from what I tell you, I will deny it and castigate you. The Vatican can be the Lubyanka—without the laughs, eh?"

"Paolo, I give you my solemn promise I will say nothing. I will treat this as sacredly as a confession."

He whispered in this hoarse voice that I always remembered, "I work for the Vatican Intelligence Agency, which is the successor agency to the medieval Inquisition. All Vatican City employees sign an agreement to cooperate on any matters which could affect the

Church. They assigned me to not only serve as your work-study coordinator but to keep an eye on you."

My reaction: *Is this a bad European stage drama? Or, maybe this is just their form of corporate espionage like in America?*

"Paolo, all this cloak and dagger—over research for my Master's Thesis?"

"No. You raise excellent points in your thesis drafts. In fact, I share your views on the need for a new, more profound Reformation. But the Church has weathered theological challenges for two thousand years. Papal offices could bury your thesis findings with reviews and committees and some official declaration would seem to respond but in reality would sweep it all away."

"Then what?" I asked. "What's the threat?"

He rested his right elbow on the table and leaned his face into his hand, obscuring his mouth. But he did not mumble.

"Let us hold the menus up to our faces as if we wish to order something else. Nod your head, if you can hear me and keep looking at the menu."

I raised my menu. I nodded. My face tightened behind the fancy printed paper. I nodded my head again, not knowing what else to do. *Why is he throwing all this at me? And, if it's true, what am I supposed to do with it?*

"You are not just any graduate student. You serve the Archbishop of Washington D.C. who has direct contact with U.S. power centers. You may not be on good terms with this one, but he is old and who is to say what his successor will be like? What if his successor were to take a turn to the left, and what if you became his confidant, and what if you had important historical information? Perhaps you would be Archbishop someday, eh?"

His eyes focused on mine. "Our Church has major confessions to make including all of the atrocities you have uncovered first-hand. I have copies of files that show Church complicity in helping high ranking Nazis escape to South America after the War; materials that reveal Church collusion with the Mafia in financial affairs; files on the corruptions of the Kennedy family from the Nazi-supporting, liquor running, stock market manipulator Joseph Kennedy, to the amoral dissipations of his sons.

"Your Camelot hero, Jack Kennedy, even brought prostitutes into the White House and shared a girlfriend with a Mafia chieftain. The Marilyn Monroe affair was merely one scandal. Your Kennedy Camelot fashioned a brilliant public relations construct as thin as a Hollywood set, to cover the iniquities."

He damned the behavior further by repeating and breaking that one word into four: in-ick-qui-tees.

An old-fashioned, meaty term—"iniquities"—for sins that cover a lot of territory. That was my reaction.

"If the Church does not make the statements of 'I Confess,' then you should use my files to force the issue with the Vatican or through American channels. Confession is good for the soul, eh? The Church must confess or she will have no soul left."

Paolo delivered his chorus of scandal non-stop.

"My revelations are not partisan. The patriarchs of the powerful Bush family and the Koch family supported Hitler before the war. Koch helped construct a major oil refinery in Nazi Germany that was personally approved by Adolf Hitler. Your Richard Nixon committed treason in 1968 to gain the Presidency by sabotaging the almost finished Paris Peace talks. The war went on for another seven years, doubling American casualties."

He handed me a thin manila file folder with three sheets of paper in it. He said, "Here's a NODIS file. Do not ask how I got it. Remember, I work for Vatican Intelligence. NODIS means 'no distribution' beyond who's listed in American security circles. It's a higher classification than 'Top Secret.' With NODIS they can check leaks. This file should never see the light of day . . . unless."

At this point, I think I was beginning to understand what "unless" meant.

I spied the red circled part on the first page.

Kennedy triumphed because of a mixture of luck, risk aversion, and deft public relations. Khrushchev's initial instruction to the Soviet commander in Cuba, General Issa Pliyev, on the night of October 22-23 was clear: "If there is a U.S. landing, use the tactical atomic weapons, but not the strategic weapons until there is an order. He later changed this to an order to use missiles without atomic warheads. If communications had been cut off between the two, or if Pliyev had not obeyed, there is high probability that a U.S./Soviet Union nuclear exchange would have occurred.

It unmasked the old Cuban Missile Crisis from eighteen years earlier. It was scary bad.

I couldn't hand the file back to Nasrani fast enough. So much blood drained from my face, I could pass for Tonto's friend, Kemosabe, without the mask.

"Gabriel, I must find a way to move these documents with you back to Washington where they may do good. From now on we will meet in open spaces and change our movements at the last minute. You need a tour of Rome which I can provide. My insights will give perspective to your work."

I asked, "Are you sure this isn't about my research on the early Church and the Council of Nicea in 325 A.D. and Constantine's Credo?"

He said, "Look who you have on your Thesis Review Committee: a Spanish Fascist and then Ratzinger, inheritor of the Inquisition, although they refurbished the name of the enterprise and updated their tactics for the 20th century. They will let you continue your theological wanderings but keep you . . . how do you say it—on the ranch? Or is it on the reservation? And then there is Brahm, who will do Ratzinger's bidding."

"Close enough. I get the picture. *Yeah. In my case, it's a small ranch on the reservation, next to the railroad tracks. That crack confirms this guy knows a lot more than he's telling. Nice metaphor, given my New Mexico roots. My respect for this guy is growing . . . and my curiosity.*

Nasrani spread his hands and ironed them along the thighs of his expensive gray Canali trousers. He was poor but wore expensive clothes, probably his only pair of dress pants. The Italian manner.

"Next week we'll meet, same day and time, but at the front door of St. Peter's. And, one more thing . . . Gabriel . . . "

"Yes?" I said.

He smiled as if smiles were out of season, which they usually were for him. "We'll talk about it then. It has to do with my family and you must keep it secret."

I wondered, *does Confession really cover secrets as well as sins?*

CHAPTER 18

Sistine Chapel Secrets

"I saw the angel in the marble and carved until I set him free."
MICHELANGELO

THIS DAY, PAOLO WANTED TO show me part of the Vatican Library, located at Cortile del Belvedere, the famous courtyard in Vatican City Called the Numismatic Cabinet or Medagliere of the Vatican Library, the Paolo Nasrani lecture says, "It preserves coins, medals, plaques, seals, tablets, engraved stones, sulfur and plaster casts, and other similar materials. The collection includes about 300,000 pieces."

Waving his right arm in a circular sweep, "The work of the Department consists of inventorying, classifying and cataloguing this material, and making it available to scholars."

He steered me over to the ancient coins section in the corner, in their wood and glass cases. His eyes lit up for some reason. He smiled, "That's a rarity," as he pointed to ancient coins from Jerusalem.

"Some of these are the type that Judas threw at the High Priest," he said.

Then we looked at Roman coins of the Republican Period; Roman coins of the Imperial Period; coins found in the Roman Catacombs; Byzantine coins; and finally Pontifical coins, the largest collection in the world.

We broke off at that point to walk over to the Sistine Chapel.

"Gabriel, it is fitting we meet here under the panels of the Sistine Chapel."

We stood directly beneath God creating Adam.

"We must find a way to forward my files to you back in the states—hidden messages like Michaelangelo's in the frescoes. Michelangelo painted the Sistine Chapel in twenty-five consecutive months in which he labored, a man possessed, from July 1508 to August 1510. He brought to life 343 figures, painted more than 600 square meters of the ceiling."

He paused, looking hard at me. "Listen to everything I say so you can repeat it verbatim if questioned."

If questioned?

I knew the Vatican Museum contained four miles of displays from ancient statues to modern paintings. The jewel was Michelangelo's glorious Sistine Chapel.

Paolo gave me a particular look, at least I think he did, when he shared Michelangelo's personal history. "He was secretly gay. Given the Church's position on homosexuality, I find that ironical," he said. "In fact, expurgation—a cleansing, if you will—of Michelangelo's life began immediately after his death. His grandnephew, Michelangelo il Giovane, in 1623 published an edition of Michelangelo's poetry in which all the masculine pronouns were changed to feminine pronouns, and this remained the standard edition for nearly two hundred and fifty years."

Paolo added, with a half-smile, "I think that's all rather desperate, eh? But those were the times. And here's another irony for you. There are pieces of St. Peter's Basilica that the Romans looted from the Temple of Herod, also known as 'Solomon's Temple.' Herod performed a major rebuild before the Roman destruction.

"Remember this tourist trivia," he cautioned, "in case anyone asks you what I told you in our meetings." He was repeating himself, I guess to make sure I got the message.

I sensed Paolo creating an operating cover—"tour guide for the nosy American priest."

"But *this* nugget of tourism is just for you," he said. "Notice in the Sistine Chapel how many figures are from the Old Testament on that marvelous ceiling. Why? Some believe Michelangelo was making his statement of reconciliation between Christian and Jew."

Paolo spoke whisper-soft, as tourists walked around us, chattering, jostling. Tired children complained, amidst an olfactory cacophony of smells: cigarettes, colognes, perfumes, shoe leathers and sweat.

We spent fifteen minutes under *The Last Judgment*, one of Michelangelo's masterpieces. Paolo noted, "This painting shows the souls of the dead rising up to face the wrath of God. The pope chose it as a warning to Catholics to adhere to their faith in the turmoil of the Reformation. Michelangelo tucked away hidden meanings and symbols because he questioned many matters in his day and he could not confront them in the open.

"One playful example—Michelangelo's self-portrait shows in the painting on the drooping skin of a face held by St. Bartholomew. Here is a footnote for you. Think of Michelangelo as a medieval pornographer. His statue of David, which is not here but in Florence, is too brilliant. You've seen the pictures. He poured more than artistic love into that piece."

At this point, confused and a little paranoid, I wondered what message, if any, there was for me in Paolo's tour choice. *Nothing is what it seems. Could that be the message?*

Then we walked over to Michelangelo's *The Pieta*, located in the right aisle in front of the first chapel. Carved out of a single block of Carrara marble, it took Michelangelo two years to complete the statue. It stood five feet, nine inches, with perfect proportions of the life-size bodies and their relationship to each other, especially the timeless grief of the young mother holding her dead son after he has been taken down from the cross. I doubted she thought of any possible resurrection in that moment of total pain bordering on complete despair.

"Come, let us step over to that white marble column where we can see better."

Paolo and I walked Wizard-of-Oz abreast to the other side of the chapel.

He didn't seem to move his lips. In a whisper, "Here, an item that if it ever gets out would blow the dome off St. Peter's."

What could be that bad, given what I've already heard from him and uncovered myself?

Nasrani's face testified, in *my* parlance, *This is some serious shit.*

"The Church conceals a pattern of worldwide pedophilia among its clergy."

"What! What're you talking about?" I said. "I mean . . . there's always somebody out there with issues. We had one wet-eyed smarmy-type back in my seminary. But everybody steered clear of him."

Paolo replied, "Not random. Not a bad apple in the barrel. Widespread. Bad. Real bad. Most dioceses. Let me repeat that. All over the world, eh?"

"How could something that terrible remain secret?" I said too loud, which made Paolo look around and cock his ear. I listened too.

All I heard were comments from a nearby American touring group. The men's mix of golf shorts and Hawaiian shirts confirmed their patrimony. Most of the women wore modest skirts to hide overfed frames. They all listened to Aldo.

Aldo was providing tour guide services, different from Nasrani.

"Aldo, you keep talking about this René Sance and all the paintings and nice things he made. Where does he live? Can we meet him? How about an autograph?"

"Aldo, has Michael Angelo done anything recently? I get a kick out of his work. Maybe he's got a gallery, if it's not too expensive?

"Aldo, is this where Jesus fought the lions?"

The group moved towards the statue of St. Sebastian, pierced with arrows, "Aldo, I didn't know you had Indians over here too."

But, the real keeper was:

"Aldo, why's that guy hanging on the cross and who is he?"

I couldn't even laugh. I could only look at Paolo who rolled his eyes and said, "All the time. We hear this *all* the time. Last week they asked the tour guide if the epistles were female apostles. Someone else wanted to confirm that Joan of Arc was the husband of Noah."

I could see him relax as he verified no interest in us.

"Bishops move the child molesters to different parishes after someone makes an allegation. The bishop will warn the priest, sometimes get him treatment—which never works, by the way. The bishops have to protect the credibility of the Church. The numbers are staggering. And then the bishops caution the victims and their families that they must remain silent, under the pain of sin. 'One cannot defame the Church of God.'"

That last comment dripped with disgust. He added, "My mind-movie replays a Church-Tin-Man with no heart. Secret Vatican analyses predict the scandals will break in the U.S. first because of your more open society and the secularized news media. Priests, maybe even bishops, could go to jail. The Vatican strategy is to buy enough time for this to become old news. You know, treat it like the Inquisition—'well, that was in the past;' and 'God's Church is made up of men, and men are weak and men sin.'

"In your America alone, our estimate is ten thousand minors have been violated. More than four thousand priests have committed these crimes. It is approximately four percent of your priests. Your bishops protected the priests, not the children."

Then he asked me, "Are you tired yet?"

I replied, "I was tired five centuries ago."

He continued. "The faithful will tolerate silly hellfire threats and the false demands of religious dogma. They will not accept the loss of their children. No one would. They'll purchase indulgences, but will not forsake their young ones to the molestation of priests, even if the robe-wearing bastards invoke God. Again, Gabriel, these are not isolated instances of some men doing bad things. This scandal is rampant, systemic, and covered up."

He looked at me, rifle-steady. "Even if this becomes public decades in the future and even if the pope himself apologizes, things will never be the same. This is bigger and badder than popes having mistresses or selling indulgences. We know what a guy named Martin Luther did about those abuses back on October 31, 1517."

There was a slight tremor in his left eye. From my poker days back in Laurel, I knew it was a tell, but I couldn't read it.

Paolo saw the shock on my face. He mumbled, "Yo sé que me sé, mas de esto callar me he. I know what I know, but will say nothing about it."

Why did I still have the feeling I wasn't seeing the full picture with Nasrani? And, why did his eyes have teeth in them now?

What's driving this guy?

CHAPTER 19

Who Is This Guy, Really?

> "Hath not a Jew eyes? Hath not a Jew hands, organs, dimensions, senses, affections, passions?"
> *MERCHANT OF VENICE*

MONDAY MORNINGS ARE THE WORST for crowds of tourists: noisy, wandering around, lost, on a mission to take in 2,000 years of history before lunch. The din made it difficult to overhear conversations. Nasrani preferred that.

We met at the bottom of the ninety-foot high solid granite obelisk in the middle of St. Peter's square, facing St. Peter's Basilica. He thought it would be easier to identify "non-tourists" that way, out in the open.

Nasrani briefed me on the obelisk and I had to take it in, to maintain our cover of tour guide and tourist.

"It's more than three hundred tons," he began, "and was erected in Egypt more than 2,000 years ago. The history it has seen! Emperor Caligula moved it to imperial Rome. It has witnessed the slaughter of Christians during the persecutions, and the torture of Protestants by the Inquisition."

We walked the square. The tour was over, but Paolo kept pointing here and there to maintain the charade.

He wasn't obvious about it. His eyes flickered left, then right. Sometimes, they just stared straight ahead but were taking in 180 degrees worth of scenery.

I had no idea of who or what to look for. Paolo said it wouldn't be a guy in an olive-colored trench coat, as he tracked the people around us.

It could be a student, a priest, a tourist couple, or a woman and her child. The key was to take a mental photo, move on to another location and take another mental photo and compare. His technique called for us to twist and turn from location to location.

What happened after a while . . . "You know, Gabriel, let us not waste any more energy on 'gotcha," as you Americans would say. Assume we are being watched. If anyone comes too close to us, we will stop talking. Stay a distance of ten feet from anyone and keep our voices low."

"Gotcha," I said. I thought Paola might appreciate some American clergy humor.

"Your research findings are most provocative," he said. "You challenge. You question. You wield historical research like a cudgel against tradition. If your thesis ever received popular acclaim, it might trigger another Reformation. But I know the Church can absorb your 'idle theological speculations' as they will label them, before burying them in the archives which conceal so much."

Maybe it was the matter of fact way Nasrani had described potential surveillance that unnerved me . . . as if it was another day at the office. Maybe it was, for him.

He went on. "They will award you your Master's Degree in Theology, despite threatening current orthodoxy. The Vatican does not want to risk offending the Washington hierarchy, not with the financial support the United States provides to the Church. You are not in the hierarchy yet, but will be one day because I know they are evaluating you."

"What?" I said. "How do you know that?"

He ignored my question.

"Come. Keep moving. We have stayed too long in one place. Watch for tourists who seem to follow."

Paolo's revelation of the widespread pedophilia had sickened me as I flashed on the wet-eyed, tongue flickering, history teacher back in my seminary. He often invited me to his room to listen to jazz and "to discuss things." Never went.

Then Paolo took me beyond where we had gone before. He gave me a typed sheet folded in half in the middle of the tour book he handed me. It read in bold outline format:

* **NAZI RELOCATION ASSISTANCE from the Vatican—50% of person's assets charged for relocation services:**

  Klaus Barbie, Franz Stangl, Adolph Eichman, Dr. Joseph Mengele. Direct and indirect assistance to 30,000 others.

* **MAFIA FINANCING AND THE VATICAN.**
* **NEW POPE JOHN PAUL I POISONED TO PREVENT SHAKEUP AT VATICAN BANK.**
* **VATICAN NETWORK OF GAY CLERICS BLACK-MAILED.**

I gambled.

I gambled because my intuition told me there were too many pieces missing in this puzzle I was spending so much time with, a so-called linguist named Paolo Nasrani.

So I said it. "Hold on. As you expect, I'm shocked over this criminality. But why tell *me*? Who are you really? It will give me more insight if I know the true Paolo Nasrani."

He looked a hard look at me, peering through his black framed non-prescription glasses which spawned a scholarly appearance.

He wore them frequently. His phony lenses were one of my discoveries.

"Now, Gabriel, walk more. Follow my lead as I change direction to keep the same people from coming too close. We move. We keep our voices low."

He had already raised a Vatican tourist brochure to his mouth, pretending it was an idiosyncratic gesture, chewing the top corner.

"This will be under your sacred seal of confession. Yes?"

"Yes," I said.

He said, "Al confessore, medico, e avvocato, non tenere il ver celato. Hide not the truth from your confessor, your doctor or your lawyer. Eh?"

"Yes," I said again.

"And you will die before revealing anything from the confession? Yes?"

"Yes, Paolo, yes. I said yes and mean it."

"You will forfeit your eternal soul if you break the sacred seal of confession, eh?"

"Yes, Paolo."

"Listen to me. Show no expression."

"I'm listening."

Just as I was beginning to question Paolo's real motivations . . . I suspect he suspected what I was thinking. *Why would someone take such risks merely because he felt frustrated in his career?*

It was an 'a-ha' moment for me and revealed the peeling onion of European history, layer within a layer within a layer. Nasrani elaborated on his family's obligation to preserve their history. That was the term he first used—"their history." It traveled farther back, with more detail than he let on at first, to the time of Jesus of Nazareth.

"I am Jewish," said Paolo.

"What!" I didn't mean to be that loud.

"I told you, no expression," he said.

"You should have told me all of this."

"I just did."

"I mean earlier. I should have known this earlier."

"Why?" he said. "You know it now. Are you with me or not?" I flashed on a Jesus-Peter moment in the New Testament.

"Yes," I said, not as strongly as Peter promised his Lord. After all, Peter went on to deny the preaching rabbi three times.

After I heard this family secret, and after the other Church revelations, I sensed there was more.

I found out. There was more—much more.

Are Jews covered too under my seal of confession?

The Year 3793, Hebrew Calendar

<Spring, Jerusalem>

CHAPTER 20

The Argument

"Judas, I know what you are doing."

I looked into those deepset brown eyes that went on forever. They always exuded a special warmth for me, or so I thought.

He trusted me. He turned over the money to me. *Does he know . . . this Rabbi Yeshua bar Yosef?*

How does he know?

"Rabbi, what do you mean? And when will you allow me to buy new sandals for you? Your feet are raw and cut. Those women had to anoint them the other day with special oils. *Is that what you want? Do you need special attention? How does this prepare us for The Revolt?*

"The funds we've given you, Judas, are for the poor when we travel. I have told you to ignore our expenses. We can rely on the people. But the widows, the lepers, the orphans—they have nothing. Do you understand?"

I kept silent.

"My mother, besides teaching me to read the scriptures, also taught me the art of numbers. Your numbers do not add up, Judas."

"Well, Rabbi, I—"

"No more lies, son of Iscariot." *He's never called me that before?*

"You are one of my favorites among the chosen. I admire your fire and your love for our people, oppressed by the Roman invaders."

"Yes, Rabbi. You know my heart burns with hatred for the Roman scum. They slay old men, women, and children and proclaim a great victory to their Emperor. Women and children they do not kill, they enslave. The comely ones, they use to fill their brothels back in Rome. They consider *us* barbarians while their prized roads and aqueducts flow red with the blood of conquered peoples."

Yeshua looks at me, pained as if I am one of his sheep caught in a thorn bush. I know he worked as a shepherd in the hills when he was not helping Yosef with his carpentry work in the poor villages surrounding Nazareth. I am not one of his damned sheep and I will not be treated like a sheep by the Romans in the land God gave to us, the chosen people.

"Judas, it would be better if you stole the money and spent it on the fleeting pleasures of this world for yourself. But you spend it on weapons, planning your uprising. Have you not listened to my message of love from the Father? Even our enemies—we *must* love our enemies."

How does he know these things? I have not shared our plans for the revolt with him. "Rabbi, remember, it was *you* who made the whip of leather cords and beat the money lenders, just last week. *You* overturned their tables. The money exchangers have complained to the Jewish leadership about *you.* I fear what they may have in mind. I hear things."

"Yes. Those accursed money lenders perverted our sacred Temple and made it a den of thieves. It was not Romans who desecrated my Father's house, but sons of Israel."

Jesus's eyes blazed even still at the remembrance.

"The money-changing fees prevent the poor from worshipping at the Temple of Solomon. I witnessed this same outrage against our people when I was twelve, while I participated in a discussion of the scriptures at the Temple. I never forgot."

Looking at me again, his arrow-eyes penetrated my soul as he spoke. "God can forgive me for my anger at the money-lenders. I injured no one, only their avaricious pride. My Father is a God of love *and* a God of justice. The oppressed *will be* vindicated."

That is the good news our people need—justice, not love. Maybe the Rabbi will help us against the Romans? I feel the energy growing in him these past three years as if he has the sun in his veins.

We were on a walk outside the city walls at the foot of the Mount of Olives heading to an orchard owned by the wealthy Joseph of Arimathea. He hid his wealth by putting it in the hands of sons and nephews. One did not raise one's head too high during the Roman occupation.

Called Gethsemane, Joseph had opened the orchard to the people as a walking garden, asking only that his ownership be respected. There was little pilfering.

"I have seen your power, Lord. I thought at first you were a prophet with a new, hidden message to unite our people under the eyes of the Romans. Who can argue with someone who says 'love your enemies?' The Roman spies in the crowds reported back to Pontius Pilate. He laughed away their concerns. I knew you were more than a prophet when I witnessed you raise Lazarus from the dead."

I remembered how friends of Lazarus were angry that you had not come in time to save him. When we arrived at the tomb, no one would come near because the stench of decay in the summer was so strong; no, more than strong, it was sickening.

"Rabbi, how did you know? *Which of my treacherous colleagues informed on me?*

He said, "I may not know the when the end-time is, but I know you store swords for your violence. You betray my message."

"You do not understand, Rabbi. We Zealots need your power to match the endless troops they will muster to put down rebellion. The ruthless Romans will recall legions from across the empire, if necessary."

If you have the power to change water into wine and walk on water and raise the dead, then you can call on YHWH to send armies of fierce Archangels to fight along side us for our freedom. This is a hallowed moment. The people unite behind you, even though your message is full of forgiveness, peace, and weakness. If we can take back our land, then the Almighty will establish a wall of Seraphim around us that not even the invincible Roman armies can penetrate.

Our YHWH separated the Red Sea for Moses. He will surely protect his people, once we unite.

If you and your Father do not do this, we shall perish from this earth. How can you be the Messiah if you turn your teachings to yourself and away from the Jewish people? We know that someday YHWH will install his kingdom on earth. Love will not accomplish that.

I will force the issue. The time must be at hand. Now!

<SPRING, Passover, JERUSALEM>

CHAPTER 21 Conspiracy

THE SWEET SMELL OF ALMOND blossoms—the first trees to bloom after the winter rains—wafted through the thirty acre Temple complex.

That night, scented oil lamps played sinister shadows on the walls of the Temple's meeting hall which overlooked the Court of the Gentiles. Three men consulted in the light flickers of the room.

Joseph Caiaphus, the high priest, decided, "Pay him the thirty pieces of silver. A cheap price to reveal the Messiah, if that is what he is. If not, the Romans will crucify him for stirring up the people. The fool."

Since the meeting in the corner of the large hall was not a public one, Caiaphas had removed his blue headdress, which matched the blue robe fringed with golden bells. Over his robe, he wore a colorful vest-garment embroidered with bands of gold, purple, scarlet, and blue.

Ahijah, an important priest in charge of drink offerings at the Temple, expressed his concern. "What about his follower, this Judas Iscariot? He knows what we are doing. If the Romans torture him, he may tell them we conspired against Rome." Lower in rank than the High Priest, he dressed in his ankle-length, seamless tunic of white linen bound at the waist.

Caiaphas responded, "Do you consider me a fool? I sent a messenger to Pilate and told him we are ferreting out a rebellious plot by this Nazarene and his ragtag followers. Since I am appointed by the Romans, I must keep them informed." The wolfish expression on his face showed his soul—willing to do anything to survive.

"Pilate's messenger offered to reimburse me the thirty pieces from the Roman treasury. It was an insincere gesture. He knew and I knew. It was part of our diplomatic ritual."

From his throne-chair, Caiphas studied his fellow Sanhedrin. He spoke again. "It is our monthly payments to him from the Temple Treasury that place the expensive wine and food on his banquet tables and maintain my position. It keeps the Romans from stealing everything. They figure as long as the cow is providing milk, why kill the cow?"

"Yes, but if this Iscariot is taken and persuades the Romans otherwise?" said Simon, a key figure of the Jewish Council known as the Sanhedrin. Caiaphas served as the head.

"Simple," said Caiaphas. "If this so-called Rabbi Yeshua bar Yosef is the Messiah, YHWY will never let anyone capture him in Gethsemane. Legions of angels will deliver him from the Romans and our palace guard. The Romans will perish like the Egyptian army that tried to recapture us when we left our slavery and crossed the Red Sea."

He stood up, gathered his expensive robes around him and began to pace; unusual for the High Priest who never expressed any emotion.

"If he is not the Messiah, then we will know that night and I have arranged for Iscariot to commit suicide to quiet him."

"I am uneasy about this," said Simon, who had heard the Rabbi preach at the wedding in Cana. He recalled the excellent wine. "Spilling innocent blood?"

Caiaphas stopped his pacing and stood over Simon, glaring at him.

"Do you not understand? It is better that one man dies to protect our people. The Romans always suspect us of having secret alliances with these Zealots. We must sacrifice one of them occasionally to allay their suspicions. I must cooperate with the occupiers or the people will perish."

Simon looked away and then up at Caiaphas, still standing over him.

"You are correct, Caiaphas. We cannot survivc a revolt. The Romans cannot be defeated and would raze our holy city as an example to the rest of the world. That is how they maintain 'peace' in their Empire. They think nothing of annihilating an entire people. In Rome, they are all wicked and rich as if they were the Babylonians and Egyptians combined."

After Judas betrayed Yeshua bar Yosef to the authorities in the Garden ... nothing ... nothing happened. No opening of the heavens. No descent of Seraphim. No miracles. Just brutal beatings and bloody whippings of The Master. Rome had triumphed again.

That night, Judas flung the coins back at the High Priest in the Temple, which was not only disrespectful, but since he had done it in front of others, it guaranteed his immediate death.

Caiaphas whispered to the chief of the guards.

They followed Iscariot out of the city, seized him and hanged him in the same Garden of Gethsemane where they had arrested Jesus.

Over the next days, Caiphas spread the word that Jesus could not be The One because he was dead—a foolish fraud—and his disciples had fled and were cowards.

Rome: 1982

CHAPTER 22

49 Begats

> "I have made a covenant with my chosen one, I have sworn to David my servant:
> Forever will I confirm your posterity and establish your throne for all generations."
> PSALM 89

"I AM A DIRECT DESCENDANT of the man known as Judas Iscariot, if you want to know the truth."

I did a too-loud "what!" and Nasrani warned me with his eyes and a grimace.

"But, how . . . how would you . . ." I couldn't find anything else to say. I couldn't even find the air.

He looked at the nearby group of nuns taking pictures of each other across the way. His eyes narrowed into slits. He was assessing whether we might be included in their picture frames.

"I am the forty-ninth begat. We have maintained a secret oral tradition in my family going back to the time of Judas. We cite the male head of the household, generation after generation. If there is no son, we go to the closest nephew." He put his hand on my elbow and steered me to the right in the open atrium.

"The Gospel of Matthew begins with the lineage of Jesus. There were fourteen generations from Abraham to David, fourteen from

David to the exile to Babylon, and fourteen from the exile to the Messiah. This established the legitimacy of the bloodline of Jesus, according to the prophecies. So the Christians say."

Nasrani executed a quick scan of the area and looked back at me.

"The coming of the Messiah would change the world. Now, given the scandals we have discussed from genocides to pedophilia . . . does it sound as if the world has changed?"

His face said *you know I speak truth.*

"Nineteen hundred years after the arrival of the Nazarene, in one century alone—the twentieth—there was more slaughter than in all the previous centuries. I am not seeing the arrival of salvation and redemption. I think you are starting to wonder too, eh?" He made a sudden move.

"Now, over here Gabriel, we have the . . . "

When Nasrani suddenly interrupted his own discourse, I knew we would change direction. He had seen someone who made him uneasy.

We had started this walking tour in the atrium of St. Peter's Basilica, under a sky where the clouds were shredded like old Kleenex. By itself, the atrium was larger than most churches. Five famous bronze doors led into the Basilica itself.

Nasrani said we would tour the Basilica another day because it was two football fields long and covered six acres. It could accommodate sixty-thousand standing worshippers.

"Besides," he added, "I have a reputation for thoroughness to protect, eh? I must provide you with the best touring services. Remember as much as you can to quell suspicions about our time together."

"But why would you hide the—"

"Why? Why? You ask me after the history you have uncovered? Can you count how many times you Christians would have exterminated my ancestors over the centuries—you who preach love, if our Jewish roots were known?" Fierce anger in his urgent whispering unsettled me. I understood.

"Especially the Iscariot connection? To survive, that's why! To not be dragged from our homes and burned alive. That's why! Eh?"

Burned alive. The phrase stuck in Nasrani's head. It was part of the history of the begat poem he had been forced to memorize. It took him six months. The males had to master the poem before age thirteen and before their secret, always-secret, Bar Mitzvah.

I grasped what was at stake for him: his job, the welfare of his mother and his two sisters; and maybe his own personal safety. The last possibility seemed unreal, but in light of his recent scandalous revelations, it was not only a possibility, but I began to think . . .

Everyone now looked suspicious.

That young couple across the street, holding hands, glancing our way—but they moved on.

The taxi driver who sat at the curb, no fares, reading the newspaper. But, he never looked at us.

"Many members of my ancestral family from Palestine to Europe practiced as Christians, but they kept their Judaism secret.Was Jesus a Christian? Of course not. He was an observant Jew. Saul of Tarsus helped create the new term 'Christian.' Saul persecuted the early Christians and then introduced anti-Semitic elements into his writings to his congregations in various cities. I have often wondered about his aggressive psychology. You see it in his letters. As you Americans would say, 'he doesn't cut anybody any slack.' Maybe he had anger management issues or unresolved issues with his father. Who knows, eh?"

"But how did you maintain all this information, generation after generation?" I asked. "Are you saying you're the forty-ninth direct generational descendant of the original Judas Iscariot?"

"Yes. We utilized an ancient oral practice of poetry and mnemonic devices to aid the long-term memory. Eh? It resembles the ancient

Greek ballad, *The Odessey*, and the Arthurian legends. But this, this is accurate and a secret to our family. Each generation has a Hebrew symbol or name and a two line poetic couplet which preserves the name of the male head and something of descriptive relevance, and maintains the rhythm of the epic."

I started to open my mouth, but nothing came out.

He continued. "We also draw on various literary and poetic devices used in the Psalms and in literature over the ages."

"Like what? I mean, how did that work?" I said.

"Allegory, allusion, analogy, archetype, chaism, comparison, imagery, metaphor, parallelism, personification, repetition, simile, and symbolism. We have a long story to memorize and tell. We need different tools to help remember."

I was impressed. I knew some of these literary tools. I had used them in my sermons back home. But chaism?

"How do you remember all of the tools and what's this chaism thing? Never heard of it."

"First, I memorize and master the tools in alphabetical order. No mystery there, eh? It is my responsibility to select the best tool for my generation and to prepare the two lines of my generational story. A chiasmus, as a rhetorical device, dates back to the ancient Greek and Roman civilizations. Its traces have been found in the ancient texts of Sanskrit and also in the ancient Chinese writings.

Here's an example from Greek literature.

'It is not the oath that makes us believe the man,
but the man the oath.' – Aeschylus, 5th Century B.C..

Here's something more relevant:

'My father Shemuel, slain by the Romans
in the revolt that dispersed God's people.
We hide in Egypt for now.
Aaron ben David, the Third Begat.'"

Nasrani looked at me, gauging my reaction.

"Of course, in Hebrew," Nasrani said, "it rhymed. That's not the best example of a chaismus, but it is the poetry from the third generation, the grandson of Judas. It uses 'ben,' the Hebrew for 'son' instead of 'bar,' the Aramaic for 'son.'

"So . . . let us walk back this way." Paolo jerked a turn to the left in the ancient atrium and apologized for the sudden move. "Forgive me," he said with cheerful insincerity.

"Gabriel, if you betray me and put me and my family at risk, I will say I fed you these fictions in order to—"

"Well, Paolo, since you've gone there, how do I know what you are telling me is true and not stories for tourists?"

Paolo replayed my New Testament knowledge of Judas, with some strange twists and turns. He explained how Judas was among the favorite of Jesus's twelve apostles. Jesus's trust in Judas was only exceeded by his affection for the young John.

Judas had an elongated right earlobe with a vertical skin line on the lobe.

Jesus gave Judas charge of the group's funds.

There was an ancient Church tradition referencing the national zealotry of Judas.

Paolo confirmed Judas' secret membership in that revolutionary sect, the Zealots, who plotted to overthrow Rome and restore the glory of King David. In fact, Judas intended to force Jesus' hand with his betrayal. Judas had been with The Master for over three years. He had seen the miracles.

That's what they were.

Not a magician's slight of hand.

Not shadowy mind-tricks.

They were powers exercised from another place—not of this world. Judas witnessed Jesus growing in his powers month after month. But, Judas felt his own passion for the revolution against Rome thwarted by his rabbi's message of love.

Judas needed the other-worldly power this god-man possessed to match the Roman troops and their swords, which they used with no hesitation, always looking to make examples of someone. Dissent in one part of the empire could spread and must be put down.

Then Paolo said, "There was a betrayal by the Iscariot, but not the one people have been taught. My ancestor arranged for the Nazarene to be turned over to the Roman authorities so Yeshua could demonstrate his power and begin the people's revolution."

Paolo stopped. He casually looked around. Satisfied, he went on.

"Judas did not know if the divine manifestation and liberation would come in the form of plagues visited on the Romans, as in ancient Egypt. Or, would legions of God's angels descend to slaughter the Romans and their Jewish leadership lackeys? Or, would the people themselves rise up, inspired by the carpenter's son?"

Paolo allowed the ghost of a smile to haunt his face. "As you know, the Jewish people did rebel decades later. The Romans slaughtered one million of them and destroyed the Temple. That was a larger proportionate Jewish genocide than the Nazis nineteen hundred years later. That was Rome's message of 'peace' to the Empire.

"Your Church misrepresented our genocide as God's displeasure for we Jews not accepting his son as the Messiah, just as the early Christian church deemphasized the Roman responsibility for the death of your Jesus. In those early centuries, the Christians were not looking to further aggravate Rome, the world power. The Jews were an easier target, and even your New Testament is clear who executed Jesus. Eh? Not the Jews."

Paolo tugged at the left French cuff of his shirt, stiff with starch, extending out one and a half inches from the expensive Canali wool suit coat, for which he told me he had never paid retail, and when I returned a questioning look back then, he had said, "Joke."

Paolo continued. "I will tell you when the exact moment came to pass, according to our family history—when it all changed. Eh? When the great betrayal took place, and I am not talking about just Judas Iscariot."

Nasrani leaned into me with a strong whisper. "Peter raised his sword and severed the ear of the high priest's servant. The Master ordered Peter to put his sword away and The Master miraculously reattached the servant's ear.

"A critical instant. Jesus, through this action, betrayed the revolt. He meant his message of peace, even if it cost him his life. Still, at that last moment, he continued to demonstrate his divine power. All of the apostles knew of Judas' zealotry and when he appeared at the Garden with the soldiers, they knew the time of betrayal approached.

"The Judas kiss signaled the Jewish uprising and The Master rejected it.

Iscariot abandoned the message of love the so-called god-man brought. He wanted to slay Romans, not love them.

"But Gabriel, come back to today. Iscariot's betrayal was nothing compared to the betrayal by the Catholic Church. Jesus says there is no law but to love God and neighbor. Nothing else. Period."

Paolo tugged at his starched right shirt sleeve to align it.

"Your Church and your silly credo have given us a formal catechism of seven hundred and eighty-one pages. It competes with the Torah and all its lengthy written arguments.

"You know your Church atrocity litany now, as I do: Crusades; Inquisitions; corruption; the continual slaughter of the people of Jesus' bloodline; the burning of witches and books. Worst of all, imposing a culture of spiritual terror, totally obsessed with sin and eternal damnation, contrary to the 'Good News.' Can you believe it? A church institutionalizes terror by threatening eternal damnation to unrepentant followers and to non-believers. Where is the message of love in this?"

Nasrani held both cuffs in front, confirming alignment and nodded to himself.

"The ironies . . . the ironies. So tragic. Can you imagine in God's eyes, the blasphemy of saying that the pope, one man, is infallible? Even Jesus was wrong about some things.

"Then, in typical Roman Church fashion, they try to walk back the 'must believe' doctrine of infallibility by qualifying it: 'Well . . .

it is only in matters of faith and morals, and it is only applicable when performed in the context of the sense of the Church body.'"

A slight Nasrani headshake from one side to the other. "I cannot translate that silliness, and I perform translation services for a living."

Nasrani makes a good case. That is the church's party-line. Sounds weak when he describes it that way.

Nasrani continued, "This man from Nazareth proclaimed a message which transcended all—greater than the Renaissance, greater than science, greater than democracy—all of it."

And here he leaned into me, his smart Italian tailored coat brushing my sweatshirt, and with a lowered voice, "He was *not* God and he was *not* the Messiah!"

Nasrani face featured a far off look, ready to succumb to the gravity of living. It was as if he wasn't present, in our present, but maybe looking across forty-nine generations?

"I think you believe me, but let me provide you more information," Nasrani said.

"More information?" I said. "I'm still trying to wrap my mind around what you've told me before, and just told me today." *How can there be more? This is already unbelievable.*

"Go ahead."

"Look at my right earlobe," he said.

I looked. *Seems normal to me; slightly elongated; nothing weird.*

"Do you see the single line crease running up and down the earlobe?" he said.

I looked closer. There it was, like a prematurely old man's wrinkle, but one running vertically parallel with his body.

"Every male member of my bloodline has that crease, that slight fold, in the right earlobe. *Every* male member."

He seemed amused at my surprise.

"Gabriel," he said with that look again, "there's more. Ever hear of the Mortara case?"

"No," I said.

"The Jewish boy kidnapped by the pope in 1858. For me, that is three Begats ago. For me, recent history. He was a third cousin. No one knows this."

"Huh?"

This Nasrani was one surprise after another. He said, "Edgardo Mortara, six years old, was taken from the family home on June 23, 1858, in Bologna, in the Papal States. He was one of eight children of the Jewish couple named Salomone and Marianna Mortara."

"Why did they take him?" I asked.

"Pope Pius IX authorized the police seizure because Edgardo had been secretly baptized as an infant by a servant girl when Edgardo was ill. There were no witnesses and there were questions about the truthfulness of the girl. Some accused her of looking for financial gain.

"The entire matter became an international incident. There were twenty New York Times editorials against what had taken place."

"Unbelievable." What else could I say?

"Edgardo was adopted by the pope and entered a seminary in his teens."

I said nothing.

"According to canon law, which was law in the Papal States, non-Christians could not raise a Christian child, even if the child was their own."

What ran through my mind was the scene where the disciples prevented children from seeing Jesus because they thought he was too tired. That's when he said, "Suffer the little children to come unto me." Or something like that.

Not only were the new disciples up to their old tricks with this pedophilia scandal Nasrani had told me about, but kidnapping kids? What an outfit! And I'm part of it?

"Gabriel . . . "

"Yes?"

"The pope defended his decision against critics, again in a speech in 1871, 'Of these dogs, there are too many of them at present in Rome, and we hear them howling in the streets, and they are disturbing us in all places.'"

How does he know all of this verbatim, with total recall? Paolo, I suspected, was more than smart. He was probably camouflaged-brilliant. And, if I were him, I'd know this too, verbatim, but I wouldn't be able to keep my composure. Of course, he's had practice over the years, hasn't he?

"Jeezsus. . ." It slipped out. I rarely took the name in vain. It was a professional pride thing for me.

"No *Jesus*, Gabriel. *Our* Jesus would never do this. Would never allow this."

I heard him. But, *"our Jesus"?*

"And, there's more."

I wanted to turn my back on "more." I looked at him, expressionless. I was out of expressions.

"Edgardo Mortara entered the Augustinian order, was ordained at age 23, and adopted the name *Pius.* Father Mortara was sent as a missionary to Munich, Mainz, and Breslau to preach to the Jews there.'

I didn't say it this time. I knew there was more.

Nasrani finished the story. "He was unsuccessful in convincing Jews to convert. You know how hard-headed we can be."

Paolo answered my next question before I asked it.

"I tell you these things because you are a spiritual person. A religious person follows the teachings of his church; the spiritual person rightly follows the guidance of his soul. Eh?"

Of course, there was even more, but no time for Nasrani to share. The old stories would stay within the family—

After the sun went down on this beautiful spring day, with the bluest sky, the kind where God shines down on the just and the unjust, there would be two hundred and eighty dead Jews laying outside their homes, if the homes were still standing and had not been burnt to the ground by the raging Catholic mob, in the small village forty miles from Krakow, Poland.

The bodies were symbols of a historical irony. From the founding of the Kingdom of Poland in 1025 through to the early years of the Polish-Lithuanian Commonwealth created in 1569, Poland was the most tolerant country in Europe. In some places, it was known as the "paradisus Iudaeorum," Latin for "Paradise for the Jews." Over centuries Poland became the home to the world's largest Jewish community of the time. Three-quarters of all Jews lived in Poland by the middle of the 16th century.

There had been three hundred and seventeen Jews in this small nameless village. A few heard early rumors and fled. Some were warned by Catholic neighbors who planned to take their homes before the evening mob could burn them down.

Some Jews always escaped, especially if the pogrom rampaged at night. This one had to happen at night because maybe God couldn't see it as well then? And, it had been such a fine day after the long, harsh winter.

Jacob Abramovich knew Jewish history well, part of his family obligation in being the 34th Begat. He had cultivated Catholic friends knowing this day might come; if not this generation, maybe the next. The important thing was to protect the bloodline.

And, of blood—

It looks and smells differently.

Fresh blood has a sickening moist, sweet, metallic odor and can look like bright paint, depending on the light available, if there is any.

It is not bright red for example next to the heads of people in the night, more blackish lying next to the raging fire consuming their plundered homes.

And, when blood congeals and dries from overnight, it turns a rust color with not much smell, except for those piles of stripped bodies where the blood still stands in pools—better not get too close.

And now the village was going to have to clean up and figure out what to do with the bodies.

The village would not have to explain to anyone about the atrocities—the looting, the raping, the butchering with clubs and knives and farm tools—because the authorities had given the wink and the nod.

Local nobility owed too much to the Jewish money lenders and the best way to resolve the debt was stirring up the people with a pogrom that would chase the Jews and their accounting records out of Poland and into Russia. Besides, Poland was Catholic; Russia practiced heretical Orthodoxy and did not recognize Rome.

This 34th generational descendant of the Iscariot had left the village late that afternoon with his young wife and two small children in the wooden cart pulled by their horse. They told everyone they needed to visit ill parents in Warsaw.

They moved with haste as the dusk at their backs tinged red.

CHAPTER 23

Researching Credo

"The opposite of faith isn't doubt; it's certitude."
Father Gabriel Garza

Gabe's official Vatican map reports that the pre-500 A.D. section of the archive, in the main building, runs under a major Vatican street. The lighting is dim; it is humid, and no one has wiped the shelves down for decades. He sneezes on the dust, a thin layer of gray snow everywhere.

Gabe locates the file drawer with microfiche from the era of the Nicene Creed, adopted by the Council of Nicea in 325 A.D. The microfiche references an 'Emperor's Credo.' *I've never heard of 'The Emperor's Credo.' Need to check this out.*

Two hours later. *Finally, something. I've been going through these damned microfiche rolls most of the afternoon. This slide on the roll is showing a copy of the Emperor's seal.*

A prefatory statement announces that the Emperor, in preparation for the Council of Nicea, has ordered that a basic statement of Christian beliefs be approved. This credo must reflect the life and Gospel of Jesus of Nazareth and should unify the Christians in the empire.

The preface also certifies that since the early days of the Christian religion, bitter disputes wracked different communities of believers, whether or not to follow the Jewish laws; and debates over the humanity and divinity of Jesus. All professed Christianity.

Constantine declares in the Emperor's Credo: "It is in the interest of God in heaven, and his representative on earth, the Emperor, that there be a binding statement of beliefs to unify God's kingdom on earth. There cannot be divisions within God's people."

There are obvious political advantages to this statement for the Emperor because it strengthens the power of his reign.

This credo, pre-dating all official creeds proposes a natural, easy-to-understand manifesto, capable of uniting *all* Christians. The implications stun Gabe. No more need to argue how many persons in the Godhead; or which person is subsumed or equal to. This says if you believe in a loving God, with Jesus the Messiah as his special messenger, and that the only law is to love God and neighbor, and that you will be raised from the dead, as Jesus was, then that's the whole ballgame. Work out your best interpretations of how to love God and neighbor. It is recommended that you follow the example of Jesus, the carpenter's son out of Nazareth. Discuss it, if you wish, but those who adhere to the simple credo are Christian.

The insights from this early credo strike like lightning when read together with the earliest books of the New Testament and Gabe's archival research:

+ Jesus was a devoted Jew and practiced his Judaism.
+ Jesus preached first, if not exclusively, to the Jewish people.
+ Jesus and his disciples believed the end of the world was near.
+ The early followers of Jesus were considered a Jewish movement within Israel.
+ Saul of Tarsus, later known as St. Paul, became instrumental in taking the Gospel to non-Jews.
+ What Paul preached to them was based on his own visionary experience. Paul's revelation from Jesus took place seven years after the crucifixion. This was in contrast to the original apostles who spent years with Jesus in person.
+ There was bitter debate in the early Church about whether the message of Jesus was for Jews only, or for gentiles as well.

- + Jesus never intended to found a Church.
- + There is no evidence that Jesus was seen as God in his lifetime.
- + Paul described "God was in Christ."

Jesus was not a god-person inhabiting a human body or a divine visitor to earth. He was a human being through whom God manifested himself.

An early reference in St. Paul's First Epistle to the Corinthians, says "Let there be no factions." *Looks as if they were having problems with factionalism way back then, too.*

Anything within the confines of The Credo is bona fide, true Christian. Gospel means "Good news." Take the good news to the world.

Could this ancient credo provide a platform to unite all Christians? How powerful might that be? How do I clarify what the "good news" of the gospel proclaims?

Catholic theologian Hans Kung presented a compelling insight. A colleague of another reform-minded theologian, the former Monsignor Joseph Ratzinger of Germany, Kung had served as an expert theological advisor to members of the Second Vatican Council until its conclusion in 1965.

Kung outlined how there were different Christian denominations going back to the time of Paul: " . . . we should undoubtedly identify the Catholics with the party of Cephas . . . the Eastern Orthodox would be the party of Apollos . . . the Protestants would certainly be the party of Paul . . . the Free Churches would be the party of Christ himself, free from all the constraints of the other Churches, their authorities and confessions . . . "

Kung concluded with: "A Church is identical with the Church of Jesus Christ only to the extent that it keeps the faith with Jesus and his cause."

If this simplified credo, with these Kung insights, could make it onto the world stage, could there be a new Christian reformation, without the killing of hundreds of thousands as in the Reformation of the 1500's? Could there be a new unified Christianity? What would that mean for the world?

Updating the words and phrases of the credo into contemporary English isn't the challenge. Nasrani's linguistic toolbox could handle that.

From studying the source documents, it is now clear that the ratified Nicene Creed, not the Emperor's Credo, promulgated a compromised statement of belief to pull the factions together.

Father Garza reports back to the credo task force.

"The Emperor himself approved this final political declaration defining Christian belief. He wanted one religion to support one empire and one emperor. As the archival history details, Constantine was a bloody emperor, recognizing the rapid growth of Christianity. Cynically, Constantine knew he could play up the part about 'Render unto Caesar what is Caesar's, and unto God what is God's as a universal requirement for obedience from his subjects. Behind the scenes, Constantine worked with Bishop Eusebius to create the doctrine of the earthly authority of God made manifest through the Emperor—a statement that this was the natural order of the universe. That statement did not make it into the new creed itself, but it did become a prevalent Church-State philosophy for hundreds of years throughout what became the Christian empire.

"I know, I know—rather convenient for the Emperor."

Several team members raise their heads from their note taking.

Gabe looks around. His blue jeans and sweatshirt contrast to the room full of black cassocks. *At least they're listening.*

"In today's time, Constantine's Credo could be read as a liberating document saying feel free to have your own sects. Stay within these boundaries and you are Christian in your belief. No need to slaughter each other over theological nuances."

Gabe notices Paolo Nasrani taking rapid notes as he speaks. Nasrani sits in more and more meetings when Gabe presents findings.

Father Garza continues. "My research leads me to conclusions I did not expect. In Jerusalem, or Rome, or Washington, or Moscow, or Beijing— this Yeshua bar Yosef, raised in the dusty village of Nazareth, presents a definite security risk—to all authority, at all times."

All eyes fix on Father Garza. He has deliberately used "Yeshua" instead of "Jesus."

"If Yeshua came back today he would be put to death: by the Americans; or the communists; or the Muslims; or the Mafia; or the military industrial complexes; or even the churches; maybe especially by the churches—not only today, but at every point in history.

"This original Gospel message threatens all human institutions and governments and churches and synagogues and mosques. God and love of neighbor reign supreme over everything else? He who brings this message must be silenced!"

Garza has raised the volume on that last sentence for dramatic effect, to take the measure of the room. Furtive glances are exchanged around the antique wood table. Nasrani looks up from his frantic note taking and smiles, just a little.

Father Garza raises a different Yeshua possibility, but shares it only with Paolo Nasrani, not the task force. Was Yeshua gay? Garza has always controlled his personal orientation through his vow of chastity. He has seldom slipped over the years. Yeshua was Jewish, through and through. Yet, he never married? This certainly contradicts the strong Jewish tradition of producing children, a commandment from God to Abraham.

The ancient Jewish culture practiced strict sexual segregation. Yet, it's clear from the Gospels that women were drawn to this Yeshua as a person and without any sexual inference. They felt valued by Yeshua, compared to their culture at the time—never threatened or diminished by him.

In the Gospel of John, it refers to the disciple whom Yeshua loved. Is it a translation issue with different meanings for "love" or something else?

Gabe says nothing because it would transgress an unspoken boundary. Some might even react with violence.

I need to check with Nasrani. He's our languages guy, he can help me. In several ancient languages, there are various translations for the word 'love.' Some mean erotic love; some mean close friendship; some mean family relationships. I hope Aramaic doesn't have as many meanings for the word "love" as the Eskimos do for "snow"—they have fifty different words for "snow."

I asked Paolo. "Could an 'outsider' orientation have helped Yeshua from Nazareth look at the world and society and the nature of man and God in a new radical way, a way which identified us all as sinners needing redemption—whatever sin and redemption were? Wait a minute! That's the point; that's *old* Church talk. Yeshua didn't emphasize sin, rather a call to be better. And, there *was* the promise of another life.

"Maybe he understood, without the benefit of contemporary science, the impacts of nature and nurture on each individual. That's why the only one to render judgement should be God, not the Jewish law or the Pharisees, or a Roman church hierarchy of supposedly-celibate, old men. What do you think?"

Paolo says, "Father Gabriel, since you ask these questions, you might be interested in a secret Church rebuttal of a 1930's book by Arthur Darby Nock."

Paolo, sensing my interest—or orientation—secures the Nock book. Just before he hands me the book, at the next week's meeting, a sheet falls out and floats under the table.

I observe the sheet upside down on the ground and see fancy gold leaf that reminds me of Archbishop Doolin's church letterhead.

No surprise there. Church officials could use the same logos, just as they are all trained alike and think alike.

Paolo summarizes the book for me. "Nock raises the possibility that Saul of Tarsus was a deeply repressed gay man. Paul's epistles contain an anti-feminine tone; he is himself unmarried, as noted in First Corinthians. He speaks several times of a 'thorn in his flesh.'

"The psychology behind Saul's conversion could have its foundation in the new religion's proclamation that all are included in God's love, and nothing can place us outside of that.

"Of course, Saul, formerly the strict Jew, now Paul, liberated by the good news, spreads the message of universal love, without limitations, to the world. God can work in mysterious ways. Eh?"

I too had heard that somewhere.

We had no further discussions of Nock.

A Paolo Nasrani might suggest that Father Garza does not anticipate how the night side of human nature—the one that would crucify Yeshua in any epoch he might appear in—would receive this unsolicited opportunity for massive Christian unity. Problems, perhaps?

What if Garza came to the same conclusion as Rabbi Heschel that God is greater than religion? Greater than any religion, every denomination, every time-bound ecclesiastical manifestation?

A Paolo Nasrani, with his several faces, might suggest too that Father Garza adopt caution and pay attention to the American gonzo journalist, Hunter Thompson. Thompson shrieked, "It's clear to me—and has been since the age of 10 or so—that most people are bastards, thieves and yes—even pig-fuckers."

Religious synthesis could be so threatening that the end would justify the bloody means.

What Nasrani knew—threats need to be removed. He and Garza must continue to be very, very careful.

CHAPTER 24

Credo vs. Credo

"They do me empty reverence, making dogmas out of human precepts."
GOSPEL OF MATTHEW

"You are not a human being in search of a spiritual experience. You are a spiritual being, immersed in a human experience."
TEILHARD DE CHARDIN

FATHER GARZA TAKES THE TASK force to school on what he has put together.

The Emperor's Credo declares:

WE BELIEVE IN THE ONE GOD.
GOD IS A LOVING GOD.
JESUS WAS BORN OF THE HOLY WOMAN MARY.
GOD WAS POWERFUL IN JESUS OF NAZARETH.
JESUS PROCLAIMED THERE IS NO LAW BUT TO LOVE GOD AND NEIGHBOR.
THE ROMANS TORTURED AND CRUCIFIED JESUS.
GOD RAISED JESUS FROM THE DEAD TO SHOW THE WORLD THE TRUTH OF HIS MESSAGE.
WE MUST FORGIVE EACH OTHER.
THERE IS A LIFE AFTER THIS ONE.

Father Garza compares the emperor's short statements to the official, compromised credo coming out of the Council of Nicea, which history labeled The Nicene Creed:

> We believe in one God, the Father, the Almighty, maker of heaven and earth, of all that is, seen and unseen.
>
> We believe in one Lord, Jesus Christ, the only Son of God eternally begotten of the Father, God from God, Light from Light, true God from true God, begotten, not made, one in Being with the Father.
>
> Through him all things were made. For us and for our salvation he came down from heaven: by the power of the Holy Spirit he was born of the Virgin Mary, and became man.
>
> For our sake he was crucified under Pontius Pilate; he suffered, died, and was buried.
>
> On the third day he rose again in fulfillment of the Scriptures;
>
> he ascended into heaven and is seated at the right hand of the Father.
>
> He will come again in glory to judge the living and the dead, and his kingdom will have no end.
>
> We believe in the Holy Spirit, the Lord, the giver of life, who proceeds from the Father and the Son.
>
> With the Father and the Son he is worshipped and glorified.
>
> He has spoken through the Prophets.
>
> We believe in one holy Catholic and apostolic Church.
>
> We acknowledge one baptism for the forgiveness of sins.
>
> We look for the resurrection of the dead,
>
> and the life of the world to come. Amen.

Father Garza looks now at his Church's official creed with hesitation. *Where is the mention of the devil, or birth control? Or being gay? Did I miss something? These two creeds are such different documents! What happened?*

Father Garza shares his theory with the task force, based on his months of tedious research in dirty file rooms with poor lighting. "Constantine convened the Council of Nicea. He invited three hundred bishops, and paid the traveling expenses of many. The bishops, having suffered under Constantine's predecessors, were a sorry lot; missing limbs, eyes, and generally in poor health from torture, but strong in spirit.

"Constantine insisted on a brief, simple statement that would unify everyone. Bitter theological quarrels about nuances of the Trinity held no interest for him. His credo offered a religious-political statement resolving differences in a declaratory fashion. The final product of the Council would carry penalties for those who did not sign on.

"But how to reconcile the original simple Emperor's Credo with the compromised product of debate and negotiation from Nicea?

"The Gospel of Mary, quoting Jesus, says, 'Go then and proclaim the good news of the realm. Do not lay down any rules beyond what I determined for you, nor give a law like the lawgiver, lest you be confined by it.'

"This gospel was written as early as The Gospel of Matthew or maybe later, about the same time as The Gospel of Luke. The person of Mary is presented as a confidant of Jesus and a leader of the disciples after Jesus leaves them. Mary's teachings focus on being true human beings."

Father Garza has had time for nothing else but this research, not even time for his daily breviary obligations which take an hour a day he no longer has.

What Father Garza does not say: *This Mary-Gospel means that everything beyond The Good News is symbolism, pageantry, myth, embellishment, and Phariseeism!*

It makes sense for people to organize themselves to spread the good news, and to create a way for the communities of believers to support each other through this vale of tears we call life. Someone, or something, must be the legitimate interpreter and depository of beliefs and doctrines—right?

If you must do a Bible, seven sacraments, priests, a mass, go ahead, if it helps you through the dark night of the soul. But, don't mandate it. Don't confuse the icing with the cake.

Father Garza continues his report back to the work group. "Here's the bottom line, my friends:

"One God.
"One Message.
"Too many messengers.

"Above all else, do not kill each other over interpretations of The Message. Remember, the whole law and the prophets, and the churches are subsumed under 'Love God and neighbor.'

Father Garza edges closer to a dogmatic cliff. "My continual reading, studying, and praying on this research confirms the truth of a minimalist theology for Christianity—back to basics. God is the unknowable. We cannot comprehend Him (or Her or It). An old Jewish saying testifies, "If I were to know HIM, I would be HIM." Yet, some Christians insist on decreeing three persons in a Godhead? Why not two? Or twenty-two?

"From science, we know that in the earth's far past, 99% of all species on the planet were wiped out. Geologists discovered how the earth has lurched from one terrible disaster to another. Astronomy pictures a universe of random violence. The stardust making up humans comes from metals created by supernova explosions, the destructions of other worlds. Were those exploded worlds previously inhabited with life forms?

"Here's the description of God by one of the guest lecturers from India at Catholic University down the street from my Washington, D.C. parish.

God is a huge elephant.

We are ants.

The ants residing on the elephant's tail say, 'God is a rope!'

The ants on the elephant's large rounded legs say, 'God is a thick tree!'

The ones on the tusks say, 'God is a spear!'

The ones on the ear of the elephant proclaim, 'God is a hairy rug!'

Each perspective of the ants is a different religion.

"Another lecturer, this one a Jesuit from South America, advocating liberation theology, joked that when he died, the first thing he was going to say to God was: 'Where were you in Auschwitz?'

God would reply, 'Where was man?'

Could the Jesus message be even more basic? There is God who loves you and there is a reason for this vale of tears.' That would be a profound message by itself because all science proves otherwise—there is no purpose for this existence. Science says we are all part of a cosmic, random-chance playground, driven by Darwinian rules. We inhabit a biospheric blue rock hurtling through a random, violent universe, without meaning."

Father Garza concluded with, "That's all folks—for today."

When Father Garza puts his Church research together with the theological science of the French paleontologist Father Teilhard de Chardin, he concludes that if Jesus came today, he would still preach his message of love of God and neighbor—all else is measured against that.

Yet, the findings of Chardin would see Jesus explaining life in terms of advanced physics, too. It would be something like: "Here's how you have evolved as the creation of the universal presence, The Cosmic Consciousness. We intuit this presence; sometimes, we experience it indirectly. We are all driven by impulses that are part of evolutionary patterns. We are called upon to be better in order to evolve."

For example, the compulsion of every cell to reproduce to "live forever" drives human behavior, although it is not recognized in the conscious mind. Human minds read this as "desires" or "drives." It is deeper than that.

Christianity is the call for humanoid mammals to take the next evolutionary step to a higher state of consciousness. In his combination of paleontology and mysticism, Chardin predicts the integration of all personal consciousness as the second coming of Christ. He views humanity as the axis of the cosmic flow, the key of the universe.

Jesus sensed the overwhelming constraints that evolution, cultural norms and DNA put on each person, although he did not have the science at the time. Yes, all were called to "salvation," but how to measure each person's progress toward salvation depended on what kind of baggage each brought to their life journey. And, why did it have to be "measured?"

The Gospel of Mary, unrecognized in the official New Testament texts, contradicted the fire and brimstone that was preached in the Lord's name. Sin is presented as an illusion. The new life in Christ makes sin negligible.

His poker playin' friend named Murph, back in Laurel, Maryland might say people's salvation depended on what kind of cards they were dealt at birth, and what they did with those cards.

That's what Father Gabriel Alphonso Esquivel Garza thinks, too. He suspects that theologian-paleontologist Chardin would agree with him and the Murph. Gabe could hear Chardin: "The problem the Church had, he said, was that she continues to live in a universe in which the rest of us do not."

CHAPTER 25
Secrets

"A chi dici il tuo secreto, doni la tua libertà. To whom you tell your secret you surrender your freedom."
PAOLO NASRANI

WE MET AT GIOLITTI'S, ROME'S most famous ice-cream establishment. It was only a five-minute walk to the Pantheon. We took the black wrought iron table and chairs outside on the patio. We always sat outside now.

Today, the pollution created a sky that was blood-colored, as if from a thousand cuts.

Paolo preferred the street noise, and church bells and vendor bustlings—cover for conversations. The tourists always moved by at a steady pace. Anyone slowing near our table would stand out, except for the waiter. We went silent when he took our orders.

The truth—I still felt shock at what Paolo had shared with me in previous meetings. Heavy stuff.

I tried to lighten up our meeting. "Paolo, at least I *know* Jesus was Jewish, for sure."

Paolo looked at me through his phony non-prescription glasses, not knowing how to react.

"Jesus went into his father's business. He lived at home until he was thirty. He thought his mother was a virgin. And his mother thought he was God."

Paolo returned a wan smile.

Guess not all American humor translates well. Timing is important too.

Should have learned that from Murphy's W.C. Fields imitations at the poker club back home.

So I added, "By the way, no one calls me 'Gabriel'. Anyone who doesn't call me Father Garza, calls me Gabe. Only my mother calls me 'Gabriel.'"

Wagging his finger at me, "I call you 'Gabriel.' You make me think of Psalm 151: 'And YHWH will direct the Archangel Gabriel to blow his mighty trumpet before all peoples, believers and non-believers, so that they shall see clearly, and their false gods and their false beliefs shall be unmasked. This revelation shall change the world and the Lord will be justified in the truth.'"

I know the psalms from the Old Testament, many verbatim. I thought there were only one hundred and fifty of them?

Paolo shared more blockbuster revelations with me, barely moving his lips, raising his eyes to me without raising his face. He admitted it was piecemeal. He possessed transcripts, affidavits, and bookkeeping records, but also gossip and secretly overheard conversations. It covered a lot of territory from the Mafia, to funneling CIA money to Solidarity through the new pope. *What a cast of characters!*

Nasrani confided, "Pope John Paul I died on September 28, 1978, after only thirty-three days in office. Rumors whispered he was poisoned and insinuated the Mafia and dark Vatican financial dealings. The pope was asking too many questions. Worse, he planned major financial changes. You never mess with the money."

There was a slight tremor in his left eye, "That which happens in Rome, they wish to keep in Rome, eh?"

Then, "The KGB was plotting ways to discredit the new Polish pope. They were preparing to intimidate former staffers back in Poland into saying he had an affair with his secretary and an illegitimate child."

With this, Paolo smiled and said, "Well, at least he was wired the right way . . . sorry, Gabriel." Then Paolo removed the grin as if he was afraid someone would see his face and suspect him of humor. For some reason, he seemed to think that would be a mistake.

John Paul II's election in 1978 changed things.

In Poland, it began. Not in East Germany or Czechoslovakia. Then the freedom push spread. Why in 1980 did they lead the way in Gdansk? Why did they decide, now or never? Only because there was a Polish pope.

There were rumors of young Polish clerics within the Vatican, who on nomination declined to be ordained, and then left the church without notice, leading to conjecture that they were, in reality, KGB agents.

And . . . new speculation. The Polish pope was cooperating with President Reagan and the Saudis to bring down the Soviet Union. Ron and Karl worked the political and spiritual angles. The Saudis planned a timed collapse in oil prices that would cave the economy of the Soviet Empire. The Soviets were propping up a paper-thin economy with major subsidies from their massive oil sales.

Other Nasrani files hid explosive Kennedy materials. Camelot had been tarnished over time back in the States but still commanded reverence. The public considered Edward Kennedy a possible national candidate someday. If the true Kennedy files were ever revealed, political ambitions would be stomped into the ground by the light of day.

My hope in the Polish pope faded, like my fascination with Camelot. He was walking away from Vatican II reform, and Camelot would be disinterred with its decay evident to everyone.

Paolo briefed me on our all-too-human Church institution which did what many institutions do—look out for itself. From Pius XII forward, the Church metastasized into a savvy international holding company with a maze of offshore holding companies used for money laundering by the Mafia. There were rumored slush funds for Italian politicians. This American archbishop, Paul Marcinkus, who was running the Vatican Bank often said, "You can't run the church on Hail Marys."

Paolo's sources predicted the collapse of Italy's largest private bank, Banco Ambrosiano. They advised Paolo that the Mob planned hits on the investigators looking into the bank's irregularities.

Banco Ambrosiano's chairman, Roberto Calvi prepared to make a run for it. To where, Paolo didn't know. All he could say, "When certain people are after you, the world is too small, eh?"

I looked off into the distance. What could I do with this information? Maybe, as Paolo suggested, I could bide my time, wait for the right opportunity. Maybe these findings could create another Woodward-Bernstein moment for ambitious reporters and force major Church reforms?

But how much of these revelations were truth, half-truth, or poetic license?

I read the notes again that Paolo had slipped to me inside the large tour guide. *Unbelievable!*

Paolo spoke to the look on my face. "This world is a wicked place."

One of the members of our work-study group, on a limited budget, had recommended Dolce Maniere, a buzzing basement bakery. He recommended the fresh panini, slabs of pizza, pastries, cake and obscenely cheap cornet—Italian croissants. He guaranteed I couldn't go wrong. So, I suggested it to Paolo, my treat—a rarity.

But Nasrani frowned and shook his head when I suggested it. I thought maybe it was the distance, twelve blocks from the Vatican. I realized later when I walked by. It was the downstairs close quarters and the possibility of being overheard.

We settled on another place, more open, with the patio on the street, similar to the other restaurants. Although the skies were clear, there was the sound of thunder, a bit dim and distant like God trying to clear his throat.

I worked it early into our conversation, more explicit than my previous hints—"why?"

"You want to know why, why I tell you these scandals?" Paolo said. "To show how serious I am. One misstep by you, one thoughtless word, and my family and I will disappear. Not sure who would do it, but it would happen.

"I knew you would ask my motivation. It is religious, eh? Are you surprised? Yes, I am Jewish by secret heritage. I have no apology for that. But, I believe in part of the message that Yeshua delivered. The Gospel of Thomas affirms this, not the Gospel of John.

"The Gospel of Thomas does not proclaim that Yeshua was a pre-existing entity with God the Father, as the Gospel of John would have you believe. That is blasphemy. God is unknowable and beyond our comprehension. You cannot know that which is by definition unknowable.

"The Gospel of Thomas provides the key insight. There is a pulsing seed of God in each person. We must take care of each other because we are all part of the wonderful oneness, although I have reservations about the 'wonderful' part."

Nasrani's eyes burned my face.

"And I like the message of love and forgiveness that Yeshua brought. I believe it because I *want* to believe it—not because I *have* to. I do not accept *my* 'an eye for an eye.' and I do not accept *your* 'no salvation outside the Church.'

"This is where I agree with your favorite theologian Hans Kung, whom *your* Church keeps trying to excommunicate. As he says, these basic Christian beliefs make me a better human being and give my life more meaning."

"What am I supposed to do with all these secrets, these files?" I said.

Paolo sat a little taller at our table on the outside patio at the new cafe, then leaned towards me and looked right into my eyes. "If you want to know the truth, start a true Second Reformation. But this time, take it all the way. We must remove this reliance on ritual that so dominates your Roman Church and my Judaism, even to this day. Our God is too big to constrain with rituals, rules, and doctrines."

Paolo ended, "My loathings are simple: stupidity, genocide and religious myths. Selah."

Then there was the elderly, nondescript couple, studying the window across the street with its cheap merchandise. *I could swear the last time I saw that old guy, he was wearing glasses and a hat.*

Last week, I identified a twenties-something fellow with sunglasses leaning against his powerful looking red Benelli motorcycle, smoking, bored. But he left when Paolo and I left, and then he disappeared as I walked to my apartment with the dead end alley entrance.

I saw him go by on the street behind me, without looking back. From my side view, I thought he was smirking.

I asked Paolo about the motorcycle guy with the imagined smirk at our workshop meeting the next day. His response, "Probably." Then he added a chilling, "They wanted you to see him so you won't notice the others."

"The others?" I said.

Paolo gave me that Italian shrug with the head tilt and the raised palms. It meant *who knows? What can we do about it? What do you expect?*

He said, "Now do you believe me? Gabriel, you're not in the U.S. or Kansas any more. Eh? Watch out for black Fiats with special plates that have SCV on them, Stato dell Citta del Vatican—Vatican City."

Boy, that's one articulate shrug. That's what I thought.

I didn't pay attention before. Too busy. Now I took mental pictures of my apartment in the morning.

In the evening, still there . . . coffee stains on the top page of the thesis draft, just as I left it. But it had been moved two inches from the little pencil mark on the table under the papers.

That troublesome cabinet door above the sink that never closed all the way because the wood was warped—was closed.

My mattress wasn't squared off on the bed the way I had made it.

Sweet, sweaty Jesus.

CHAPTER 26

Nasrani

"The vocation of the Jewish people is to listen to God in all his manifestations and to be a people of God in the midst of other peoples."
PAOLO NASRANI, THE FORTY-NINTH BEGAT.

I WEAR DIFFERENT HATS AND perform various jobs to support my family. I have other names, too.

I convene the research teams. I expedite theses. I provide translation services. I serve as tour guide when needed. And, I do other things.

So, I arranged for the Garza thesis defense in Constantine's Room. I closed the room to tourism when the review committee met. Some Vatican museums have a reputation for inconvenient hours and galleries closing without any notice. Today, we would live up to that reputation.

The room was on the upper floor of the Vatican museums. The room displayed frescoes designed to look like tapestries proclaiming Christianity's victory over paganism.

On the wall to the left of the entrance, Constantine addresses his soldiers and sees the vision of the cross. I sat under the fresco of the baptism of Constantine, opposite to the wall which held the Emperor's historic vision. I twitched facial movements from time to time to make it look like I was paying attention.

Everyone thought Raphael painted the frescoes. He didn't. I knew that. His assistants painted them during the Italian renaissance. It was my job to know these things—and more.

Once in a while, I play my little games. Just like Paolo Nasrani is not my real name. "They" would understand how poetically sardonic my assumed names are: "Paolo" for "Paul" and "Nasrani" which means "the Nazarene."

The Arabs have a term for this "camouflage." They called it "taqiyya." It means that deception and concealment are permissible when they are necessary. So, if a Muslim were to find himself in the midst of a group of Christians, and in danger should he reveal his Islam, he should say that he is a Christian. What does it matter? The truth can be elastic? Eh? So, I am a Jew in the midst of a group of Christians.

Of course I want them to view me as religiously respectful.

In truth, what I am respectful of is the potential of this Father Garza's thesis which can take us back to the turning point of the new Christian Church in 325 A.D. Then, the church began its unfortunate transformation into an imperial power with the trappings and formulations of a Roman enterprise.

CHAPTER 27

The Thesis

THREE LARGE BLACK BINDERS, ONE for each member of the review committee, announced Father Gabriel Garza's Master's Thesis. The bold print on the first page inside the binders said, ***A HISTORICALLY BASED EXAMINATION OF ORIGINAL CHRISTIAN BELIEFS*** **[Back to Basics, Using the Credo as a Means of Christian Unification].**

The thesis summary:

> **Based on direct source research from the Vatican archives, and a professionally executed historical methodology including the books which became the early Gospels, we can establish a valid statement of early Christian beliefs which can serve to unify Christianity and accurately reflect the message of the Jewish Jesus of Nazareth.**

Wordy, but that's how they do things in academe, Gabe thought. You just have to figure out the game. I've always been pretty good at that. Probably some "Indian-survival DNA."

Since Father Garza had enjoyed direct access to Vatican documents dating to the early centuries of Christianity, he presented his thesis with a sense of authority, perhaps like the child Jesus in the temple preaching to the rabbis.

The three-member thesis review committee shifted in their seats and glanced at each other, not used to graduate students speaking on Church history with such competence. They had received their draft copies a month earlier. This was the formal unveiling, usually followed by a choreographed inquiry taking two hours over espresso and pastries in a collegial atmosphere as they welcomed the Master's candidate into the ranks of Church academe.

Instead, the chair of the Committee, Archbishop Alonso Quijano from Granada, Spain on a six-month sabbatical to Rome, opened with a cross-examination, no welcoming pleasantries.

He wore a stern expression full of conviction, designed to intimidate. Gabe had seen it before and done better by his old boss, Archbishop Doolin.

Paolo, in an earlier cafe chat, recalled to Father Gabe that Granada had been a seat of the Spanish Inquisition.

Quijano carried himself with that regal authority than only a slim, 6'3" Spaniard can command, because the Spanish generally come in smaller sizes. "Father Garza, I studied your thesis with great interest. Your scholarly research and citations are flawless. You quote original sources."

The pupils of his eyes were as black as a snake; his mouth thin and cruel like a poorly healed knife wound. Quijano reeked of stale cigarette smoke. Yellow stained his teeth so badly to make it appear that Spain had not yet discovered dentistry. But then, he came from the land of Franco where there were no elections to contest, hence no need for good teeth and hair. His right two fingers were a permanent nicotine brown, as were the nails. Nasrani had also said in an earlier cafe conversation regarding the Archbishop's habit, "Amor, tosse, e fumo malamente si nascondono. Love, a cough, and smoke are hard to hide."

"Based on the conclusions you present, please advise this Committee why we should not immediately initiate proceedings against you as a heretic? Father Garza, if this thesis represents your theological perspective, why are you a priest or why even remain Roman Catholic?"

Any other thesis candidate might have been stunned, but Garza was on full alert. He had even worn his black cassock and a borrowed roman collar for the occasion. No blue jeans and no Redskins sweatshirt today.

Father Garza, veteran of trains running next to his New Mexico house, frigid seminary winters in Michigan, and the violence of his impoverished Washington parish, quipped: "Your Eminence, since Adolph Hitler was Catholic, and was in a monastery as a young man and considered becoming a priest, I would hope there is still room for me here."

At once, the other Committee member, Cardinal Joseph Ratzinger, who had served in the German Army as a youth, but was from an anti-Nazi family, choked out: "I am familiar with that era and I am also personally aware of how many blessed members of the clergy were slaughtered by that devil in human form and his evil minions."

This is just like being back with the Archbishop in Washington, Gabe thought. *Better fix this, fast.*

"Forgive me, your Eminence and Cardinal Ratzinger. I should not have been flippant. We Americans can be like that. Begging your pardon, let me explain," said Father Garza. "May I?"

"Please do," said Quijano, a rictus for a smile forming.

"No," replied Cardinal Ratzinger. His eyes blazed with injury. "We need to clarify the matter of the Nazis and the self-righteous remarks made by Father Garza." He remembered how, at age fourteen, he had been conscripted into the Hitler Youth, but refused to attend meetings.

Ratzinger hesitated. He turned to the third thesis review panel member. "Antonio, respond to him. I am too angry." Monsignor Antonio Brahm, another tall lurking-type, had both German and Italian roots. He was from Basel, Switzerland.

"Father Garza, the German people bear the responsibility for electing Hitler with forty-three percent of their electoral vote. Many believed their only choice was between Hitler or the godless communist hordes from the East with their endless People's Committees.

"Once Hitler came to power, he constructed a total dictatorship, complete and ruthless. Your comment about Hitler and the generals being Catholic—it was like the Mafia in the United States taking over the government. They are all Catholic, are they not? At least, the Italian ones. How much dissent would you have with a one-party Mafia government?"

Ratzinger's face was still flushed, but it was Brahm raising the decibel level. "How many people would speak against it, Father Garza, and what would happen to them? Capisce?" He gave Garza a chilled-steel look.

Brahm's use of an Italian idiom contradicted his pale face and thin bloodless lips. His black hair was cut short and he wore glasses with gun metal rims. An unconvincing manner of deference left the impression of a German general posing as a waiter.

It flashed through Brahm's mind. How could he explain his beloved Germany and the ... the contradictions? How his father's family had to leave Germany in the closing days of the war and resettle in Switzerland where he had arranged accounts and friends from earlier years, just in case.

His father told him about visiting Berlin in the 1920s. He observed violent communist protests in front of the Chancellory Building. His father pointed out, how, despite the rocks, bottles and tear gas that filled the air, no one stepped over the low railings marking off the grass and flowers. That would have violated the German sense of order.

When both the communists and the fascists began burning books, his father, who knew the German history of the Thirty Years religious wars, said to his mother, "Antonia, first they burn the books. Then they burn the people. We must be careful."

A friend of the family, Dr. Erich Klaussen, a noted Catholic leader, was killed by the Nazis and his body cremated. They sent his ashes to his wife by registered post.

Brahm, the father, told his son Antonio—his name was a concession to his beautiful Italian mother carrying watered down Borgia DNA from long ago—that he could imagine Mrs. Klaussen receiving and signing for the package, not knowing what was in it.

Germany is polite. Germany is an orderly country. It is part of their "Kultur."

Willi Schmidt, a music critic in Munich, was shot because he was mistaken for Willi Schmidt the storm trooper, who had been executed earlier in the day in an internal Hitler purge.

The German State was thorough.

One night, with the curtains drawn, and in a low voice, his father explained German character to Antonio. German culture was a mere veneer. The pagan barbarism, sulking in the German forests that had checkmated the Romans 2000 years ago, was always threatening to show its ugly head and overwhelm them.

Antonio's cousin, a fourteen-year-old boy with Down's syndrome, was taken away by the Nazis and put to sleep as part of the race purification.

Right before his older brother was forced into the Hitler Youth at age fourteen, their beloved parish priest had confided after Mass to Antonio's father. "I fear the Nazi regime is the greatest threat to Catholicism since Martin Luther. They are trying to replace Christianity with the mythic false religion of National Socialism."

Perhaps someone overheard the conversation who was not friendly to the sentiments expressed. The parish priest disappeared a week later. The rumor: he had been sent East to a work camp. This was at the time when Antonio began to wonder what his father did. No one was exempt from the war effort. His business trips to the East took more and more time and he came home upset every time.

How do you explain this to an American in the 1980s? thought Brahm. America, a country where, if you do not have two cars in the driveway and a color television set, you consider yourself deprived. They had no concept of sickening, lightning-to-the-spine fear.

"Lest you become too self-righteous, Father Garza, the Mafia has also been influential in the American government, going back decades. Your late President Kennedy, so admired in his cloak of Camelot, hid his Mafia ties. Vatican intelligence knew that the Mafia procured women for him. He even shared a girlfriend with a Mafia leader."

"I beg your pardon, Monsignor Brahm, those are nasty rumors spread by people who hated Kennedy and what he stood for, and I find that offensive, with due respect, sir!"

"Father Garza, do you think I would make such a statement if it were not true, or if I did not have evidence? Brahm looked over at Ratzinger.

Archbishop Quijano pushed his way back in. "Gentlemen, interesting, but not relevant to our mission today. Please return to my original question."

Leaning forward across the dark polished wood table dating back to the time of Spanish Cardinal Tomas de Torquemada, "Perhaps you misunderstood me. It was a serious question. Father Garza, I do not see where your thesis findings are in conformance with church teaching."

Garza replied: "My thesis builds on historical facts from my firsthand research in the Vatican archives. It includes the books of the New Testament with the most accurate translations of their original languages—Mr. Nasrani helped with that—and some ancient texts not accepted into the New Testament."

Garza looked down at his written outline for prompting and continued.

"I do not place much credibility on the writings of the early Church Fathers, which came between 100 and 300 A.D. The Church Fathers were already generations removed from the time of Jesus of Nazareth and too much a captive of their own respective cultures.

"Since the most authentic voice we have is the New Testament, I paid close attention to it, especially the writings of Paul," Father Garza continued. "You know as I do, that Paul's writings make up most of the New Testament. Yet, he was not one of the original apostles and never knew Jesus in person.

"My conclusions are that the credo Emperor Constantine proposed, to unify the Christians in his empire, is closer to the original Jesus message than what we have inherited today.

"Jesus of Nazareth did exist, of course. God, this Cosmic Consciousness that we cannot fathom, was in him in a special, powerful way. I believe God resurrected him in some form and he continues in another dimension. His message was love God and neighbor, however that translates, despite what we see and experience in this reality. The good news of this Messiah is so radical that it challenges every man-made institution, government, and religion.

"If Jesus came today, he would not recognize the Catholic Church as something he created. First of all, he had no intention of creating a 'church.' He believed in the consummation of the world in his lifetime. He never required membership in a church as a condition of entry into the kingdom of God."

The pastries and espresso cups sat, orphaned, at the end of the table.

Father Garza continued, "Secondly, Jesus would view the Church today as imitating the stifling mandates of the Judaic Law of the Pharisees and Sadducees that he was so critical of."

He heard his pontificating tone. *Better sound less self-righteous.* He paused by looking at the pastries. *Last thing on my mind is sweets.*

"Jesus would be understanding of this Church as a human enterprise trying to do the right thing, but sinning in the process. He would recognize that sin for what it is and forgive it. He always forgave the sinner who repented, in the name of his Father.

Father Garza noticed Archbishop Quijano looking out the window.

"With respect, the premise for my thesis becomes more acceptable if you see the Holy Roman Catholic Church, like us, called to be better.

"We all recognize the good that the Church has done. But, some of her sins are, to use our Catholic terms, 'mortal sins': the two thousand years' persecution of Jesus' people, the Jews, leading to this century's Nazi Holocaust; the torture, trials and executions of heretics; the Crusades; the burning of witches; wars of religion; colonialism; unholy alliances with repressive and dictatorial governments extending to our own times; creating burdensome, silly prescriptions for the faithful such as not eating meat on Fridays; the selling of indulgences; and the list goes on.

I don't want to sound like I'm reading a grocery list. "When I examine the history, every century spews forth its own Church atrocities; not a few isolated failings, as I was taught as a youth."

Quijano's gaze, smoldering, returned from the window to *the heretic.*

"Gentlemen," Father Garza went on, "the conclusions I have reached from over eighteen months of research would be supported by the work of Father Hans Kung, who served as a principle architect of the theological agenda of the Second Vatican Council. As you know, he is considered an outstanding Catholic theologian."

Quijano did a pursing twist of his lips and hissed: "I know Kung's work. He excels in asking sly questions which impress the laity who are not educated in these complex theological questions. That's why everyone needs our Holy Mother Church to interpret God's word, His message, His will."

Quijano almost launched with his emotions, but checked himself and didn't say, *I will do whatever is necessary to take our people to the true*

God: ornate Churches, seven sacraments, celibate priests, fancy robes, sacred scriptures. I will feed their imaginations and even their fears with hells and devils. I will muster all the bells and smells I am able.

Instead, Quijano continued his dark glower: "Since we must speak with forthrightness in this proceeding, Kung is a heretical wolf in the sheep's cloak of a theologian. He could trigger another bloody Reformation worse than Luther's!"

Quijano fought for control, deep in his anger. It had been decades since empathy crawled out of his eyes.

"If it were up to heretics of his ilk, we'd cast aside two thousand years of tradition. Kung would say instead of being a single, divinely founded institution, our Church reflects many different communities, whose origin is human and historical. If so, then where are we?"

The other committee review member, Cardinal Ratzinger, a professor of theology at the University of Regensburg, in Bavaria, Germany, had also served as a consultant to the Congregation for the Doctrine of the Faith, in Rome. He had been a colleague of Kung's years ago but there had been a rift.

The Congregation lay claim as the successor agency to the particular Church enterprise known as The Inquisition. Gabe had made the historical connection early on. *I assume they've repainted and changed the carpeting since the 1400s to make it look better. Still the same old thing.*

Ratzinger did not reenter the fray. He seemed just disappointed.

Brahm said, "Father Garza, the implications of what you have presented go far beyond what Luther and all the other heretics have proposed over the centuries. If we look at Luther's historical record, he kept seventy-five percent of what we regard as Catholicism. In fact, with all the changes taking place with Vatican II, in another twenty years, you won't be able to tell the difference between a Catholic, Episcopal or Lutheran service.

"Father Garza, what you posit is beyond the simple heresies the Holy Mother Church has had to fight over the years. What you suggest is so revolutionary, why stay in the Church? Why be a priest?"

"Your Eminences, I never said we don't need a church. To use an American idiom, we need to keep our eye on the ball. We need to reaffirm the message. We need to acknowledge this institution as a human one and keep it honest. When it preaches and carries out the message of the Christ, the spirit is in the Church. When the Church acts as the Antichrist, to use a sound theological term, the spirit of God is not there."

Quijano gripped the sides of his chair, knuckles white.

Father Garza assessed. He adopted a flat, non-aggressive monotone. "With the Reformation, theology and doctrinal debate in the Church became defensive and restricted. Then, everyone had to tow the line on a particular mode of thinking, or they were proclaimed heretical. As we know, the Church's prescription for heretics was fatal."

Ratzinger was taking notes. Quijano's eyes were now fixed on the far wall over Garza's left shoulder, the corners of his mouth downturned, breathing in short gasps.

Father Garza pressed his case. "I've been a priest, working with people long enough to know that we need the structure the Church can provide. The Church will encourage our community of believers, striving to live according to the message of the Gospels. Maybe I should belong to a stripped down, Protestant version of Christianity, but we are all emotional creatures as well. *This* is the tradition I was raised in. It is rich with history and ritual. I want to remain a part of it because it is who I am, my identity as a person. If I were being reincarnated, and could choose my religion, I'd come back as a Lutheran Jew; that's a reformed Jew, not orthodox or conservative."

It's a good summary of where I'm at. Hope it doesn't sound brash or insolent. I see Nasrani, sitting against the far wall, has come alive, sitting ramrod straight, and shooting laser-like eyes. And I see that Quijano's mouth has turned down even more; if it went further, it would fall off his face.

Father Garza continued. "Don't confuse the Roman Catholic tradition and its overwhelming medieval trappings, which I find enchanting by the way, with the Gospel Message. They are not the same. To be a Christian means acceptance of his message and striving to imitate Jesus. Profound in its simplicity."

Archbishop Quijano, his face now a brooding, elongated El Greco portrait, shook his head at the heretical American cleric, knowing how the flames of a burning pyre would feed on his fat. "Father Garza, you have abused the archival privileges of Holy Mother Church. You now jeopardize your immortal soul by continuing to manipulate historical research to justify heresies."

Garza thought of the historical pictures of the Inquisition. *This guy could model the latest fall fashion wear from the Inquisition—basic black. I can see Quijano strutting the runway, eyes flashing dark looks at everyone. No, correction—the eyes would be shark eyes that didn't reflect light.*

A fiery Latin temperament, which he suppressed most of the time, took easy-going Gabe temporary prisoner. "You're telling me that I must accept the Church's version of the Gospel and if I don't, I will go to hell? If there is a hell?"

He tried to tone it down, but couldn't.

"What kind of God do you worship? That's not my God and I didn't become a priest to threaten everyone with eternal damnation! I became a priest to tell them that the Cosmic Consciousness that underlies all reality is a loving entity, although it may not appear that way; especially with the random violence that astronomy has uncovered as the pattern of this universe. Put that together with the Darwinian behavior of life forms and you have a recipe for a brutal existence.

"Jesus said we are all in this together and need to take care of each other. People must hear the 'good news' to get through this 'vale of tears' we call life. Christianity calls on us to be better than we would normally be. You preach a God who makes creatures so they can be tortured forever? Have you read the same Gospel Message that I have?"

Archbishop Quijano jumped from his seat, face drained of color, his eyes slashed cavities of dark, ready to toss Father Garza out of the room. Quijano had been especially offended by the obituary that Garza had included in the appendix of his thesis to leaven the seriousness of his presentation. Quijano exposed the religious smear.

It had read:

OBITUARIES JERUSALEM 33 A.D.

Jesus Christ, 33, of Nazareth, died Friday on Golgotha, outside Jerusalem.

He was crucified by the Romans. The causes of death were exhaustion, severe torture, and loss of blood.

He was the son of the late Joseph of Nazareth and Mary, his devoted mother.

Self-educated, Jesus spent most of his adult life as a carpenter and teacher.

He also worked as a non-traditional medical doctor. It was reported he had healed many.

To the consternation of Jewish officials, the body has disappeared, coinciding with reported appearances of the deceased.

In lieu of flowers, the family has requested that everyone try to live as Jesus did. Donations may be sent to anyone in need."

Garza had plagiarized most of it, but couldn't remember the citation. He had wanted to use it to bring out the humanity of his Jesus. *Not such a good idea after all. Now I have a Church archbishop on my case, ready to stroke out from me giving him heretical coronaries.*

Responding to the blasphemies, written and verbal, Cardinal Quijano spat, "Any decent church would have burned you at the stake years ago! You defile the blood of martyrs over nineteen centuries. Christians endured horrible tortures for their beliefs and you turn it into some pseudo-spiritual, scientific psycho-babble! How else do you explain 2.1 billion Christians world-wide, if that is not the hand of God?"

"Archbishop, with all due respect, there are 1.6 billion Muslims; 1 billion Hindus; and the Jews have been around forever. I think the standard for measuring truth is in the message and the results from that message. If it's based on numbers, then the Muslims and Hindus own equal claim. I don't think their message has the same truth as our belief."

"Bastardo!" the Archbishop replied.

Father Garza said, "Tu olvidaste que yo soy bilingual tambien." *You forget that I am also bi-lingual. I know the lingo too, you medieval throwback. Recheck my last name.*

Father Garza assumed high tea with Archbishop Quijano was over. No one had touched the forlorn pastries, the espressos, or the tea.

By their next meeting, Nasrani had performed major damage control through private conversations with Brahm and Ratzinger.

Archbishop Quijano composed himself somewhat when Nasrani apparently criticized Garza before their committee meeting, "Ovejas bobas, por do va una, van todas." It meant, " Silly sheep, where one goes, all go."

Quijano heard one thing. Nasrani meant something else.

The smoke-reek still assaulted Garza's nostrils. He could tell Quijano tried to cover it with a cheap cologne. With the nicotine, he smelled of burnt orange peels.

Garza couldn't help but wonder. *A guy who smokes like a chimney, with enough smoke to announce a pope? Well, at least he goes in the alley and doesn't fog up our meeting room.*

"Father Garza, your historical short-sightedness so reflects your American world view, and the arrogance of the New World," Archbishop Quijano began. He sounded polite, but Gabe heard gritting teeth.

"The Church's failings live in the history texts for all to see and to second guess. But are you so blind? Have you not thought this through? Compare these historical aberrations—missteps—to what good the Church has done for so many millions in their daily lives!"

"But Archbishop. . ."

"Shut up and don't interrupt me again!" He glared at the priest wearing his irreverence like so many ignorant Americans. *They have no appreciation for the challenges and nuances of history—and yes, the difficult choices that leaders must make.*

"The Church has been God's vehicle to proclaim through his only Son that there a just and loving Presence. All men and women are called to serve God.

"We brought this message to a world that recognized only brute force; the strong took whatever they wanted. Rome was the Nazi Germany of its day. Yes, they built roads and aqueducts for drinking and bathing, but they annihilated anyone who stood in their way. That is why these Christians were persecuted for centuries under the Romans. Christianity raised too many questions, as it does for every government, in every time.

"Everyone knows about the martyrs in the Coliseum killed by the wild animals. But those martyrs were only a small percentage of the Christian population. Many more had their property confiscated. Many families were sold into slavery, their wives and daughters sold to brothels, a fate the Romans considered humorously ironical given the Christian belief in the sanctity of marriage and sex. It was easier to be a martyr for a short time of glorious torture for Our Lord than to live a life in complete poverty or sexual slavery.

"But, the Roman era of blood, conquest, and slavery, found itself hungering for the Gospel message. There was no stopping the thousands of secret conversions to the new Christian sect. If you cannot defend God's anointed institution for delivering his message, because you perceive some minor rituals to be outdated, then leave—leave now!

"For the record, Father Garza, I am familiar with Chardin and his poetic musings describing how the Creator intended to let his creation come to him and merge into a universal perfectness. But he ignored a major factor in his scheme: Man has free will and often chooses evil. Our recorded history demonstrates that man does not become nobler as he evolves, but uses new knowledge to work even greater evil. Chardin was too optimistic. Only by following the Gospel can man achieve union with God. We cannot save the world. Even Our Lord could not save the world. That is why we must pray."

Squinting and locking eyes on Garza, Quijano shouted, "Now, whatever else you do in that unholy abomination you call a thesis, be sure to reflect what I have said!"

Luckily for Father Garza, it was a team review.

Cardinal Ratzinger seemed intrigued, despite his forlorn look.

Father Garza had cited Ratzinger's esteemed theological colleague from Germany, Father Hans Kung. Leaders in the reforms of Vatican II, both Kung and Ratzinger proposed a fresh review of the Church's theological underpinnings.

Ratzinger's theology suggested that God speaks to us through the Church today and not just through the Bible.

Ratzinger committed to salvaging Father Garza's thesis; *and perhaps his soul? No; that is too dramatic. Garza already follows in the Lord's footsteps. I don't agree with Quijano's harsh condemnation. But I could suggest that Brahm help save Father Garza's thesis . . . and maybe his priesthood?*

Ratzinger understood Garza's points and respected the passion behind them. His father's outspoken criticism of the Nazis had sent the family to an internal exile. As the Allied front drew near in Germany, Private Joseph Ratzinger deserted from the German army.

As a young professor of theology, Ratzinger had been viewed as a rebel, protesting the medieval confines of Thomism, a systematic way of Church thinking which had lasted for centuries. The irony: Thomism, when first introduced, was attacked by the Church's contemporaneous hierarchy.

Years after World War II, Ratzinger held the second chair in dogmatic theology at the University of Tubingen, in Germany. One of his students, a fervent Marxist, challenged Ratzinger in his classroom.

Marxism was the European young people's philosophical flavor of the post-war decades. Ratzinger had assumed that the construction of the Berlin Wall on August 13, 1961, would have dampened leftist ardor. The Wall exposed the true face of communism, one would think.

"Herr Professor, why did you not attack the Nazi regime? Why did you not work to overthrow Hitler!" the student had shouted in class, full of self-righteous anger, at the age of nineteen, and twenty-three years removed from the heavy steps on the staircase early in the morning, the Gestapo's favored time to meet less resistance, but still enough daylight for the neighbors to see and be warned.

Professor Ratzinger put a weary smile on his face: "This is not part of the course outline for today, but I will comment. Who was I going to shoot? My Lieutenant? He had a wife and three kids and was a former bank clerk. He despised the Nazis as much as I did.

"The Russians were sweeping in from the East, looting and raping. Any woman who was raped only once was fortunate. We knew this was taking place because we had returning wounded veterans in our ranks. They recuperated in our anti-aircraft platoon.

"One had a duty to defend the Fatherland, not the Nazi regime. It was a tragic time."

Ratzinger refocused his thoughts and returned to the present: "Archbishop Quijano, please permit Antonio, with some advice from me, to work with Father Garza over the next months. I am confident we can correct his thesis to reconcile the political elements of the Nicene Creed, which Father Garza has uncovered, without having to challenge the Church's essential doctrines.

"I recommend this in light of the commitment Father Garza retains for the message of Jesus. I don't think we need to look for heresies that may not be there." *You, Father Garza, are a critic of the system you work in. In the end, you belong to it . . . and to us.*

Father Garza appreciated Ratzinger's intervention but could feel his own attitude hardening. *I don't need an M.A. in theology to preach in the missions of Africa or South America or wherever they might threaten me with exile. If they want to threaten me with an overseas assignment, so what? That's what the Holy Ghost Fathers do, serve the missions. No more bullshit about contraception and how many persons in a godhead! No wonder there had been a reformation, even though one of his religious teachers in the seminary had attributed its actual origins to Martin Luther's constipation.*

Hell, I'm ready to lead "Let's Do the Reformation All Over Again, Part Two." It would be bigger and badder than Part One which starred Martin Luther and one-half of Germany filling in as extras.

Garza's research had uncovered two other controversies:

*There was no historical evidence for unbroken papal succession, a finding that created interesting theological roads to travel down.

*The same system of Papal Courts that condemned Galileo three hundred years ago, was still in operation.

Could they come after me now—or in the future? How would they do it?

When he walked home at night to his apartment, Gabe stayed in the center of the alleys. He didn't like the shadows.

CHAPTER 28

Who Murdered The Kennedys—All Of Them?

"Chi fonda in sul popolo, fonda in sulla rena. Who builds on the mob builds on sand."
OLD ITALIAN SAYING.

RATZINGER AND BRAHM REVIEWED THE linguistics comparisons made of the credo by Father Garza. Ratzinger sat in on the first meeting. After that, no more.

The new Polish Pope, John Paul II, had appointed Ratzinger on November 25, 1981, to be the Cardinal-Prefect of the Congregation for the Doctrine of the Faith, formerly known as the Holy Office. In the sixteenth century, it was known as the Roman Inquisition. Ratzinger no longer had time to review mere Masters' theses.

Garza puzzled. *That's the same outfit that silenced Galileo and burnt Bruno. What's going on? I thought Cardinal Ratzinger was one of the good guys? Maybe the pope wants Ratzinger to dismember this Inquisition legacy, this crime against humanity and reason?*

With the help of assigned languages expert Paolo Nasrani, the team studied each word of the credo, analyzing ancient Greek and Latin texts against the English translation.

Garza couldn't resist, "Monsignor Brahm, excuse the digression, but since our last meeting, I was wondering where you got your information on alleged misbehavior by President Kennedy?"

"I have been fortunate during my ecclesiastical career to have Cardinal Ratzinger as a mentor," Brahm said. "He views me as a younger brother. In the 1960s, Karl was a theological adviser to Vatican II, along with Hans Kung. In that capacity, he ended up working with all parts of the Vatican, including Vatican intelligence, the unit known as Sodalitium Pianum. I served as an assistant to him. I was privy to everything—*every thing.*

Brahm looked at Garza and then at Nasrani, framing his coming request with raised eyebrows.

"Signore Nasrani, would you excuse us? We'll resume the translation checks shortly."

"Of course," said Nasrani, rising from the seat at the table he shared. *Hmm. My family goes back to the time of Yeshua in the Holy Land, and they dismiss me? A Swiss-German barbarian and a mixed race mongrel from across the ocean?*

After Nasrani closed the door, Brahm resumed. "In its heyday, Sodalitium Pianum opened mail, monitored bookstores for heretical literature, and engaged in other clandestine activities. They were supposedly disbanded in 1921, but instead went underground and devised an informal intelligence service to analyze current affairs. The Cardinal stayed close to the Intelligence Unit to monitor the activities of the ultra right wing in the Curia which was determined to destroy the deliberations of the Vatican II conferences."

"What? You mean all that rumored Church spy stuff at Vatican II was true?"

"With sadness, I must say yes."

"We did not fear debate or contrary opinions. I helped Ratzinger insure there was no blackmail, violence, or other intimidation. Even people who have taken vows, when they think God is on their side, will engage in unscrupulous acts. Sodalitium is expert at what they do."

Brahm's face fell at the recollection. "I urged Karl to not accept the appointment. I predicted it would tarnish his reputation as an ascending, brilliant theologian and could brand him as a mediocre Bavarian Church bureaucrat. The Curia and the other Vatican institutions are formidable."

"Do they know who killed President Kennedy?" Garza asked, dipping his toe in the intelligence waters.

"Yes."

"Who did?"

"Who do you think?"

"Well, back in America, the chief suspects for years have remained the Russians, for the humiliation of the Cuban Blockade; Castro, for the Bay of Pigs invasion and the U.S. attempts on his life; the Mafia, for Bobby Kennedy's anti-racketeering crusade; the CIA; and even LBJ, lusting for the President's chair. Nobody knows."

"Are you *sure* you want to know?"

"Yes."

"It was the Mafia. Joseph Kennedy, the President's father, worked with them when he was a bootlegger. There were rumors that he tipped the Mafia off before the stock market crashed in 1929. Kennedy got out of the market before the crash. Some say he manipulated it. That, we don't know.

"Joseph Kennedy was one of the wealthiest men in the country at the time. He helped buy the election in 1960 for his son Jack, through the Chicago and West Virginia political machines.

"When Bobby went after Jimmy Hoffa and racketeering, the Mob viewed this as betrayal, far worse than being an enemy. With an enemy, you reach accommodation so that it does not interfere with business. Betrayal cannot be forgiven."

The dust in the room made Gabe's nose itch. He wanted to sneeze. He held it, pinching his nose. *I might never get this chance again. I can't interrupt. This is unbelievable!*

"Lee Harvey Oswald was one of two shooters. He was in the book depository building.

The second shooter positioned himself in another building across the street with a better angle on the presidential car. Oswald didn't know about him. He wasn't supposed to.

"Oswald, with his exceptional marksmanship as a former Marine, killed Kennedy. The other back-up shooter wasn't needed. The game plan insured Oswald would be blamed. The New Orleans Mob killed the second gunman a year later on a boat six miles from New Orleans in the Gulf. They shot him and tossed the body overboard with weights.

"Oswald's pro-Cuba activities, his having lived in Russia, and being married to a Russian woman would distract anyone from reading the assassination for what it was, a Mob hit. We are not sure, did Oswald know in fact who he was working for?

"We do know that Jack Ruby associated with the Mafia. He killed Oswald before he could be interrogated. Sam Giancana and Jimmy Hoffa, with suggested ties to the assassination, were themselves silenced years later:

"Giancana was killed on July 19, 1975, the night before he was to testify before the Church Senate Committee. They shot him six times around the mouth, heavy Mafia symbolism. Each member of the Senate Committee understood.

"Hoffa disappeared two weeks later on July 30. He knew too much. He was trying to regain his former Teamster position as President and threatened to talk if he didn't get what he wanted. He also threatened the Mob's access to the Teamster pension funds. They needed that capital to expand Las Vegas where they could launder the money from their prostitution rings, drug sales, extortion and other racketeering. The Mob expected Las Vegas to generate billions every year and sidestep the IRS.

"Hoffa was crushed in an auto compactor in Hamtramck, Michigan."

Gabe sat unblinking, looking at Brahm. *God, my heart has stopped beating.*

"In Europe, we are amused at how Americans make fun of the Mafia's influence in Italy. How do you think your J. Edgar

Hoover stayed in power so long, especially with his unusual sexual proclivities?

"Hoover wielded secret files on friends and foes. He had more than that, according to my sources. The Mob kept him on their payroll. Every time he went to the Maryland or California tracks, he won large sums of money.

"Why do you think he spent so little Agency resources fighting the Mob? He acted for years as if it was just a minor criminal nuisance. Sorry for the extensive history lesson, Father Garza, but you asked."

Gabe nodded, quiet.

"The Mob perpetuates back door access to the corridors of power because it is willing and capable of anything, *anything* to get what it wants.

"The Russians and Cubans wouldn't dare do it. They knew killing the president would be war. When the Russians first heard of the assassination, they were terrified there had been a right wing military coup, and a nuclear launch was imminent. The U.S. military exerted enormous influence, even though it theoretically reported to President Kennedy.

"Castro had the motivation. After all, the Kennedys and their CIA had plotted his murder. What many people don't know is that there were tactical nukes still in Cuba after the Russian ships were turned back by the U.S. Navy.

"Castro had told Moscow he wanted to continue to confront the U.S. after the height of the Cuban Missile Crisis. Castro was willing to launch. Moscow considered assassinating Castro to prevent a war they did not want. Moscow had trained Castro's security personnel. Three of his bodyguards reported to the KGB.

"Castro was so enraged at going from a near first-world status with nukes, back to an incidental island in the Caribbean, that he swallowed half of his unlit cigar in a tirade against his Soviet sponsors. They rushed him to the hospital to have his stomach pumped."

Gabe leaned forward, holding his breath.

"The CIA wouldn't carry out an assassination against Kennedy, even though they worried about the President's anger after the Bay of Pigs when he threatened to break the Agency into a thousand pieces.

"LBJ was unscrupulous as far as his career was concerned, but he wouldn't go that far. He knew secrets always come out. Besides, he didn't want to confront an outfit that specialized in extreme ventilation of the twelve-gauge variety. They might come in, blazing, and you end up on the floor, leaking. Nobody wants to leak.

"I would suggest *this* for your consideration, Father Garza."

"Yes, Monsignor?"

"There is a principle of logic and problem solving known as 'Occam's razor' which I will paraphrase. When you are presented with multiple explanations, look for the simplest one."

Gabe felt lightheaded with this onslaught of secret information. "What about Bobby Kennedy?" he asked.

"The Mafia hated Bobby, but they considered Jack the head of the snake. If they took Jack out, Bobby would have no power. They could handle LBJ, who viewed the Mafia as just another political interest group, one with unorthodox political tactics.

"They never considered a scenario where Bobby would win the Presidency. They conceded him the Senator's seat in New York to keep him out of the way. They weren't too worried because in the Senate Bobby had ninety-nine other prima donna colleagues to work with. Bobby wasn't good at working *with* people.

"The Mob knew LBJ would lock up the Presidency for the next eight years. During that time, they would find ways with LBJ's help to tarnish the Kennedy image. Damaging leaks of improper personal behavior by Kennedy would leak, first as sensationalized rumors in the tabloid press.

"But the rising power of television trumped the old political machines. Bobby replicated his late brother's Irish good looks with a full head of hair and straight, white teeth . . . and the magical veneer of Camelot.

"When LBJ didn't run in '68 and Bobby won the California primary, they had to kill him right away before the Secret Service provided the mandated extra protection.

"The heads of the Five Families had received disturbing confidential information from an informant high up in the CIA. If elected, Bobby planned a black ops which would take out the heads of the Five Families at once in what would appear to be a bloody mob warfare incident. Such an internal criminal stratagem showed up a decade later in the *Godfather* film.

"Then, when the successor Mafia generation stepped in to take their place, he was going to play them off one against the other. The Mafia would never recover. Bobby swore to his brother, Ted, he would destroy the Mob—damn any consequences.

"Bobby's middle name was 'vindictive.' He had adored Jack. He calculated that if the public ever found out about his bloody vengeance, he would explain this as an official action in a matter of national security to protect the United States from internal treasonous threats. With Bobby wearing the inherited mantle of Camelot, the public would applaud. The irony, of course, is that the Mob does pose your country's most serious internal threat."

"How is it possible for you to know these things?" said Garza. *How can this not come out in public?*

Brahm replied, "Let us say that I am telling you a story, my way. I have sources. If I burden you with evidence, you risk becoming a target. Shall I continue?"

"Yes. Please. Sorry."

"I understand," said Brahm pressing his lips together in sympathy. "Sirhan Sirhan attended several Kennedy rallies across the country, waiting for the kill order. The night Bobby won the California primary, Sirhan received his command. He executed Bobby Kennedy at the victory party in L.A.

"As a Palestinian, Sirhan viewed Kennedy as an American Jewish lackey. His Mafia handlers encouraged this view but they also hypnotized Sirhan several times so that he could remember only segments of what led up to the shooting. He could recall his hatred of the pro-Jewish Kennedy but not the details of who directed him. Years later, memories returned, but by then Sirhan was considered a rambling lunatic from his solitary confinement and dismissed, except by those who carefully tracked these things, like Sodalitium Pianum."

Sympathy played on Brahm's face for the naive American cleric. *Tough Washington, D.C. neighborhoods are no match for the violence and betrayals in the corridors of world power.*

"Brilliant in its way," Brahm went on. "Impossible to trace the assassination to the Mob. Who would believe it? Bobby had been murdered by a deranged Palestinian who hated the Jews and hated Kennedy for his support of Israel. That contains historical ironies. Bobby's father, old Joe Kennedy, was anti-Semitic, and in the beginning supported Hitler. Your President Roosevelt had to rein the elder Kennedy in."

"This is hard to take in all at once. I guess . . . I'm . . . stunned," said Garza.

"Remember Occam's razor. Who had the strongest motivation and the most to gain? A sitting President and his brother, heir apparent, eliminated in five years? What do you think the statistical odds are of that happening by random happenstance in a relatively safe democracy?

"I predict that in the next ten years you will see books published by 'Mob insiders' or Mafia relatives. They will reference Kennedy ties to the Mafia, their immoral private behavior, and the possibility of Mafia involvement in the assassinations. It will be a calculated campaign to desensitize the American public to the truth of what happened. It will also enhance the reputation of the Mob as an untouchable power and part of the American political landscape, lurking in the shadows, something to be feared.

"You have already witnessed a piece of this strategy with the release of the popular movie, *The Godfather*, along with its sequels. With Mafia influence in Hollywood, do you think this movie came out by accident? All of a sudden, this obscure writer $20,000 in debt, Mario Puzo, pens a best-selling book?

"No, the movie humanizes the Mob with Brando's and Pacino's superb acting talents. It creates acceptance for Mob thuggery as part of the American cultural landscape—a brilliant public image coup for their criminal enterprises."

Brahm's steel blue eyes looked into Garza's face. Garza blinked hard.

"Knowing the vindictiveness of your American Mob, I make a prediction. They will not be satisfied with the removal of the two Kennedy brothers. They will bring down as many family members as they can in the coming decades. They will use women, alcohol, drugs, car accidents, suicide, and cancer injections. It will be spread out over time with no apparent pattern. It will become known as the Kennedy family curse or something similar."

"My God, Monsignor, how can you say this?"

"Remember where my family came from, like Ratzinger's, and what I have already witnessed in the most Christian of nations next to my beloved Switzerland. As to sources, I cannot comment further on that. We will regard this as a casual talk between us, yes?"

"Yes."

Gabriel Garza never got headaches. Now, he felt a terrible pounding in his head. *Was this the truth, a half truth, or poetic license?*

On his way back to the apartment at dusk, despite his throbbing head, he still noticed the nondescript couple studying nothing in the shop window across the street too long and how, when he passed them, they refused to look at him, but set up their pace behind him.

CHAPTER 29

One More Watergate File

WHEN I DRAGGED MYSELF BACK to my apartment, it was 7:30 p.m. It had been a very long day as I labored up the forty-eight steps.

A small note on blue paper was taped to the door. It said: CHECK YOUR READING FILE.

I knew it had been written on an anonymous typewriter by someone wearing cheap latex exam gloves. I knew who that someone was.

Nasrani had left papers for me to study and then return to him the next time we met. The hiding spot was the hollow interior of the worn cabinet door below the kitchen sink. It could be pulled apart by yanking on the small nail in the middle and then pushed back into place. Nasrani rarely used it anymore.

He no longer picked my door lock since I had given him a key.

Curiosity trumped my exhaustion.

Another note, stapled to the file, said:

I think you recognize this. Key excerpts only but most interesting. The unexpurgated transcripts will not come out for decades, if they ever do. I show you this to prove what I have access to. Your countrymen would be appalled but this is how things are done in the corridors of power from popes to presidents. I included several notes.

I could visualize a Nasrani smile with no warmth as he placed the file.

This file folder had a faded logo, but you could still see the remnants of an American eagle and the flag. Several letters were so aged they were missing. D ARTM T OF USTICE. The tab on the file was clear enough: Presidential Tapes 1973.

I suddenly felt several years older than yesterday. I opened the file.

[These excerpts show the White House trying to set up Attorney General Mitchell to take the fall.]

March 20, 1973, 6:00 p.m. . . . .

HALDEMAN: . . . Ziegler's theory is based on what the press guys say—convinced that what they're after is Colson on criminal. They think he's the highest guy they can get on criminal in the White House. Mitchell [is] on the outside. Now, there—the worst—it isn't—the worst you can get is damn bad out there.

NIXON: It's Mitchell.

HALDEMAN: Because if Mitchell was the authority.

NIXON: He's the Attorney General of the United States.

HALDEMAN: As Attorney General of the United States, and—

NIXON: The President's campaign manager. That's pretty goddamn bad. That's damn near as bad as it is out there. Do you agree with this? . . . .

. . . .

HALDEMAN: See John Dean's whole approach as I understand it—this is when we went through it out in California for two full days. What came out of is his whole premise—his basic approach to this is one of containment. Keep it in this box and he thinks he can. And that box goes on the theory that Liddy did it without authorization from above and Liddy's been convicted of doing it. Liddy was the responsible guy at the campaign organization. He's the highest guy that they've got. The other people were employees of Liddy's.

[Famous "cancer on the presidency" reference.]

March 21, 1973, 10:12 a.m. . . . .

NIXON: In other words, your judgment as to where it stands, and where we go now.

DEAN: I think that there's no doubt about the seriousness of the problem we're—we've got. We have a cancer—within—close to the presidency, that's growing. It's growing daily. It's compounding. It grows geometrically now, because it compounds itself. That'll be clear as I explain you know, some of the details of why it is. And it basically is because, one, we're being blackmailed, two, people are going to start perjuring themselves to protect other people and the like. And that is just—and there is no assurance—

NIXON: That it won't bust.

DEAN: That that won't bust.

NIXON: True.

DEAN: So let me give you the sort of basic facts, talking first about the Watergate, and then about Segretti, and then about some of the peripheral items that have come up. First of all, on the Watergate: how did it all start? Where did it start? It started with an instruction to me from Bob Haldeman to see if we couldn't set up a perfectly legitimate campaign intelligence operation over at the reelection committee.

NIXON: Mm—hmm.

. . . .

DEAN:—the most troublesome post-thing, because, one, Bob is involved in that. John is involved in that. I am involved in that. Mitchell is involved in that. And that's an obstruction of justice.

NIXON: In other words, the fact that you're taking care of the witnesses.

DEAN: That's right. Uh—

NIXON: How was Bob involved?

DEAN: Well, they ran out of money over there. Bob had three hundred and fifty thousand dollars in a safe over here that was really set aside for polling purposes . . .

. . . .

DEAN: . . . But it raises the whole question of Hunt now has made a direct threat against Ehrlichman as a result of this. This is his blackmail. He says, " I will bring John Ehrlichman down to his knees and put him in jail. I have done enough seamy things for he and Keogh that they'll never survive it.

NIXON: What's that, on Ellsberg?

DEAN: Ellsberg, and apparently some other things. I don't know the full extent of it. Uh—

NIXON: I don't know about anything else.

DEAN: I don't know either, and I [laughs] almost hate to learn some of these—

NIXON: Yeah.

. . . .

DEAN: —which will not only go on now, it'll go on when these people are in prison. And it will compound the obstruction of justice situation. It'll cost money. It's dangerous. Nobody, nothing—people around here are not pros at this sort of thing. This is the sort of thing Mafia people can do: washing money, getting clean money, and things like that we're—we just don't know about those things, because we're not used to, you know—we are not criminals and not used to dealing in that business. It's—

NIXON: That's right.

DEAN: It's a tough thing to know how to do.

NIXON: Maybe we can't even do that.

. . . .

DEAN: I would say these people are going to cost a million dollars over the next two years.

NIXON: Could you get that?

DEAN: Mm-hmm.

NIXON: You—on the money, if you need the money, I mean, you could get the money. Let's say—

DEAN: Well, I think that we're going—

NIXON: What I meant is, you could get a million dollars. And you could get it in cash. I know where it could be gotten.

DEAN: Mm-hmm.

NIXON: I mean it's not easy, but it could be done. But the question is who the hell would handle it?

DEAN: That's right. Uh—

NIXON: Any ideas on that?

DEAN: Well, I would think that would be something that Mitchell ought to be charged with.

NIXON: I would think so too.

DEAN: And get some pros to help him.

. . . .

DEAN: . . . But some people are going to have to go to jail. That's the long and short of it, also.

NIXON: Who? Let's talk about that.

DEAN: All right. I think I could, for one.

NIXON: You go to jail?

DEAN: That's right.

. . . .

NIXON: Tell me—talking about your obstruction of justice role, I don't see it. I can't see it. You're—

DEAN: Well, I've been a con—I have been a conduit for information on taking care of people out there who are guilty of crimes.

NIXON: Oh, you mean like the blackmail.

DEAN: The blackmail. Right.

. . . .

NIXON: I think you may be overplaying, but who else do you think has—?

DEAN: Potential criminal liability?

NIXON: Yeah.

DEAN: I think Ehrlichman does. I think that—I think—

NIXON: Why Ehrlichman? What'd he do?

DEAN: Because of this conspiracy to burglarize the Ellsberg office.

. . . .

June 4, 1973, 10:05 p.m. . . . .

NIXON: Both you and he—he just throughout until the twenty-first, didn't say one damn word that—indicated that either of—he mentioned that Ehrlichman's involved with something about the Chappaquiddick thing. And I, and there's nothing wrong with that.

HALDEMAN: Mm-hmm.

NIXON: You know the Chappaquiddick thing?

HALDEMAN: Well, that was with that Tony or something, huh?

NIXON: Huh?

HALDEMAN: With that guy Tony?

NIXON: Yeah.

HALDEMAN: Yeah.

NIXON: And so what the hell is that, that we—that an investigation was conducted? He says that's a problem for Ehrlichman, he said. That's a problem.

HALDEMAN: Those are all, what he's talking about there, are—

NIXON: Have nothing to do with Watergate.

. . . .

When we met again, I handed Nasrani the file wrapped around a bottle of wine in a gaily colored bag holding the gift. He thanked me and said: "Interesting reading?"

"Why did you give me that file?"

"I heard you and Brahm discussed Kennedy issues."

"How do you know that?"

"Gabe . . . eh?" accompanied with that articulate Italian shoulder-shrug.

I said, "Well . . . yes. Watergate was nine years ago and rumors and bits and pieces have come out. But that's the first time I've ever seen it put together that way."

"See anything unusual?" Nasrani asked.

"The whole thing's . . . I meant it almost sent a president to jail."

"Yes, yes," he said. But if you read it very carefully—

"The Kennedy thing?" I said.

"What about it?" Nasrani said.

Then it fell into place, why the file and the Brahm conversation. I said, "Kennedy, Chappaquiddick, and a guy named Tony?"

"Want the story behind that?" asked Nasrani.

"One more horror story? Give it to me."

Nasrani reconfirmed for me what a wicked, wicked place this world is. "Tony worked for one of the Families in New York. The transcript might lead you to believe he was only supposed to keep an eye on the Kennedy compound. But he had other instructions and a free hand. He was very well paid with the understanding that if he got caught, he would be cut loose. They would disappear him. The Mafia doesn't have a witness protection program for its people."

"What are you saying, exactly?" I asked.

"With his car lights off, this Tony followed Teddy and his date for the evening. When they came to the one lane Dike Bridge, Tony slammed into the rear of Kennedy's 1967 4 door Oldsmobile Delmont 88 with the license plate L78-207. Kennedy applied his brakes but still went over the side of the wooden bridge with no guardrail. The car plunged into the tide-swept Poucha Pond.

"Tony left the scene immediately, because there's always someone around, even in a remote area late at night. He figured either Kennedy would drown or have to explain the unexplainable, if he survived."

Nasrani pulled out another shoulder shrug. That should have said it all, but he added, "Camelot was not about who the Kennedys *really* were, and it was not about who you Americans *really* were. It was about how America wanted to see itself. The irony—the original Camelot was a failed myth too."

CHAPTER 30
Still Shrouded In Mystery

First, Gabe made a gift of Quijano's favorite Italian pastries at their final meeting, four chocolate covered cannoli.

Then, Gabe pinned the small silver medal to the outside of his cassock, displaying Our Lady of Fatima, given to him by his mother for his First Communion. He always carried it in his wallet. The medal advertised *tradition*.

Finally, Gabe created a new thesis title: *On a Unified Christianity: A Comparative Analysis of the Nicene Creed, the Protestant Reformation, and Vatican II.*

This rewrite put his previously stated church positions in a more acceptable context of future theological challenges guaranteed to be debated over the next fifty years, triggered by Vatican II. Father Garza anticipated new lines of inquiry which questioned how the Church could prepare for coming controversies.

To help frame the issues, he quoted Paul's First Epistle to the Corinthians: ". . .that you are quarreling among yourselves. This is what I mean: 'One of you will say, I belong to Paul, another I belong to Apollos, still another, Cephas has my allegiance, and the fourth, I belong to Christ.'"

Father Garza used the Pauline reference to acknowledge the different denominations in the early days of Christianity. He put his own quote on the table: "We *all* belong to the Christ."

At academic arms-length from himself, Garza could now explore the concept of the Church as a sinful human institution, responsible for a series of historical atrocities, but devoted to bearing witness to the good news that Jesus brought. He quoted Hans Kung and his one-time colleague Karl Ratzinger, along with the theories of French Jesuit Pierre Teilhard de Chardin.

The Church needed to redeem itself through its evolution. One way to start that ball rolling was to strip everything away, except for The Credo, the old one from Emperor Constantine.

This ancient creed could unite Christianity, put the past behind, and move toward the ultimate Cosmic Consciousness.

Finally, Father Gabriel Garza shared his recent personal experience with the review panel, aimed at Quijano.

Father Garza's Vatican pass guaranteed his access to all Vatican archives and Church facilities.

He requested a personal briefing by Church experts at the Cathedral of St. John the Baptist in Turin, four hundred and thirty-seven miles from Rome, which housed the reputed burial shroud of Jesus. The shroud of was one of the Catholic stories his mother told him about. Now, he could visit it up close and personal.

After he traveled by train to Turin and rested for a day at the local rectory—Vatican credentials opened all doors—Garza received an update. Local church officials told him the timing was excellent.

A detailed examination of the shroud by an American team had just taken place. The team had found no evidence of forgery although a carbon dating analysis showed that the piece of cloth tested went only as far back as the medieval period. However, the tested fragment may not have been part of the original shroud, but a cloth portion added to the edges of the original.

An original research methodology had been suggested by an unusual source, the art community. A well-known artist, specializing in antique reconstructive art, viewed the shroud. He concluded that the image on the shroud was the result of the product of decomposition of dead gases interacting with the material of the cloth—a partial explanation only. They still couldn't justify the photo-negative image on the cloth, since no one understood photography until the time of the first permanent photograph in 1826. The medieval mind could not conceive of photography. So, scratch the suspicion of one medievalist playing with photographic plates.

Scientific experts from different disciplines examined the shroud: chemistry, biology, medical forensics, and optical imaging. There were outlines of flowering plants on the shroud. Examination revealed that the plants would have come from the environs of Jerusalem during the months of March or April.

They couldn't explain it.

Gabe had read up on the shroud before the train trip. He expected one more phony artifact the Church imposed on a superstitious peasantry. But in deference to his mother's pious upbringing, he'd check it out for himself.

The shroud's linen cloth displayed an imbedded image of a man who appeared to have suffered the same wounds as Jesus, as described in the New Testament Gospels. The shroud measured 14.3 feet by 3.7 feet.

Devout Catholics believed Joseph of Arimathea wrapped the body of Jesus in the shroud after his crucifixion by the Romans. The image on the shroud was that of a muscular man, tall for the times, between 5 feet 7 inches, to 6 feet 2 inches. The man-image had a beard, mustache, and shoulder-length hair parted in the middle.

In 1898, an Italian photographer, Secondo Pia, took the first ever photograph of the shroud. In his darkroom, there was a visible image of the negative plate. Negatives of the image give off an appearance of a positive image.

Gabe said he had taken a personal confidant with him on the trip to the Turin Cathedral—*skepticism*. But the guards saw only Gabe. His Vatican pass in the fancy black leather wallet permitted him to stand next to the hard plastic container displaying the shroud. Normally, fifteen feet was the closest the public was allowed.

Viewing the Shroud, especially the face, yes, especially the face, Gabe experienced . . . awe. With difficulty, he pulled his gaze away. *Meet the security risk known as Jesus of Nazareth,* was all he could think. His head filled with helium and the church canted to the right.

Rubbing his hand on the back of his neck . . . *How could I feel something from an old piece of cloth? Has my imagination slipped into overdrive? Is it the ambiance of the church and the other visitors? Maybe I'm just tired from a long trip?*

This is spooky . . . a warm, loving strangeness. I can't seem to reason it away. What if this is the face behind that phone call from Jesus I received back in the rectory years ago? Never did figure out if that was a dream or not.

The briefing report he had read on the train to Turin offered Gabe one compelling theory. The high definition of the image was caused by an energy source acting from inside the shroud.

The Russian researcher, Alexander Belyakov hypothesized that an intense but short flash source, which lasted some hundredths of a second, could explain it. Others suggested a burst of directional ultraviolet radiation. The theorists refused to identify the source of the energy.

There is something about the face. It isn't the long-haired, smiling, "be-your-best-friend," homogenized portrait in my children's prayer book. This face has pain with strength, character.

In his bones, in his gut, Gabe believed. And that's what he told the committee.

The final piece of the strategy for winning Quijano's thesis approval—Father Garza's short commentary on the nature of miracles. He believed in them.

He noted the progress in science and the understanding of how modern man can manipulate matter. Physical miracles weren't all miracles, merely applications of advanced physics.

The authentic miracles were not the physical ones. Genuine miracles effected the changing of a man's heart. Those merited the resonance of blowing trumpets. Changing stones into bread was easy, or would be, someday. The hearts of men, just take a look at the atrocities in human history, offered the unexplored frontiers.

And, he added a new point, counter-point near the end of his thesis. Father Garza, with sincere conscience, summarized the theological controversies of a post-Vatican II world in this fashion:

The traditionalists, as represented by Archbishop Quijano and Archbishop Ratzinger show a Christ whom the Church proclaims him to be—not a political activist, but the Messiah who lived, died and proved his messiahship by being raised from the dead.

Father Hans Kung believes the Church needs to be saved from sinister Roman reactionaries who have perverted Christianity.

The traditionalists would charge Kung with subservience to passing intellectual and political fashions. Christ promised that the gates of hell would not prevail against his Church. Thus, there is no need to save the Church from Borgia popes, incompetent bishops, sexually predatory clergy, financial scandals or a Concordat with Hitler. The church is already saved.

Perhaps one smidgen of intellectual dishonesty—Father Garza did not footnote that he still agreed with Hans Kung.

The pastries, the Fatima medal, his revisions to the thesis, and the story of the shroud might win Quijano over—barely.

CHAPTER 31

Bi-Polar Nation

> "Bipolar disorder, also known as manic-depressive illness, is a brain disorder that causes unusual shifts in mood, energy, activity levels . . ."
> *National Institutes of Mental Health*

Ratzinger and Brahm were clean. No Jewish blood or atrocities on their hands. Except . . . that I remembered something.

My ex-seminary roommate and current poker club colleague, Owen Friel, told me, before I left for Europe, that if there's a nation that could qualify as bi-polar, his vote would go to Germany—hands down, without reservation, no hesitation. Game. Set. Match.

He said, "I don't say that just because I'm 100% Irish, offspring from that wind-swept, desolate, priest-ridden land of potatoes and British atrocities."

He had stories: from his father; extensive historical reading; and an unusual experience.

A party put the ribbon on the package.

Unbelievable.

So, I told this story to Paolo. It may have been my suppressed Gentile guilt bubbling up as apology, saying I think I understand . . . a little bit.

Owen Friel went to this Saturday night party in Gaithersburg—just your standard, friends-party in a small town north of Rockville where he worked. He knew this international couple—she was from Cuba; he was from Puerto Rico. Normally oil and water don't mix, but they did, pretty well.

The thirties-something couple had invited a potpourri of folks from their federal agencies. She worked at the State Department; he worked at the World Bank.

Owen chanced upon two unusual cocktail conversations in the same evening.

After he had told me his story, Owen had given a look as if warning of coming bad karma. Europe was the place our ancestors had left, a cesspool of continual conflict.

Bored, ready to leave the party at 10:30 p.m., Owen started a chat with the effervescent woman in her thirties with the striking yellow-blond hair, sky-blue eyes, and that lipstick which looked redder on her than any woman in Washington. Nice nose, not too large, not too small.

Owen had summarized declaring "good bone all over the face."

He also observed the green sheen of her stylish silk dress, cut above slim knees.

His story came with a mini-lecture on hair color: "The difference between white-blond and yellow-blond is one of tone. White is cold; yellow projects warmth. Yellow-blond says sunshine; white blond is polar night."

I thought if he was that caught up in her hair, no wonder he approached her.

Owen was divorced then. So he paid attention to those things. No harm in talking to a pretty lady whose eyes sparkled, but be careful because a large handsome man was standing next to her.

Owen fought down the urge to pet her face with his eyes.

Owen said to her, "I noticed people here from different countries and I couldn't help but pick up on your accent. Mind me asking?"

With a friendly gaze, "Not at all. I am Helga Siberbauer and this is my husband, Alphonso Arias. I am German, from Argentina."

Owen had learned his World War II history at the knee of an expert. Owen's father was D-day+5 which meant he had hit the beach five days after June 6, 1944.

"So, are you originally from Germany?" he said.

"Yes, my father emigrated to Argentina after the war."

Okay, she mentioned the war. Just ease into this. Don't want to turn this friendly cocktail party into an interrogation.

"Really? You know, my father was in the war and served in Germany. In fact, he got a bronze star for helping plan the crossing of the Rhine River. Do you know what your father did in the war? Where he was?"

Let's see what kind of political pablum gets served up. Damn! She looks like one of those German women on the beer garden posters.

"He was in the SS. He moved to Argentina after the war to avoid all the politics."

Owen's smile dimmed, undergoing a total eclipse. *Avoid all the politics? Never heard that one before. There was a lot more to the SS than "politics."*

"In the SS? Well, didn't they have a reputation for doing nasty things?"

"You must understand. It was war. Horrible things happen in war. Most of what they said about the SS was propaganda by the victorious Allies. No one knew what was going on. Under Hitler, no information was available."

Her now-direct gaze returned a slight chill. The previously sunny smile slipped from the movie-star-quality face.

Her husband, handsome Hispanic-son-of-Argentina, now a U.S. citizen, in an expensive tweed sports coat, joined the conversation.

"Yes, Helga is correct. I work for the State Department, the Diplomatic Corps, and am well versed in history. Atrocities were committed by both sides."

Owen heard dismissive tone. *Did he just toss a bloody history of slaughter into the boring dustbin of history? And, how did this guy get into our State Department? Let me try something here.*

"Well, I work in Rockville down the road and we have a bright Maryland state representative, Al Dominguez, whom I meet with during the legislative sessions. He's a rising political star. He's also Cuban and would fit right in with the international flavor of this party."

Owen leaned into the couple and lowered his voice.

"He's Jewish. Can you believe how global the Washington region has become?"

Helga glanced at her State Department husband. Her mouth had become thin and cruel like a well-healed knife wound.

"Al told me his wife was born in The Camps, during the war. When I met her, thin with deep-set eyes, she struck me as wearing a tragic air, a scarf of despair, even before he had shared her background with me. Her eyes told me she had known real sorrow. Just my impression, of course."

U.S. diplomat Alphonso Arias said in a low undertone: "They had their chance."

I misheard. He didn't say that. I must have misunderstood.

"I'm sorry. What did you say?" feeling a prickle at the back of the neck.

"The Jews—they had their chance to get out of Germany."

Despite the time spent at Murph's on Friday nights practicing poker faces, Owen's visage crumbled, turning a red color, not in the Crayola crayon box. "I see. Just where, exactly, were they supposed to go?"

"So. . . it's Owen, right?" I read smug on his face and a red-for-danger light came on inside my head.

"Owen, I can tell from your expression you are one of them." A half smile tried to escape the tight corners of his closed mouth. *Or, is he starting to curl his lip at me?*

"One of whom?"

"Those Gentiles who guilt-trip over what happened to the Jews. Do you want to talk frankly?"

"You know, Mr. Arias, I've always believed that what folks are doing to the Jews this week will probably be done to me next week."

"Owen, come now. I suspect you are a student of history like me. You know the origins of the State of Israel, right? Western powers made a present of Arab territory to a Jewish lobby. No one consulted the Muslim and Christian natives."

Owen said, "Your offhanded comment about their chance to leave Europe is offensive. I studied my Jewish history from two experts, Leon Uris and Simon Wiesenthal."

"You are reading the wrong things into what I said. I find the Jews a fascinating people. I would never advocate the extermination of an entire people. That would be monstrous. You may think because Helga's father served in the SS that he initiated special actions. Under the Nazis one did what one was told, or else, and these actions were necessary for the times.

Owen's face retained its rich crimson, still not within the range of Crayola normality.

"I know that is a joke in the American lexicon," Arias said. "'I vas only following orden.' If you didn't follow orders you were a dead man. They sent good Germans to the camps just for telling anti-Hitler jokes.

"They all followed orders. They were Germans! Because of that ironclad discipline, they were able to take over Europe and major parts of Russia."

He waved his lecturing hand as if conducting a historical orchestra. His expensive sports coat was getting on Owen's nerves, while dandruff on the tweed shoulders twinkled under the room's lights.

"There were no judicial proceedings for not following orders. If you disobeyed, you were shot. They had special SS units who executed deserters on the spot; no last cigarette and blindfold. You were dragged over to the nearest wall or ditch. It was a brutal time.

"If you were a high ranking officer you would be shot and your family back in Germany would be sent to a concentration camp.

"I know enough American history to dampen your fires of indignation. Let us examine your national self-righteousness."

His brown-eyed gaze locked onto Owen's face.

"The current estimate is that 20 million Africans died in transit over the three centuries of the slave trade. America and its Christian churches supported it with twisted Biblical references, or looked the other way.

"Everyone knows what happened to the native Americans. They were driven west to create more 'living space' for the White man. The Germans did the same in the East to create more living space for the Aryan race. Is it so different because the Indians were nomadic and the Slavs were settled? Both populations were considered inferior and almost eliminated.

"The remaining Indians were put on reservations. The Germans referred to their reservations as concentration camps, because they did not have the wide open spaces of the American badlands. In fact, I read that Hitler admired the way the Americans had handled the Indian question. They were removed, exterminated, and forgotten about, with only an occasional nostalgic footnote in the history texts. Today, Indian likenesses adorn tee shirts and sports teams because they are now harmless.

"Personally, I think Hitler ensnared himself in the Jewish question. He should have stayed focused on establishing a new order for Europe and defending against the Bolsheviks in the East. He diverted enormous logistics to the Final Solution to say nothing of the loss of Jewish scientific talent that fled to America before the war."

Waving the arm some more, "Again, I am an admirer of the Jews. Do you think it is an accident or a mere coincidence that two of the world's greatest religions are from these people? I work with many Jews in the State Department and other federal agencies. They possess a fierce work ethic and a commitment to education.

"I have been in conversations with Jews downtown where one says 'It can't happen here,' meaning the United States. The other one says 'of course it could happen here.' Then, they turn to me because I have a doctorate in European history and am an uninterested Gentile, and ask me what I think."

"I respond by saying, 'History never repeats itself—exactly. But it can run in rhythms. You have to examine the variables in place at the time.'

"That is what I say."

He pointed his finger at Owen which seemed to smirk like his face, and which Owen wanted to break-off and stick where the sun didn't shine. "Ahh, but that is not what I think. Do you want to know what I really think, Mr. Friel? Do you want to hear?"

"Yes," said Owen.

"The other Jew in the conversation then says, 'We must be careful. It could happen here, too. We must not overreach.'

"Friel, volumes of bitter history in that one word: 'overreach.' He is correct because that is what I have concluded too. 'It' could happen here if they overreach and overachieve and overrepresent themselves in this self-identified Christian country."

Owen worked at maintaining radio silence. *Had truth just raised her head?*

Then Owen responded, "I know this crap goes back centuries with the Christian charge that the Jews killed Christ, which is bullshit."

"Friend, you miss the point. That reveals partial motivation for the persecutions. The whole truth exposes the Jewish people as too smart, too ambitious, and too hard-working. Also, they set themselves apart as the perpetual outsider, creating an easy target."

Arias continued with his lecturing tone. "One example from my doctoral studies: In the Middle Ages the Polish King Boleslav invited the Jews in. He gave them special rights and privileges. Many Jews could read and write. They were excellent bankers who could keep the economy healthy. Most of the Christian population was illiterate peasantry.

"Remember, in that earlier Christian tradition, it was a mortal sin to lend money, to charge interest. That did not apply to Jews since they were non-Christian. They were so masterful at money lending that if a nobleman became too indebted, he would start a pogrom and erase his debt by killing or exiling his bankers.

"The Jews also bred resentment in the general population for their role as tax collectors and overseers of property for the nobility."

Arias continued: "Every place the Jews settle, they excel over time. Prosperity sows the seeds of their inevitable destruction. Look at the Jews of Babylon and Egypt. Daniel, the Jewish Prophet, ended up being a key advisor to King Nebuchadnezzar. The other non-Jewish advisors to the king were jealous and had him thrown into the den of lions to be eaten alive.

"Moses held a special place in Egypt where the Jews had been slaves for hundreds of years. That does not happen normally. See? Permit me to suggest what is at work here. It is beyond the Jews and beyond American and European history."

"What is it, then?" Owen asked, giving him a weary half-smile.

Arias said, "Normal people can do unimaginably terrible things. Injustice is the normal, unchangeable state of things. Always, they will kill you if they can."

Arias had Owen's attention. Owen knew history, but not the way Arias was presenting it.

Helga Siberbauer Arias, she of the blue gemstone eyes and slight German accent, knew more than she told Owen; more than she had even told her husband.

It happened when she was four years old.

She spied the large, weathered leather luggage on the bed which was usually locked in the closet. Her father had searched through it the night before, after a whispered phone call. He left the house in a hurry early the next morning.

They felt at home in the German community outside Buenos Aires. But her father always watched for strangers, especially anyone who came into the neighborhood asking questions.

She remembered her father having beers with a friend from the Fatherland, who, slightly drunk, responded to her father, "Ja, Oberstgruppenfuhrer."

With a pitiless tone in his voice she had never heard before, "Werner, you fool! Don't ever use the old SS titles. I pay local police to keep us safe. One slip and Jew agents will be all over us!

He growled in a fierce whisper, "That fucking Jew pig Wiesenthal is relentless. He has my records. The war is over but those bastards have sent kill teams looking for our brothers-in-arms. If we had completed the task, there would be no one looking for us.

"Israel Carmi himself, from that Jewish Brigade scum, may be looking for me. My sources say they have executed over one thousand loyal Nazis."

Now, after folding the luggage open on the bed, Helga picked up small heavy iron medals with their blue ribbons and silver thunderbolts, releasing a dank, musky smell. She recognized the imbedded twisted crosses but didn't know how or why she knew.

Next to the medals in the luggage was a shiny, black German pistol and shiny gold squares the size of the candy bars her father bought for her on Sundays after Mass. There were more than she could count. She could already count to fifty! Pater was proud of his smart daughter with the straw-blonde hair and the huge blue eyes.

Underneath these items, she found three small tins with screw-on tops. She opened one. Small sparkling stones spilled from it like the ones her mother wore around her neck and on her fingers when she dressed up to go to the opera in Buenos Aires. Those trips were rare. Father always worried about something he called a low profile.

Large faded manila envelopes rested on the bottom. The first one held papers with important looking seals and stamps.

Another envelope held pictures. Laughing German soldiers stood around naked girls, some soldiers lying on top of the girls like they were playing a game or tickling the girls. *Why did the soldiers have their pants down? That was not proper. You did not show those parts to other people. What was going on?*

Several pictures revealed rows of people sleeping in a large ditch. They were all stacked up on top of one another. *Why were they all sleeping there with no clothes?* Up on the edge of the ditch, next to a big pile of dirt, were stacks of clothes, with soldiers looking through the clothes.

These pictures were not good. They gave her bad feelings. She sensed these were secret pictures and she should not be looking at them.

Because Helga could count to fifty, and because Helga was smart, she put everything back in place, exactly as before she opened the luggage.

When Helga was several years older she brought one of her school friends over to the house for apple strudel, the best in the neighborhood, thanks to her mother who had brought the delicious recipes from the old country.

"Momma, this is my best friend from school."

Heidi Siberbauer nodded and smiled at the slight senorita-brown-eyed, black-haired classmate with whom Helga was arm-in-arm, in the European fashion.

"Her name is Ester Frank."

Her mother's face fell and her eyes widened, for a mere second. Then her mother-smile returned.

Helga saw. *Is she ill? I have never seen mother smile like it is strangling the rest of her face?*

Ester possessed an attentive air with a thin nose set in a hawkish face. Her school uniform made her appear even more serious.

After the snack, Ester left for her home, after looking at Helga's mother with a sidelong glance over her shoulder.

"Helga, is Ester a good friend of yours?"

"Yes, momma, she is always nice to me. She says she loves my blonde hair and wishes she could look like me. She gets good grades and always says smart things.

"Helga, do you know that she is Jewish?"

"No, I don't think so. I don't know. What does that mean?"

"Does she wear a crucifix around her neck? I didn't see one this afternoon."

"No, mama. I have never seen her with a crucifix, but I did see her wear a star on a gold chain once. She said it was special, from her grandmother who was from Germany, like us, long ago. She said she is only allowed to wear it when the family has its party with lights. She said they do it every year in December. It sounds like fun. If she invites me I would like to go this year."

"Well . . . we . . . "

"Did I do something wrong, momma?"

"Helga, it is complicated. When your father comes home, after dinner, we will sit down and he can explain things to you."

"Yes, momma."

That's when Karl Siberbauer educated Helga in the true history of their beloved Germany, not what was being taught in the schools or what she might read in the newspapers.

After Heidi washed and put away the dinner dishes, she put out plates of apple strudel left over from the after-school snack.

"As always, Heidi, your strudel is excellent!"

"Thank you, Karl."

"Helga, your mother says you had a friend over after school today and that she is Jewish?"

"Karl, she's so young," said Heidi. "Do we need to burden her now with the Jews?"

"Is there ever a good time?" he said.

"Well, Helga. Is your friend Jewish?"

"I'm not sure, Father. Mama thinks she is because she doesn't wear a crucifix and sometimes she wears a star on a gold chain."

"Helga, you are going to be a big girl soon and I want to explain things that can be hard to understand. They are important because they are why we moved to Argentina.

"Liebchen, you know what criminals are?"

"Yes, father. They are bad people who do bad things."

"You've been to Uncle Gerhart's farm. He raises pigs and crops. You've seen the pigs. Did you know that pigs are one of the smartest animals?"

Helga giggled, despite the serious mood. "Papa, you are funny. Pigs are dirty, not smart."

"No, Mein Liebchen. Pigs are smart and dirty. They can be mean too. When you are not looking they can knock you down or even bite you.

"Helga, your mother says that Ester seemed like a sweet girl and I'm sure she is. Not all Jews are bad. But it is because of their history and the criminal acts that so many of them committed that we have to be on guard against them.

"Remember, piglets are cute when they are little; not so cute when they grow up and eat everything and smell bad."

Helga's face was dimming. *What have I done wrong and what does Ester have to do with Uncle Gerhart's pigs?*

"The Jews are criminal pigs. They do bad things to other people. They grab everything they can. Sometimes, they even steal from other pigs. These people, as you know from your Bible studies in school, are the ones who killed our Lord and Savior Jesus Christ; and then they cursed themselves by saying 'blame us and our children.' Typical Jewish arrogance."

Helga nodded because she was smart she remembered all her school teachings.

"We Germans lost The Great War because Jewish bankers stabbed us in the back. The Jewish bankers in London went to New York and told the Jews on Wall Street that they were losing the war, and if the British lost, they would be unable to repay the billions of war bonds the Americans held. That's when the United States joined the war against us."

Karl reached across the table and took Helga's hand into his two large hands.

"After we lost the war, our beloved Fatherland was on its knees, poor and hungry. It took a wheelbarrow of worthless money to buy one loaf of bread. There was fighting in the streets in all the big cities, every night. No one would help us."

Karl gently squeezed Helga's hand.

"Then along came our German Messiah, Adolph Hitler. The Fuhrer recognized that we are one people, Ein Volk. He reminded us that we are one Christian nation, even though we are half Catholic and half Protestant.

"The Russians to our East were godless communists. They boasted many Jews in their ranks because Jews are a most godless people believing that good must happen here, not beyond the grave, and therefore they must set out to remake the world.

"Hitler gave us order. Order is important for Germans. With order, came hope. He inspired us.

"Your friend Steffi—remember how she hurt you with her lies and yelling at you at recess last week? That is what Jews were like, telling lies all the time. They made friends only with other Jews. They were always plotting to take advantage of good Germans. Der Fuhrer possessed the courage to call for measures needed to protect our Fatherland.

"The rules Herr Hitler imposed on Jews were not new. Wearing special clothing and not being allowed to work in certain professions were practices that Christian Europe had imposed on Jews going back for a thousand years. Can you imagine, practices going back that long and then we Germans get blamed?

"The feelings about the Jews have always been there. We Germans were honest about the problem. The French and Italians would talk it to death. Germans took action.

"Der Fuhrer told the Jews to leave Germany. Even then, they were looking for ways around the rules and arguing . . . always arguing. They still did not go so we rounded them up and put them into camps where they would have to work.

Heidi started gathering the dessert plates for washing. The jew-talk always bothered her. She agreed with Karl, but . . . *that was the past and no one cared anymore.*

"You see, Jews were like gypsies. They were lazy and stole money from people who did the work; you know, people like your uncle with his farm. He rises at dawn and labors all day.

"The Jews stole from him by changing the prices that would be paid for his crops. It made Uncle angry. This was happening all over Germany.

"You know how it is when you have a pebble in your shoe?"

"How do you mean, Father?"

"You must remove it or it gets worse and worse. That is what we had to do with the Jews."

He looked over at Heidi. "Other countries would not take Jews. So we sent them to labor camps in the East. Conditions were hard in the camps because there was a war. Germany was fighting for its life and could not spare extra food and clothing for those who did not work. Disease broke out in the camps. Many died.

"After the war, the countries who fought against Germany felt guilty for not helping the Jews more and they created a new country only for Jews called Israel. They took that land from people who were already there called Palestinians. The Palestinians were Muslims and Christians who had lived there since the time of Jesus.

"This Jew-country, Israel, spreads propaganda about Germany and the war. Do you know what propaganda is, my darling?"

"No, Father."

"It is making lies that sound like the truth."

"The Jews said we murdered many of their people. The truth? Disease and the terrible things that happen in war killed them.

"That is why I left Germany with your mother and we came to Argentina, where you were born. The Jews were telling lies and it became too dangerous for me. These people wanted revenge, even though I always followed my orders, like a good German soldier. German discipline was the backbone of our Army. A "Wehrmacht," a war machine, beats in the heart of every loyal German."

Helga was still looking at her father with her big blue eyes.

Karl tried a smile. *How beautiful she is, like her mother. It was worth it to purify the German race. We will go back some day.*

"Helga, this means you must be careful with Ester."

"Can she still be my friend? She is so kind. Did you know that her favorite saying is one she borrowed from her Aunt Anne, when she was a girl: 'Think of all the beauty still left around you every day and be happy.' Isn't that nice?"

Karl and Heidi exchanged a look—the one that parents use in the face of an innocence that will too soon be wrenched away.

"It would be better if she were not your friend. She should not come here again. It might cause problems for me. And Liebchen, you should not go through my things. The suitcases contain old war relics, reminders of a special time. As soldiers, we had a duty to protect our Fatherland. In the SS we were the special soldiers and had to do many hard things."

Karl and Heidi could see Helga's face dim. But it had to be done. When Helga was older, she would understand. By then, Ester would have broken the friendship with some typical Jewish betrayal of their daughter.

Helga would discover the Jewish rule: Jews cannot lie, cheat or steal from other Jews, only from the Gentiles, because Jews are The Chosen People.

As former SS Oberstgruppenfuhrer Karl Siberbauer explained the controversial, bloody history to his young daughter, he could smell the diesel of the Panzer III tanks and hear the roar of the Heinkel bombers overhead as the Blitzkrieg rolled East.

The dust! The dust of Poland and the Ukraine, everywhere! The SS-Liebstandarte Adolph Hitler Division hurtled across the vast plains. We were unstoppable. My divisions were gods, casting thunderbolts of destruction in our path! This was truly the beginning of The Thousand Year Reich and more living space for the German people.

The Germans knew that their agricultural improvements in irrigation, hybrids, and fertilizers would not keep up with a growing population and The Fatherland's raised expectations.

Karl knew, from a short conversation with Himmler, that Hitler had planned to seize Ukraine from the Soviet Union, starve thirty million East Europeans and transfer the food to Germany. Harsh, but necessary. Darwin rules in human affairs too, not just in the worlds of animals and plants. The battle for existence is unforgiving. The struggle eliminates that which is unfit, that which is the outsider, like the Jews. These are natural laws.

In the city of Bydgoscz, in northern Poland, Karl came upon the bodies of several hundred German nationals. They were in a line along the side of the road. The dead included women, most of whom had their dresses torn open in front, blood pooling between their legs.

Polish snipers killed the German civilians; that's what the Poles said. SS Oberstgruppenfuhrer Karl Siberbauer ordered immediate reprisals.

Helga grew older and overheard more.

When her father's soldier friends from the old country visited, and it grew late, and they drank too many beers, her father's voice took on a different tone—forceful—like he was giving orders. He spoke an anger which she did not understand because he seemed to be happy with her mother, and with Helga, and their German neighborhood.

She didn't know for sure what his job was—consulting about businesses—whatever that meant. German visitors, many with old war wounds, left small briefcases behind, always locked.

Karl's voice thundered as the Kameraden raised their beer mugs late into the evening: "Der Fuhrer's arrival was the second coming of the Messiah! How we needed him! The country was still shattered from The Great War. Berlin was a whorehouse. Unemployment and inflation crippled us. This one man appeared on the scene. He made us proud to be Germans again. He restored our precious orden!

They clinked beer steins. "To the Fatherland!"

Karl continued, "The world marveled at our accomplishments. Important people from England and the United States came to pay homage to our leader. One of the richest Americans, Joseph Kennedy, the U.S. Ambassador to England, was a strong admirer of the Reich in 1938. Kennedy was critical of the Jewish influence surrounding President Roosevelt, who had appointed him to his ambassadorial post. Kennedy understood how we were the bulwark between Christian civilization and the communist menace in the East.

"Kennedy had a solution to 'the Jewish problem.' He had developed a plan with Prime Minister Chamberlain to ship all German Jews to Africa and other places in the Western Hemisphere under the joint administration of Britain and the United States.

"The powerful Senator Prescott Bush too, was involved with companies that helped rebuild Germany between the wars.

"They feared us. Can you believe it? They bled us dry with the Great War and then starved us with crippling reparations and imposed restrictions on the size of our military.

"Because I came from a good German family and earned my degree from Frieberg, I had the opportunity to join the SS. Few people realize our officer ranks were filled with well educated, patriotic Germans who were fervent in their anti-Bolshevism. Germany was a Christian, middle-class country. We hated the idea of a Stalinist nation run by so-called people's committees.

"Of course, in the soldier ranks you have all kinds. I remember a Private Otto Volker from my hometown in Flamsche who was drinking with his fellows and I overheard his conversation.

"Private Volker said, 'I tell you. I know what the Jews did! They must be destroyed! In 1928 and 1929 they carried the women off and raped them and cut them up and drank the blood. Every Sunday in their synagogues they sacrificed human blood, Christian blood. When we smashed their synagogues we found many Christian bodies. We knew they were Christian because many wore crucifixes or scapulars around their dead necks. Their doctrine says the best deed they can do is to sacrifice Christians.'"

"These claims were silly, but I never corrected them, said Karl. "They were useful to accomplishing our tasks. I still had to conduct symbolic acts to stiffen the spine of the unit for their special duties."

Karl lowered his voice, "Before I fired the shot into the Jewish baby's head, holding it upside down in the air by its left ankle, I pronounced to the child, in front of my unit, 'You must die so that we can live.'"

Karl looked around the room, returning his voice to normal command mode. "I had witnessed hesitation in my men's faces over the last week. Population cleansing damages a soldier's spirit even when it must be executed in the name of One Christian Europe and the needed living space for the German people. This difficult duty in the eastern lands would ensure a higher standard of living for our German families for generations.

"I then threw the child's body into the large empty pit dug overnight by Ukrainian peasants for the 3,000 Jews rounded up the day before and held nearby under guard.

"The ragged prisoners wearing their Star of David were being marched to the site as I spoke to the men to fortify them for their grim task.

"Those of us who were educated understood the scientific principles of natural selection. We officially acknowledged how Jews had plagued Europe for centuries with their presence. They wheedled and conspired against we Christians. They sought to dominate various enterprises all out of proportion to their numbers. While the Jews were less than one percent in Germany, they were always overrepresented in commerce, the arts, academe, and finance. "

Glancing again around the room at Alte Kameraden, the old comrades, "Oh, finance; yes, they'd been at that for centuries."

His friends had heard it all before, but still riveted their eyes on their leader, taking comfort from old refrains, far from home, across the ocean.

"We tried another way before the camps. We urged them to leave. We told them they were not welcome. We confiscated their businesses and threw them out of their jobs. So many of them still stayed! They bleated like sheep that they were Germans and could trace their lineage back hundreds of years. Their families had been in the Fatherland for centuries, but that was because no one before us had the strength to purify Germany for The Thousand Year Reich.

"We confiscated their wealth for the war effort. There was so much of it! We also arranged for German companies like Krupp and I.G. Farben to use Jewish labor in their factories next to the camps. We removed the unfit workers."

"We had the complete support of the German people. There was no love for the Jews. The Reich sold the jew-property to loyal Nazi Party members. Those German businessmen who were lukewarm to the Third Reich became fervent supporters when given the opportunity to become rich overnight, doing nothing.

"Finally, we had no choice. We discharged our duty as ordered by Der Fuhrer. For this, we were painted as monsters. The strongest deserve to rule."

Heads nodded, accompanied with "Ja's." Scattered refrains, "Ein Volk, Ein Reich, Ein Führer."—One People, One Reich, One Leader.

He raised his arm in the Nazi salute, "Seig Heil!"

"Germany took on the entire world! The Americans damn us as thugs and murderers. The victors always rewrite history. The 'SS monster' rhetoric was convenient for America after the war when it wanted to rebuild the Fatherland to confront the Soviets. Easier to blame our Nazi party than to recognize the entire country's commitment to the cause. It lets the Americans and our fellow countrymen sleep better at night. The truth. The Truth! Many of our officers were educated, creative and technically accomplished members of Germany's intellectual elite. Even Himmler himself was well educated.

Karl raised his right arm again, but with a fist this time.

"These were good German men committed to a unified Christian Europe. They stood against the huge Jewish Bolshevik menace in the East. Do the Americans know this? Of course. That is why the American Intelligence Service helped so many of us to escape, as did the Catholic Church."

"Ja, I made it here through the Church network, before my family emigrated," said an old comrade-in-arms, missing an eye.

Karl continued, "If anyone thinks the fears of the Bolshevik hordes were unfounded, look at what the Russians did at the end of the war. They raped two million German women! They pillaged eastern Germany, shipping entire factories back to Russia. Even that war criminal Churchill referred to the horror of the Iron Curtain's descent onto Eastern Europe.

"Of course we had our low-class thugs who delighted in the killings. But then, so did the civilian populations. You would not believe how the Jewish removal activities drew such crowds in Poland.

"We had to keep quiet about the times and locations. Those Slavs turned our disposal regimens into parties with their gawking and drinking. Some even took pictures, which was forbidden. I think the sight of helpless women stripping naked and being killed excited them on some level. Maybe it was the psychology of 'thank God, it's not me.'

"What grim tasks, creating the large pits, making everyone undress without creating panic—you see, we did that by giving them no hope, and then lining them up to be shot. Sometimes, we were in a hurry and just had them lay down on one another in the pit—like sardines in the can—we used to joke. We made sure they were dead before we buried them. We wanted no victim witnesses.

"I know first hand, from talking with Himmler, that we had 42,500 ghettos and work camps. We discarded at least fifteen million who were unfit to be part of the new European Order; nine million were Jews with their conspiratorial strangleholds on commerce and finance. We took in enormous wealth.

"They accuse us of eliminating eleven million, including six million Jews. Nein! It was many more and Europe looks different today for our efforts.

"But . . . we lost the war, did we not? We had to leave our beloved Fatherland, Ja, to avoid ugly recriminations. People admire winners only. But, did we lose? Look at their healthy Aryan faces today. This new German generation benefits from the sacrifices of our population-cleansing as they accuse us of crimes against humanity. They are not held back by the millstones of the deformed, the

Gypsies, the homosexuals and the Jews. We will dominate Europe again, even with reduced borders!

"I predict we will become the economic engine for all of Europe. Decades from now, if there is a depression, these European cowards will come to us, begging for our help.

"Kameraden! The irony! Winners rewrite the history books. Christopher Columbus, the hero who they say discovered America, opened the door for the extermination of entire populations in the Caribbean.

"European adventurers who went into Central America and South America conquered those native peoples and territories. We did nothing worse than they did, except in typical German fashion we were organized and kept fastidious records. There are records of the Spanish murder, rape, and pillaging. But they are hidden in archives behind the history books touting their conquests.

"I remember one reference to the Spanish sexual slave trading. The Indians were a handsome people. The diary of the Jesuit priest noted that nine and ten year old girls had become popular that year. It wasn't clear if it was a trend at the time, or if they were all that was left.

"Mein Kameranden! You have made me go on too long. I am hoarse. We are made scapegoats so that others do not have to look into their hearts and at their history. Our time in the sun will come again."

Raising his beer stein, gesturing all to rise . . .

"To the Fourth Reich!"

"So," Arias continued with his Gaithersburg party conversation, "I know Jewish insecurity which equals the arrogance of their culture. Both are well grounded. The German experience, which we were discussing, was a combination of scapegoating and jealousy."

Owen took a small sip of his drink to hide the surprise on his face. *Where does this guy get all this information and why don't I know these facts?*

"The German jealousy grew out of Jewish success in commerce, law, medicine, the arts, and academe. Jews were successful out of proportion to their 1% of the German population.

"The Jewish population in the U.S. has fluctuated between 2% to 3% for decades. What do you think is the Jewish representation in Hollywood, or on Wall Street, or in the legal and medical professions? Certainly much more than 3%, wouldn't you say? What happens if there is a major economic downturn and Jewish Wall Street names are linked to it?"

Arias gave a short laugh—one sharp bark. "Yes, there are reasons for their insecurity."

Owen glanced at Helga, she of the blue gemstone eyes, and now a smile as cold as a pawnbroker's.

Owen still listened hard, while his face studied his shoes.

Arias said, "You may have noticed in recent years the support Israel receives from the American Christian Evangelicals. These are Christian fundamentalists, many with roots in the White South.

"Do you know their history with the KKK? The KKK agenda persecuted Blacks, Jews, and Catholics. That includes you and me Mr. Friel, and we're not Black or Jewish. If you're not part of their little select white religious group, you go to hell. If you were Jewish would you want to rely on that kind of support?"

Arias put his hand on Owen's shoulder and Owen took a step back without thinking.

"Friel, one other thing. The Germans and the Americans are so alike. Both respond violently to ideology; both seek to improve the world and often do it with military force."

Not wanting to over-react, which would lead to strong words, after all, it was just a party, Owen decided to leave the conversation and find another drink. He needed it.

I need to process what I've heard. His take on history is verbal chloroform. Damn it, how did he get to work for our State Department with those attitudes? Who let him the fuck in!

Owen's head was spinning. *These goddam arrogant Argentinians! Helga, with her gold-spun blonde hair and azure eyes, and Arias' savoir-faire aren't the ingredients of monsters, or the offspring of monsters . . . are they?*

Did the world just get more complicated?

Having decided to stay longer at the diverse party, Owen noticed a friendly looking woman, also early thirties. She projected an engaging, intelligent energy, despite the glasses and the frumpy brown, cotton-something-or-other skirt. She spoke with a pronounced accent.

Owen ventured forth again. He decided to forgo his patented, guaranteed ice-breaker of "What's up?"

Instead, "Sorry, but I couldn't help but notice your British accent. Are you from Great Britain or Australia?"

"No. I'm German. I learned English from the Brits. I am from the part of Germany that was under the British occupation after the war."

Owen did a mental double-take, "I just met another person at this same party, also with a German background."

She replied, "I know, I met her," hesitation in her eyes.

Owen felt he was tempting something sad in her. "I told her that my mother is German-American and that my father was in the war in Germany. So, I've always had an interest in Germany. Her father was in the war too. Was your father in the war?"

"No.

"Oh," Owen said.

Owen said nothing.

She said nothing.

Then, "He was in a concentration camp," she said.

"What! Was he Jewish?"

"No."

"A political enemy?"

"No. He refused to fight in the war."

"A conscientious objector?"

"No, he opposed the war and didn't agree with what was going on."

Owen had never heard of this—a civilian, non-political German resisting the Nazi state?

"But how did he even know what was going on? The government controlled the media with propaganda and restricted all information!"

"We knew enough about what was going on. My father was opposed to the war and they arrested him. People knew. It was impossible to not know."

Owen looked at her, "We never heard about German war protestors. That isn't the way they wrote it in our history books."

The woman in the nondescript skirt with the now-honest eyes said, "They didn't write it that way in ours either. It was bad Nazis who did everything, as if the German people were sitting on the . . . how do you say . . . 'sidelines?' Is that the correct word, meaning not involved?"

"That's right," Owen said.

Owen feared if he looked in a mirror, he would see his eyes spinning in his head like one of the old TV cartoon characters. "Nice to meet you, need another drink. I have to think about what you told me."

A typical Saturday night outing for divorced-Owen usually meant all verbal-social-Styrofoam and packing peanuts of meaninglessness. Not this one.

Owen bowed his head as he wended his way to the kitchen bar, again.

Jesus wept.

That's all I could think when Owen told me these stories.

Too much betrayal.

First, the Jesus message betrayed by his followers.

Then, the thousands, millions?, betrayed by the Church while Christians slaughtered each other.

And now, more extermination of The Chosen People in the modern era.

I couldn't help but wonder, WHY WON'T OUR GOD TAKE BETTER CARE OF HIS CHILDREN?

CHAPTER 32

Final Lecture

FATHER GARZA ENDURED ONE FINAL lecture from Archbishop Quijano.

"I want to elaborate on a point Monsignor Brahm made earlier about the institutional Church, a Church which you criticize, even though you are part of it," opened the Archbishop looking with narrowing eyes at Garza and with a plastic smile approximating human behavior.

"Let me provide you with facts. Seven years ago, your country lost an unjust war in Southeast Asia. Monsignor Brahm, in conversation with me over espressos last month, in the company of Cardinal Ratzinger, advised that at least one million Vietnamese—one million!—were killed by you Americans! It may be as many as two million or three million killed according to Vatican intelligence."

Brahm raised his eyebrows at Quijano disclosing their private conversation, but those were the facts he had shared with the Archbishop.

"This ossified church structure you accuse us of belonging to has for centuries promulgated "Jus ad bellum." You know it as "The Just War Theory." The rules are simple.

"For a war to be just, it must be necessary to wage against an aggressor; all the alternatives have been exhausted. Secondly, there must be a likelihood of success. Finally, the use of arms must not produce evil greater than that being eliminated.

"Remember, Father Garza, I am a product of Franco Spain, not some pseudo-liberal French paleontologist or heretical, *enfant terrible* German theologian . . . excuse me, Cardinal, I was not referring to you."

Gabe studied the intense Quijano face with its now-annoyed look, *but then, sunshine probably annoys him too.*

Quijano went on. "I understand the communist menace. I have family who were butchered by the Red Terror in our bitter Civil War. I remember as a child being repelled by my grandfather's fingernails which never grew straight after being torn out by the communists. Americans have a saying that if you haven't been a communist before the age of forty, you have no heart; and if you are a communist after age forty, you are a fool. Sometimes, you Americans … "

Quijano shook his head as he reached for his small gold cigarette lighter.

"That makes light of the horror that is communism. Over 500,000 Spaniards were killed by either the Red Terror or the White Terror. So, I have nothing but loathing for that evil system that is communism.

"I tell you, we killed our share of communists, but in self-defense. We suffered the greatest anticlerical bloodletting Europe has ever known. In the Andalusian diocese of Malaga, in just one instance, 115 out of 240 clergy were killed in the year before Italian troops seized the city in 1937. Often before their deaths, clergy were sexually tortured … "

Quijano stared at the lighter and continued. "But tell me, Father Garza, was the United States fearful of a North Vietnamese invasion of California after the so-called Gulf of Tonkin resolution? Did you think the North Vietnamese naval patrol boats would cross the Pacific and shell Los Angeles?"

Father Garza's lips pursed and his head nodded no. *Finally, something we agree on.*

"No sir, no one expected an attack on California from Hanoi.

Quijano continued, with a raised voice. "You lost 58,000 Americans and there were two million Vietnamese civilians killed?

There is the companion 'Jus in bello' in Church teachings, how to properly conduct a war. Remember, I am no friend of communists."

Quijano moved into full outrage. "Indiscriminate bombing by B-52's? Jungle defoliation and poisoning of the countryside? Napalm against civilians? The assassination of 26,000 Vietnamese by a man who later headed up your CIA, and a fellow Catholic—he will be damned. Against a country of peasants who had never set a foot on your soil?"

Quijano rubbed the lighter between his right thumb and forefinger.

"I suspect your former Defense Secretary McNamara, a war criminal, will in the future claim that those who served the Kennedy and Johnson administrations acted according to what they thought were the principles and traditions of the United States. Yet, they were wrong, horribly wrong. Your best and brightest. Yes?"

Quijano now provided a twisted smile so vicious Father Garza could have smelled it with his eyes closed.

"And I suspect your McNamara will also complain that they were too busy with other issues to fully examine what was happening as they slipped deeper and deeper into immoral war tactics.

"You are a Christian country, yes? And, Germany—pardon me, fellow panel members—was a Christian country too at the time of World War II?

"So, is the message at fault? Is it the failure of the community of believers who promulgate the message, and their institutional representatives called the Holy Roman Catholic Church? Or, is it the culpability of arrogant, sinful men who do not listen and have not listened for two thousand years?"

Again, with raised voice, "I submit that your criticism is misdirected at our religious institution which can and does err, but not in matters of faith and morals. Something as 'outdated' as the Church's teachings would serve us well if nations followed her principles.

"Then, the Jews. Always the Jews. There was that high profile Jew secretly warning Nixon before the 1968 election that peace was at hand with North Vietnam. Then your presidential candidate Nixon committed treason by sabotaging the agreement. That continued your war with peasants in Southeast Asia for seven more bloody years, all those countless additional innocent lives—in the name of power and influence! And war is good for Wall Street, yes? We know who predominates on Wall Street, do we not? So typical."

A bead of perspiration emerged on either side of Quijano's forehead.

Gabe wanted to release a you-just-don't-get-it sigh, but didn't dare. Not now.

"And those Jews of old. If anyone should have listened and recognized Our Lord, it was them! They were the Chosen People. God spoke to them through their Abraham and Moses. Jesus was one of their own. Instead, they crucified him and rejected his message because it did not conform to their expectation of a New Jerusalem on earth which would overthrow Rome."

Hearing this from his forlorn observer's seat against the far wall, Nasrani brooded, although his face betrayed nothing. *It was that gospel-writer Matthew who shifted blame for Jesus' death to the Jewish crowds. In his narrative, he roared out, "His blood be on us, and on our children!" The Christian Church had made too much out of Matthew's literary decision. It would have been better for the moral health of Christianity if the blame has stayed with Pilate, where it belonged.*

Quijano continued, "A sly, obdurate people, Jews brought tragedy upon their own heads. That is why we expelled them five hundred years ago from Spain. We would not allow them and the Muslims to abort our national resurrection and the return to our Catholic heritage."

Archbishop Quijano mopped his brow with his black silk handkerchief. He rarely talked this long, or with such passion. *But to confront a specially appointed, overseas, clerical heretic, here in Rome, in the bosom of the Church!*

"Father Garza, you of all people, with your heritage and your research on Emperor Constantine should have insights into our Spanish history. After being subjugated by the Moor for eight hundred years, we were finally free. Necessity required us to make sure there was no fifth column of Jews, or other non-believers, left behind to weaken us. Constantine wanted one God, one religion, one Emperor. We wanted the same."

Replaying the night side of his country's history had stretched Quijano's angular face tighter.

"I was born in a small village named Castrillo Matajudios, one hundred sixty kilometers north of Madrid. Translate the name of my city and you see what the mentality is. You need to ask *why*, before you start with your 'judging' which is conditioned by your New World orientation.

Yeah, I can translate that, Gabe thought. *Something like Little Hill Fort of Jew Killers. Anti-Semitism runs deep with these people. I say "these people," but I've got their Spanish DNA along with the Indian strands. He's always bringing up the Jews. I could ask him what's in his morning espresso and he'd launch on the Jews somehow. "They" probably put something in his coffee.*

Archbishop Quijano added, "As we moved into the modern era of the twentieth century, there were several attempts to change the name of my town. They failed.

"This Saul of Tarsus whom you quote, and whom I properly call St. Paul, said in his Epistle to the Romans: 'In respect to the gospel, the Jews are enemies of God for your sake … '"

Quijano saw Garza looking down, to the side, uncomfortable, and he read the American priest's body language.

"No, Father Garza, I am not some caricature of an anti-Semite, or a pseudo-Nazi in church robes. Let me tell you about the Jews. Despise them? No, I have fierce admiration for them and because of that I fear them."

He brought his voice down. "As a people, the Jews are the most cunning intellect alive, and it has been that way throughout history. We fight this enemy who, through thousands of years of schooling is intellectually superior to us. Even before the Roman empire; no, even before Rome was founded, the Jews were able to write.

"But even that statement is too modest. By the Blessed Virgin, look at the Ten Commandments—written on tablets! That's why the Jews are called 'The People of the Book.'

"You have a race of people that has been making laws for thousands of years, maybe seven thousand? From these people of Abraham issued three of the most powerful religions: theirs; our true Christianity, and this murderous, upstart Islam.

"When Egypt subjugated them, who rose to a top position of power? The Egyptian Prince, secretly Jewish, Moses.

"In Babylon, it was the Jewish Daniel who prayed East to Jerusalem, three times a day, who became an important official and survived deadly plots by his jealous non-Jewish colleagues."

Archbishop Quijano breathed hard. He pulled out the black silk handkerchief from his sleeve and mopped his sweating brow again. *These people from the New World, they don't understand, so American in their views. They must have positive outcomes, productivity, success. I have the European true view of reality. We always have tragedy with us. It comes with our human nature.*

What this Garza is criticizing is the nature of life, of having to make choices, usually between a lesser and a greater evil; not between good and evil. Both fascism and communism were bad, but fascism at least tolerated, even promoted Christianity when it served their needs. As a boy, I remember the village priests always willing to administer last rights to the communists lined up against the church wall to be shot.

"You modernists condemn Torquemada for ferreting out heretics. His tactics were justifiable according to the penal standard of the fifteenth century. There was the absolute necessity to preserve *Christian* Spain.

"The Protestant historical estimates are that the number of persons burnt from 1481 to 1504, when Isabella died, was only two thousand; not an exceptional number given what was at stake. A contemporary Spanish chronicler from that era called Torquemada 'the hammer of heretics, the light of Spain, the savior of his country, the honor of his order'."

Quijano reflected, then said, "Go back to 325 A.D. and this Constantine that you, Garza, are acting so surprised about. It does not matter what the ancient Emperor's motivations were. His approval of Christianity gave the true religion a firm political foundation. It changed the world forever. Do you not see the hand of God?

"Garza, you are offended because you have discovered that many religious myths are just that—myths. But they bless people with a vision of what should be. People must have hope. They must see flesh and blood. Chardin's "Cosmic Consciousness" will stir no one's soul. A loving Virgin Mary will.

"I suspect Spinoza's influence on this Chardin. Spinoza came into the world a Jew, in 1632, the son of Marrano parents, those types we needed to keep an eye on. Spinoza had appeal for many with his philosophy: 'God therefore cannot in any way be thought of as separate from the universe. God is in the world and the world is in God. The infinite is in the finite and the finite is in the infinite. And nature? It is a particular way in which God himself exists. And human consciousness? It is a particular way in which God himself thinks. That means that the individual self and all finite things are not simply independent substances; they are modifications of the one and only divine substance. So God is all in all.

"Do not look surprised that I quote Spinoza verbatim. One must know one's enemies. Do you even know that the Jewish religious authorities issued a cherem—a shunning—against him, and his books were also later put on the Catholic Church's Index of Forbidden Books?

"You yap like a puppy at the ankles of truth and nibble around it. You think you understand this Chardin and Spinoza mystical-poetry? You imperil your immortal soul."

"We've had our little debates, Father Garza. Mutual name-calling aside, yes, I know what you think of me—it is written all over your face."

He leaned forward. "Let us apply your so-called findings. Let us say that a member of my congregation has lost a beloved child and she is in such grief, she no longer wants to live. Every moment without her child is its own crucifixion. Who does she cry to? Your Cosmic Consciousness? Your Spinoza theoretical construct?"

Quijano's face softened and his voice lost some of its arrogant timbre. Perhaps he had seen this?

"Or, does she cry out for my Jesus and plead with him to help her with her pain and to make good on his promise of our resurrection—that resurrection he has promised and the resurrection that St. Paul says, without it, we Christians are fools.

"She may even invoke Blessed Mary and ask for a raising, like that of Lazarus. But the grieving mother knows better. Her child was not Jesus's friend, like Lazarus, and she must wait for her crossing over to see her child, the one who never experienced the joys of love and marriage and her own children, and more sunrises and sunsets."

Quijano extended his right arm, palm up, as if seeking alms. "Yes, Father? What do you say?"

Quijano's face began to harden as he continued. "Would our world be a better place without the Holy Roman Catholic Church to serve as the messenger of Our Lord? Would we have different answers—in the end? I will ask you this, too—would our world be a better place without the Gospel from Jesus of Nazareth? I *know* your answer to that. You must then ask, if you think the world would be better for it, how do you spread that message of the "Good News?"

I had to admit, Quijano made me pause. I would think about his rants, even after he signed my thesis paperwork.

What if I'm no more than an overly educated 20th-century heretic, full of what I think I know?

Maybe rules and structures are required in order to survive for 2,000 years?

What if? What if?

I need to follow my dad's advice. Do the right thing and the best you can. Leave the rest up to The Lord.

This one had been different, Paolo Nasrani reflected. He didn't sit in on all thesis reviews after they had reached the final stage before the committee.

He sat against the far wall underneath the ancient fresco by one of the Masters.

He didn't pay attention to priceless, historical pictures any longer. They were everywhere in Vatican City, like trees in a cultural forest, even in this year, 1982.

Nasrani played his professional coordinator role with practiced invisibility as an underpaid, quirky, lisping linguist. He had scheduled the Vatican room of Heliodorus, a private antechamber decorated by Raphael between 1512 and 1514. The room's name referred to the fresco on the right from where he was sitting—*The Expulsion of Heliodorus from the Temple.* Jewish history described a thief called Heliodorus who is felled by a horseman as he tries to make off with the treasure from the Temple of Jerusalem.

Only Nasrani could appreciate the irony of the fresco's subject matter, his own presence, and the cross-examination of Father Garza's thesis.

Before the meeting, in private, Nasrani explained to the Thesis Committee that he had steered Father Garza down a more traditional line of inquiry, encouraged him to update the stilted language in sacramental liturgies, and to build his thesis research around that goal. But, no. Garza had insisted in his "I'm American-and-nobody-can-tell-me-what-to-do" fashion that he would go wherever the Vatican research led him.

Because none of them could see the thinking back behind his eyes, Nasrani had apologized. "Your Excellencies, you know the Americans. Their true religion is the pursuit of pleasure and money. They profess to worship God but can be some of the cruelest people on earth. It is redemption through violence. Look at their movies—the good guy always kills the bad guy and exits with the pretty girl. This is the culture that Father Garza comes from. It is full of self-righteousness."

He paused. "We, however, know the world is beyond fixing and that is why we pray."

He added, "A chi non si lascia consigliare, non si può aiutare. There is no helping him who will not be advised."

That's how Nasrani had described it, with a laugh for somewhat longer than the remarks merited because his mouth felt full of sand. The expression on his face lacked something. It was a something once known as honesty.

When Archbishop Quijano, the Thesis Committee Review chairman, had descended into another anti-Semitic rant, Nasrani brooded. *With these people it is "jew this—jew that." Yes, always "the Jews." Well, I know things the old fool does not know. Tel Aviv holds this information close.*

The Spanish Inquisition that Quijano would have supported, had he lived then, created more forced conversions of Spanish Jews than the history books confessed. We have secret genetic studies on the male Y-chromosome. They conclude that twenty percent of contemporary Spanish males have Y-chromosomes associated with Sephardic Jewish ancestry.

There are also many Catholic-professing descendants of Marranos and Spanish-speaking crypto-Jews in the Southwestern United States and scattered through Hispanic America.

One of the ironies of my people is that the word "Jewish" doesn't appear in the Old Testament. There I go again, thinking "Old" Testament. I'm not much of a Jew any more, accepting the term "Old" Testament. When you are deep cover, you pay a price.

My real Jews take affront to the term "Old" Testament, as if it is a precursor to the new; or as if the "old" should be discarded. Christians declare us too stubborn to accept the "New" Testament.

I like the message of the Jew, Yeshua from Nazareth. But I despise the institutions men created around his message. How do you pervert the teachings of a wandering, preaching rabbi, in a fourth-rate, no-name land full of sand and create a Roman church that insists it speaks for God, who is beyond all human understanding, and then that institution proceeds to tell everyone how to live their lives and then judges their spiritual well-being for eternity? Maybe Garza's thesis and his credo findings will some day bring his church down. If the Spirit is truly there, will his church then resurrect like his Rabbi of long ago?

This Yeshua-man was God? What could be more blasphemous than proclaiming that which is beyond our comprehension has taken on a human form?

One of the most influential rabbis was Hillel who lived one generation before Yeshua. He was asked the meaning of Judaism. He responded, "What is hateful to you, do not do to others. That is the whole of Torah, all the rest is commentary—go now and learn."

When Judea fell to the Babylonians, and the people were taken into captivity, they were known as the Juda-ites (Yehudin), since they were the people of Judah. The religion they practiced was called "Judah-ism."

And then my Judaism over the centuries has taken a wrong turn, just as the Yeshua message. In the third century, Rabbi Simlai taught that were 613 commandments given by God in the Torah. He divided them into 248 positive commandments (thou shalt's) and 365 negative commandments (thou shalt not's). That is as lengthy as the Catholic catechism Garza was criticizing.

I would love to say, "The Torah commands us to not eat pork. Is that God speaking or just pigs trying to outsmart everyone?"

My God, the Jewish God, offers a shattered glass at your wedding, a quick burial when you die, no saints, no afterlife, just blind obedience to the deity who commanded Abraham to make a burnt offering of his only son.

This Yeshua, if he came back and said the law is fulfilled; now, forget the laws and help one another, both the Jews and the Christians would kill him again.

Enough of my mental meanderings.

Father Garza—you are not going to get away from us. You will continue with your doubts, your everlasting dissatisfaction with yourself and your Church. You will execute vain attempts to amend and improve. But there is no happiness for you, because you speak truth to power.

Paolo Nasrani closed his eyes for the moment.

Sh'ma Yisrael: Adonai Eloheynu Adonai Echad. Hear, O Israel, the LORD is our God; the LORD is one.

CHAPTER 33

Dead Sea Scroll

Once the smoke comes out of the bottle, you can't put it back in. That's what Father Gabriel Garza was thinking.

I remember every detail: the sweet pastry smells of the cafe; the expensive table cloth; what the waiter looked like, and how Paolo Nasrani kept waving him away from our patio seating. We always sat outside, away from the cramped tables inside.

"We have come far, you and I, my friend, eh? Still you do not wear your black cassock," said Paolo, "just your Washington Redskins sweatshirt." He reached over to squeeze and release my shoulder. He had never done that before.

This was at Il Bar Sotto il Mare, across from the Vatican museums. I had been looking forward to their seafood specialties. I had expected Paolo to share the famous menu with me, but he handed me something else. I lost my appetite.

"I know you are upset with the bloody findings of your research. Yes? They shake your religious foundations. You would step up to the challenge if history called upon you, eh? Now I will share this with you, to use when it is right and just. Look."

Paolo slid a large, manila envelope across the table, looking over my shoulder for inquiring eyes. I opened it and took out several photos of . . . metal plates?

"What are these?"

He told me.

"A number of scrolls were discovered in 1947 along the Dead Sea Coast. You have heard of these, eh? They are called 'The Dead Sea Scrolls.'"

"Yes," I said. "Everyone's heard of them."

Paolo's gaze fixed on me. Then his eyes flickered as he hesitated and performed a scan of our surroundings—more studious than previous, casual viewings inside Rome's cafes and on her streets. "Controversy still rages. Could they present a radically different view of Christianity, or confirm what is already declared? Inside 'Cave 4' on March 14, 1952, there was one enigmatic copper scroll."

"Copper? I thought everything back then was parchment or, you know, animal skins and stuff?"

"You are correct, my friend. But they utilized copper, containing one percent tin, to preserve important documents, expensive but more durable than parchment or animal skins. They could not unroll this copper piece. It looked important and needed special care. Hebrew lettering appeared on its outside and dated to 70 CE. It had to be cut apart into twenty-three strips to be read because of the risk of crumbling."

Paolo looked side to side, with studied casualness and then leaned in.

"That is when it disappeared, eh? Overnight. Gone."

"Gone?" I said.

I heard echoes of my father, 'Son, close your mouth. You're catching flies.' I closed my mouth.

Paolo said, waving the waiter away again, "Initially, the Israeli Antiquities Authority held the scroll. Then, somehow, it fell into the hands of the Mossad. Good authority informs they pay well and must have these things, eh? Part of their declared Israeli heritage—irreplaceable. They do not negotiate, I am told. They offer the bullet or the coin."

The waiter scowled. Paolo ignored him.

"The metal scroll had to be sliced open by craftsmen with special skills to remove the green sheen of corrosion. It was six inches wide and ended up being three feet long. The Mossad had the experts. The script on the plates was similar to Mishnaic Hebrew, a Hebrew dialect, but also contained some Greek. A scribe who specialized in copper most likely performed the engravings."

I glimpsed a separate document behind the photos in the envelope with a distinctive letterhead logo—*it's that Jewish candelabra thing that holds seven candles. And, of course, unusual Hebrew-looking letters.*

"What's attached there?" I asked.

"The translation."

"In English?"

"Yes, translated twice. Once, from the letters on the plates into literal English, and a second time into colloquial English to reveal the true significance of what is being said."

Paolo handed me the paper translation, the one with the easy-to-read English.

To those communities who follow Yeshua of Nazareth: I bid you SHALOM—

SIMON WAS MY FATHER, before he was Peter, before he met the itinerant, preaching carpenter who stole him away from our family. My father was a rough-built, broken-nosed, emotional man, angry one moment, generous the next. Always a good heart. I tell you to describe the man—not a myth. Yeshua turned him into . . . I do not know what. Simon would upset my mother by bringing someone home who needed a meal. His response, "YHWH was good to me today with the fish, I can be good with his people." My mother would reply, "Are you a fisher for all men or for your family?" If the person was non-Jewish, Mother would give my father a look. Strict rules govern our interactions with unclean nonbelievers. This is what my father told me about his three years with Yeshua. There were signs and wonders. He said the true mystery was the

changing of men's hearts—colder and harder than the temple stones— and there he witnessed the miraculous every day. When the Master called him, he had followed—a mix of curiosity, this man's compelling presence, and a bad fishing season which imposed boring indolence on our village. He smelled the Master's sweat. He saw the Rabbi's washed out look from sleepless nights. He saw this Yeshua scratch at the lice, and throw up when all they had to eat was bad fish. A god does not sweat, or itch, or throw up. The idea that a man could be YHWH is beyond blasphemous. It was the message that this man carried—with charisma, with authority, and with miracles from our YHWH. The message was YHWH loves us. We should take care of each other. We must strive to be better. There is a life after this one. My Simon sensed danger for the upcoming eight-day festival of Pesach, those many years ago. Before the Passover, he sent me and my young brother away to our uncle's village, a two-day journey. The air in Jerusalem discharged the energy of a Spring thunderstorm, only this storm was political. The Romans felt it. They judged political tension to be a challenge and they would do something about this man who encouraged large crowds everywhere. Jewish crowds could turn into Jewish riots. The Emperor in Rome forbade riots. Informers hid everywhere: for the Romans; informers for the High Priest; and informers for the Zealots. My father knew that Judas plotted against the Romans. He hated Romans. An aunt of Judas had been raped by drunken soldiers years ago when they wandered through her dusty village as she washed the family's clothes. She was one of the daily depredations the Jewish people suffered at the hands of these empire builders. Simon wanted his sons out of harm's way. If something triggered a Roman action—Romans were ruthless—perhaps they would spare my harmless mother and my two small sisters. Seven

Shabbats passed after Father sent us away. Mother summoned us but said we must be careful. Peter—he was Peter now—no more Simon, was being watched by the authorities, both the Jewish and the Roman. My brother and I returned home. The tortured crucifixion of Yeshua between the two thieves and the baffling rumors of his miraculous resurrection shook the valleys around Jerusalem. Mother said father had left our home. He was hiding in Jerusalem with the followers in an upstairs room. It was located off an alley near the city entrance called the Eye of the Needle, a portal so small that men stooped to go through it. Simon Peter returned to our home. We heard that The Spirit had come to the followers and they were now publicly preaching the Yeshua message in different languages:

GIVE UP YOUR OLD WAYS. REPENT. BE SAVED WITH THE WATERS.

THE END OF DAYS IS UPON US. TAKE CARE OF ONE ANOTHER.

JOIN GOD IN THE AFTERLIFE.

My Simon was gone. This new man's appearance startled me. He had the expression of one who sees something just over the horizon, full of expectation. The eyes in his craggy face shone a special light. Somehow, the broken nose and wrinkles had receded. But his full head of hair, which used to be a burnished red, had turned white. An energy marked him. He slept little. Always meeting with people and talking about what had happened with this Yeshua and what he meant for the Jewish people. Several years later, a Saul from Tarsus arrived, speaking with authority as the original twelve, sparking their anger. The twelve lived with the Master. Saul had only witnessed him in a rumored vision. The Apostles suspected Saul-Paul reported back to the Romans on my father's movements. They thought he sowed enmity in our ranks by proclaiming

Yeshua to be the Messiah, not just for we Jews, but for all people. Remember, Saul, he now called himself "Paul," had in the early days, arrested Jews for these new beliefs. Then, he worked for the High Priest. Who did he work for now? More years went by and this Paul spread the good news everywhere. He was tireless. Peter said that Paul's guilt drove him as much as the Master's message. Paul had assisted the stoning of Brother Stephen before the Lord appeared to Saul on the road to Damascus. Before my father went to Rome, he directed four trusted followers to write what had transpired with their beloved Yeshua, a true son of God. The End Days had not descended as expected and might not for some time. Paul swept the world with his letters and his travels. If there was no record from the original followers, then there would only be the views of a man who had never lived with Yeshua. Peter said he must go to Rome and preach to the influential Jewish community there. He still had reservations about reaching out to the Gentiles. Yeshua had never directed that. Was Paul betraying the message or fulfilling it? Peter lost that argument to Paul. He finally saw the hand of God. That is what The Master would have wanted—taking the message of love to all men. Paul's congregations were establishing priesthoods and hierarchy resembling the Jewish one Yeshua had criticized. Now, they were appointing bishops who would be successors to the Apostles. None of these positions allowed women. My mother reproached Peter. "Did your Yeshua leave out half of the people? Did this savior not have a mother? Why so many rules and strictures for each community?" At first, it seemed necessary because charlatans were preaching crazy things that The Master had never proclaimed. Everyone was waiting for The Second Coming, for it was The End of Days. The final words father said to me, before he left for Rome, "The Lord never meant to establish

a priesthood and sacraments and mandated beliefs. I fear these things will suffocate his message." That is what I see now as I approach my end of days, with age and sicknesses, as Rome lays siege to our beloved Jerusalem. I ask, "What will happen to THE MESSAGE? "But then, it is in the hands of The Lord. Everything is."

I looked up from the scroll translation, returning to the world of restaurant smells and the sounds of small Italian cars on cobble-stoned streets.

I said my goodbyes.

Paolo understood.

I returned to my now-claustrophobic apartment.

There were more shadows everywhere than before.

After Father Garza exited the cafe, Nasrani remained at their table, banging a tight fist against his lips. His eyes had distance in them.

This priest is shaken by what I have shared. What if he knew things I haven't told him? Did someone say, the murder of millions is a statistic; the murder of someone you know is an atrocity?

I knew of David Stoliar through our Begats, direct male descendants of Judas Iscariot. A Begat, like me, but two generations before, and he was sole witness to the worst civilian maritime disaster of World War II. The word "disaster" provides total insufficiency as the descriptive word.

He was the only survivor among eight hundred Jews fleeing the Shoah in Romania aboard a refugee ship that was barred from Palestine, interned by Turkey for months, set adrift without power, and then torpedoed by a Soviet submarine in the Black Sea in 1942.

He had been aboard an overloaded 150-foot steamer called the Struma. Britain refused to admit the refugee ship into Palestine. Turkey quarantined the vessel for seventy-one days before towing it out to sea.

When the explosion rocked the ship he was one of the lucky ones thrown into the air overboard and into the sea. The water was full of debris and numbingly cold.

The shivering sobs and helpless cries subsided as the hours went by and people let go and slipped under the water into peace.

Stoliar clung to a piece of the ship's decking, alone. When he took out his jack- knife to slit his wrists, his fingers were too numb to help him make his earthly exit and it slid into the watery depths. Hours later he was spotted by a Turkish rowboat and pulled aboard.

First, he was hospitalized in Istanbul, then jailed to keep him quiet.

Eventually, he reached Palestine and joined the British Army's Jewish Brigade in 1943.

He fought with the Israeli Army in the 1948 war of independence.

The sole survivor on a ship of eight hundred Jewish civilians . . . with no one to save them.

What would the priest say to that?

CHAPTER 34

Sign-Off

As he signed the Vatican gold-embossed approval sheet for the Master's thesis, Archbishop Quijano glanced sideways at Father Garza, murmuring, "We must have structure and organization. Without rules, there is no Church."

Garza tried to smile in agreement, but it got stuck on his face and he looked away. He recalled what Nasrani had said about Quijano at one of their cafe meetings. "He is a fanatic and the fanatic always conceals secret doubt."

During his evening prayer at Vespers back in his room, Quijano could not shake the thoughts.

What if Garza is right?

What if our Holy Roman Catholic Church acts the opposite of what Jesus Christ has preached? Garza made parallels between the Church hierarchy and the silly, self-serving rules of the Pharisees and Sadducees of old. In fact, Christ demonstrated uncharacteristic anger when he chased the money lenders out of the Temple. But, the Jews—such a hard-headed people. Could not see what was right in front of them. When someone, usually a prophet, called out to the Jews for reform, they killed him. Just like they killed Jesus.

Does this American renegade bring prophecy or heresy?

Heresy, of course!

In the day of his forebears, only ten generations back, they would have burned Garza— tortured him first to send the right message and bolster the faith of those who might be wavering. Garza is a villainous, whoreson, devil-monk.

You can't tear down and rebuild something as important and meaningful as a church without triggering loss of faith by those millions needing this anchor in their lives. It was not like Jesus said, "Destroy this temple and I will rebuild it in three days."

Why did Jesus speak in riddles? I know it was not wise to speak in direct fashion in the time of the Romans—not healthy to even be noticed. They crucified him for it. He erred in proclaiming the immediate Apocalypse which he and the early Church preached. Could he have been wrong about other things? If so, how could he be God?

Quijano gave himself another mental slap, went over to the sink and splashed cold water on his face, three times.

This Hans Kung, a self-aggrandizing papal antagonist, and the other questioning heretics—they sow doubt. Now Garza walks in their footsteps. What to do?

The next day, Quijano spoke to Paolo Nasrani, the Vatican's thesis coordinator. "Request Cardinal Ratzinger to open a file on Garza and put a copy of his thesis in it. I must approve the thesis so that I do not alienate powerful American hierarchy. Put this envelope with it. This man is dangerous."

"Dangerous, Your Excellency? How might that be?"

"Garza is an idealist and a dreamer," Quijano said.

"Eh? Why does that present a problem?"

"This world is beyond saving, except for Our Lord's personal intervention. That will not happen in my lifetime. I must protect what we have. I cannot waste my time on the world as it ought to be. Besides, the man asks too many infuriating questions."

After leaving the meeting, Nasrani read the memo inside the unsealed envelope before he delivered the package at the Vatican offices for filing.

Date: December 3, 1982
To: The Vatican File
From: His Excellency Archbishop Quijano, Archbishop of Granada, Spain
Subject: Critical Recommendations to Accompany the Vatican File Copy of the Master's Thesis of Father Gabriel Garza from the Archdiocese of Washington,
D. C., the United States (attached)

A man of God in my ecclesiastical position should not vent in such a manner, as I have done during this thesis review. I have examined my conscience to determine why this Father Garza angers me so.

All religious institutions, even if divinely inspired, can attract foolish, error-prone, and not-well-intentioned people. Should we condemn the entire institution for failing to sustain some impossibly high standard that we set in our mind for them? Bad things can happen whenever people are in charge.

Idealists—those are the ones to watch out for, especially when joined with the psychology of the true believer. They can wreak enormous damage. That is what I object to with this Garza. He is a dangerous idealist, unknowingly preparing for a lifetime of cynicism.

These cynics are guilty of filling their own minds with illusions about human nature. Suspicion and disbelief are the inevitable outcome. If we see the world for what it is and not blind ourselves by ill-founded expectations about how others (persons, institutions) are supposed to behave, we are more likely to reap and reciprocate the love that God intends us to find in the company of our fellow man.

Indeed, better to be a realist than to pass from idealist to cynic—and to be a realist who, not expecting the impossible, sees and delights in all the many small good things—and the occasional big good thing—that real people do in this work. We should labor and engage ourselves to bring out the best in our institutions, rather than denounce and tear them down.

There is a short distance only, between cynicism and nihilism.

This priest must not become a candidate for higher positions in the Church. I doubt he will continue long in the priesthood.

He is prone to raising troublesome questions and may cause harm to our Holy Church in the future.

Put a watch on this file. Make sure it never leaves the Vatican offices.

May God be with us.

Nasrani decided to lose the envelope.

The solitary Garza file would remain untouched.

One week after the Quijano Committee sign-off . . .

Gabe packed. He looked around the apartment. The cautions of the weekly Nasrani meetings imagined places for hiding miniature microphones. He had found none.

Gabe had now completed the Vatican Fellowship and earned his Master's in Church Theology. He placed a thesis copy and key research papers in a white cardboard box labeled "Vatican Thesis research files" and shipped it back to St. Anthony's.

There were other files that Paolo Nasrani, the 49th BEGAT, had given him immediately before he sealed the box. They appeared to be historical research files, nothing more—if someone looked at the labels: Constantine. Chardin. Kung. Thesis Outlines. Church-Jewish

History. Pauline Doctrine. Inquisition up to Modern Day. Mortara Case.

The more dangerous files had been sent to New Mexico earlier. "Paolo," Gabe had asked months ago, "Where could I keep these files? Given what's in them, there's nowhere they could be safe."

"Who do you trust in this world, without reservation, eh? Anyone?"

"My mother, but she's back in New Mexico, without any reservation." *Joke.*

"That is what we must do. We will send them to New Mexico. Mothers know, 'Obres son amores, que no buenas razones—Deeds are love, and not fine phrases.' Let me work out a plan for sending them without threat of interception."

"Will my mother be at risk?"

"I think not. Not at risk like her son, eh? Besides, a mother will do anything for her son. Her name is not Mary, is it?" he said with an almost-smile.

One file, a medical file, revealed that Jack Kennedy had been treated since 1940 for a series of venereal diseases and it named the paramours, including a former Nazi girlfriend. He often experienced pain while urinating, unlike the poker Knights of the Round Table back in Laurel, Maryland.

Any file reader would have thought, *so much for Camelot.*

Paolo thought, *In case Edward Kennedy ever becomes President, or his nephew John-John . . . this is contingency insurance to protect our long-term interests.*

Paolo came to the apartment to say goodbye. He suggested they step outside into the alley. Paolo distrusted walls which still might have ears. Clouds hugged the rooftops of the buildings around them.

"Some things regarding *your* Jesus, *my* Yeshua. He was a good man. I respect his message. I believe God was *in him*. But he was *not* God," Nasrani said.

With thousand-year-old eyes and a wry smile, he added, "I have trouble with *our* God, yours and mine, the one that let his so-called only son be tortured to death. He has sentenced his other children to death too, the day they were born. We are all to be executed by life. Maybe we are in the sixth day of creation—God still creating, eh? Bad timing on our part to be here now?"

This was no more simpering Italian linguist or invisible work team coordinator.

"I have trouble with *your* Roman Catholic Church—pay attention to that first word—a church whose leader sits in Rome and whose God prefers to be addressed in Latin."

No more long-lashed, olive skinned, pretend-homosexual. This was now a god-wrestling Jew carrying the DNA of zealots, and he was saying, as gently as he could, "Gabriel, Gabriel. Surely you realize now the easy part is over—discovering historical realities. But Gabriel, what would you do? What would you have your Church do? What would *your* new Church look like, eh?"

"My church?"

"You have so thoroughly criticized and deconstructed the church you serve. You must have a replacement in mind. You should save the baby, throw out the bathwater, and add a new warm towel. Maybe some talcum powder.

"Hmmm," Garza said.

"Since you are working on your *Reformation Part II*, maybe call it the *Back to Basics Reformed Coalition of Believing, Loving Communities*."

Garza said, "That doesn't quite roll off the tongue. I can't imagine what the acronym would be. But you make a point. Those who believe in the message of Jesus and want to follow his example—-what should they be called? How would they be organized? Not Christians. That term did not exist in his day. Maybe . . .?"

Paolo said, "Accenna al savio e lascia far a lui. Give the wise man a hint and leave him to act."

Garza used the goodbye opportunity to ask again. Nasrani had answered the same question, one time before. "Paolo, why did you share these things with me? What would I do with them? I'm a priest in a poor, tough parish."

"Ah, Gabriel, he who has eyes let him see what I see. You are anointed from America to study here in Rome. You work in the Archdiocese of Washington, one of the most important centers of Church power in the United States. You are walking distance to the National Shrine of Catholicism. You are in the capital of a superpower. And, you may one day be the Archbishop yourself, eh?"

"What are you talking about? I don't even belong to the Archdiocese—I'm still on loan to them from my Order."

"Gabriel, you know I know things. I have seen files, records . . . "

"Like what?" Gabe said.

"They have their eyes on you. You are being groomed."

Nasrani thought back on that conversation. It was half true. They, the Vatican and the Archdiocese, were keeping an eye on Father Garza. But it might require a direct intervention by God himself for Garza to move up in the Church he now questioned too much. The chances of clerical promotion for Garza were as remote as having a Jesuit become pope.

It might happen, eh?

As they hugged for the first and last time, and then shook hands, Gabriel and Paolo wondered if his thesis *On A Unified Christianity*

could ever create needed reform. Paolo concluded, "No son soldados todos los que van á la guerra. All are not soldiers who go to the wars."

Gabriel nodded his head thanks and held his fist up to his chest and shook it.

They both understood that the non-thesis, boxed files—Mafia financing, Kennedy murders, a poisoned pope, a treasonous President, Church pedophilia—could bring governments down.

But Father Garza had puzzled at the secret files on CIA misdeeds: The Tuskegee Study; chemical testing on prisoners by the U.S. Army and Dow Chemical; the MKUltra mind control experiments; biological agent testing on U.S. populations in cities; and the deliberate radiation of 235 American babies.

He was just a parish priest, not a savior.

On the flight back to Washington, D.C., Father Garza thought about what Nasrani had said. Nasrani had asked the right question. *What would my church look like? Would it be better?*

I could address my reservations about the Church. Another Reformation would help, one that took everything back to the basics of the Nazarene's message without all the paraphernalia of priests, rituals, papal anathemas and gold chalices. Good exegesis and common sense could move us forward.

But Nasrani's other questions were tougher:

Why does a loving God create creatures and subject them to suffering?

Why, in this reality, do life forms have to consume one another to survive?

Jesus, or Yeshua—as Nasrani would say—was a devout Jew, obviously worshipping the God of the Old Testament. Yet, that God sought to destroy his creation with a flood. What kind of God does that? And, what kind of God ordered Abraham to perform the blood sacrifice of his son to appease his divine ego?

Yeshua-the-Messiah cured the blind man, but not blindness? This is a savior?

The irony: Nasrani the disbeliever, answered key questions about the Nazarene, even if he could not fathom the mind of the God of the Jews. "Father Gabriel, this is why they crucified him, besides his challenging the money. His message overthrew the old God, and challenged the basis of the Roman establishment and all authority and Judaism itself. Judaism was now reduced to a pale precursor of the new message of love over everything. Of course they killed him. We, all religions and nation-states, would kill him again today, and tomorrow, and the day after tomorrow."

Father Garza accepted his own personal closure. All icons from ageless Catholic practices to Kennedy luminaries had been shattered with time and revelation. The world was hopelessly, helplessly corrupt, lost, and without meaning. Nothing else remained, except for the Jesus message.

In the Jesus message, one could find purpose, meaning, the strength to keep moving day to day, in the face of life's evils which included illness and death. Maybe his old nemesis back in Washington, Archbishop Doolin, was right—it *is* a mystery.

As Father Garza drifted off to sleep on the long, trans-Atlantic flight, *Can someone give me an AMEN?*

CHAPTER 35

The Notebook

"Moses dragged us through the desert to the one place in the Middle East where there is no oil."
Golda Meir

Anyone opening Nasrani's black moleskin notebook, which he fit into the right front pocket of his tailor-made pants, one of the two pair he owned—one black, one gray—would have read poems in Italian; or was it Spanish? Or, was it not quite either . . . a puzzle-form of Latin?

Efforts at translation into English would not make sense. But then, it was poetry—what would you expect?

If you possessed the Mossad codebook, you might figure it out. Each puzzle-piece letter had a numerical counterpart which in turn translated into one of the twenty-two letters of the Hebrew alphabet, made up only of consonants.

Tradecraft changed the letter-numerical relationship daily, and if you got that right, you then needed to be well versed in Hebrew to put the vowels in where they belonged.

Paolo Nasrani: self-presented translator, tour guide, study group convener, dutiful son and brother, counterfeit gay, and a pretend Christian in the Vatican colony of self-proclaimed virgins. He was also a deep undercover agent for the Mossad, the Israeli Intelligence

Service. His younger brother owned membership in Kidon, Mossad's ultra-secret assassination unit.

The Mossad possessed an arsenal in ways to kill that equalled the Mafia, the former KGB, or China's secret service. They kept at their disposal in Israel a small laboratory of poisons, sealed in vials until the moment came to strike.

They had long and short-blade knives.

Piano wire to garrotte.

Explosives no bigger than a throat lozenge capable of blowing off a person's head.

An arsenal of guns: short-barrel pistols, sniper rifles with a mile killing range.

If the victim was to be killed silently—strangulation with a cheese-cutter, or use of a handgun fitted with a silencer, or a nerve agent delivered by an aerosol or injection.

Agents knew how to break into an office, a bedroom, or any other target and plant electronic bugs . . . or a bomb. They knew "masluh," the skill of shaking off a tail, required training for all their personnel.

The women agents could use their sex to sleep with someone to obtain vital information. The link between intelligence work and sexual entrapment was as old as spying itself. You could read about Judith and Holofernes in the *Tanach*, what the Christians had dismissively labeled *The Old Testament*, millennia ago. But it took a special kind of courage and skill to acquire information in that intimate fashion.

Most agents spent two years at the Mossad training school at Henzelia, near Tel Aviv. Select students attended a special camp in the Negev desert. There, they learned to kill . . . how to use the appropriate weapon for the proper occasion.

None of this applied to Nasrani. These were not his instruments. He stayed in place and fed back reports when it was critical, like now. Above all, he protected this Mossad secret identity.

His superiors in Tel Aviv had approved Nasrani's information sharing with Garza about his Jewish background. The priest could help the cause at the right time decades into the future. His ecclesiastical destiny might ascend with the post-Vatican II reforms which no one could turn back.

Nasrani would not expose himself by accident or even by torture. But he had revealed much of himself to this Father Garza, a most interesting man. *Could he be THE ONE? The Joshua who, in our matrix of existence, could bring down the rotten Jericho-walls of religious ritual? Maybe he possesses conversos genes from his mother? It may be why her ancestors left Spain? You could succeed if you kept your Judaism secret. But in Spain, they were always suspicious of the conversos, those Jews who converted to Christianity. We Jews called them "tornadizos," renegades. As always, the covetous Christians welcomed any excuse to take over our lands and steal our wealth.*

Like the Jews, this Garza believes in a religion of deed, not creed. "Creed doesn't feed," Garza had told him. But, has Garza ever seen the mad monkey that is in all of us? Too bad he was part of that religion business which was nothing more than a way to control and manipulate.

But, like we Jews, he seems to be comfortable arguing with God. He certainly questions everything. We encourage our people to explore their own personal relationship with God. This Garza may be as our Jacob, a "God-wrestler."

CHAPTER 36
Plan B

NASRANI KNEW HOW THIS POINT was arrived at:

In 1980, with Iran seizing American hostages and the U.S. viewed as powerless after the unsuccessful rescue attempt, Israel has performed a radical reassessment of its strategic, long-term position.

What Israel sees:

The world's greatest superpower serves at the beck and call of a sand pit in the Eastern Mediterranean.

The Soviet Union will implode by the year 2000. It merely requires a prolonged drop in the price of oil, and the Soviets, so dependent on the oil revenues from abroad to prop up the failure of their collectivized economy, will collapse.

Israeli intelligence safeguards clandestine information that the new President Reagan, the new Polish pope who abhors communism and its Soviet champions, and a key Saudi prince, plot the Soviet collapse. It must appear as if the Saudi's are performing their usual market dance of driving out oil competition by lowering the price. It must be gradual. Too sudden a move could trigger radical Soviet action.

With the Soviets no longer in a competitive stance with the U.S., and the U.S. lessening its foreign commitments, Iran will dominate the region. Iran will pursue nuclear weapons. Israel agonizes over that possibility.

More instability must be created in the Middle East to demand the introduction and permanent stationing of U.S. troops. With this scenario, if the Iranians attack Israel with nuclear weapons, the fallout would kill thousands of U.S. soldiers. Iran knows that the U.S. would retaliate by bouncing rubble on top of rubble with nuclear strikes. The U.S. is the only country in the world with the grit to use nuclear weapons. They have before, haven't they?

Israeli war planners play various gaming strategies. If no ready-made pretext for American intervention presents itself, then phony rationales must be planted, perhaps "evidence" of stored weapons of mass destruction in Iran, Libya, or even Iraq? They have people in place, in Washington, to make the case for whatever benefits their interests.

YHWH gave us this land. This time we keep it.

Of course, Nasrani did not share information on the secret "Operation Exodus" and its companion "Armageddon." Those were not their technical code names, but common agency references.

Both plans anticipate another attempted Jewish genocide, this time by Islamic states, again. Why wouldn't the Jewish state prepare for such a contingency? The Egyptians, the Babylonians, and the Romans attempted their genocides as did the Christians and the Nazis. The Arab states attacked Israel in 1948 and 1973 and continued with on-going, low-level hostilities.

Israel will now begin "Operation Exodus." Tel Aviv has been secretly buying up small numbers of foreclosed homes and apartments throughout the United States as they become available. Periodic American recessions will speed up acquisition with bargain sales prices. Foreign investment fund managers take the lead, as fronts, creating anonymous REITS—real estate investment trusts—with bundled housing mortgages.

"Exodus" focuses on Florida which already has an influential Jewish population, and the Las Vegas region—both reasonable real estate prices. They are not the high profile nuclear targets of New York and California.

Tourist brochures announce that Vegas has two hundred eleven clear days a year; a winter low of thirty-six; four inches of rain a year.

They've moved in Jewish pioneers, young American Jewish couples with dual citizenship and zero assets. They provide rent-free dwellings. In exchange, the youthful couples—they've all been tested for sperm and ovary fertility—pay for the utilities and upkeep, and agree to have at least three children in a ten year period. After ten years, they can option their dwelling for half the original price.

No Arab country will own capacity to strike as far as Las Vegas. The U.S. will not permit it. But, the unvarnished Israeli assessment warns that New York or another large American city could be hit someday with nuclear suitcase bombs . . . so the strategy is to give birth to a decentralized sprinkling of Jews in key locations throughout America.

Jews know diasporas.

Armageddon: Israel takes out all her enemies. One thing triggers this plan and that is a nuclear attack on Israel. The response will be proportionate; "proportionate" in Israeli eyes—everyone will be looking at radioactive deserts in all Arab capitals.

Mecca? Israel will deliver a veritable Jericho-wall-rubble, with radiation, not Plan B or Plan C. This is Plan OMEGA. It wreaks retribution against major cities in the Arab countries that tried to annihilate the new Jewish state in 1948.

And, there is a final warhead aimed at Berlin, when all is lost. Berlin—where Hitler lost his last battles against the Red Army . . . and marriage, and blew his brains out.

The Jewish memory is long. An eye for an eye.

Nasrani owned a complete commitment to his people while acknowledging a terrible irony.

If King David attended an ultra-Orthodox synagogue in present-day Jerusalem, he would be bewildered to find people dressed in Eastern European clothes, speaking in a German dialect—Yiddish—and having endless arguments about the meaning of Babylonian text, the Talmud. There were neither synagogues, nor volumes of Talmud, nor Torah scrolls in ancient Judea.

But King David and Paolo Nasrani are the people of God and their lineage must survive. Bullets must accompany the phylacteries. If the chosen people perish, so does the earth.

Amen and Amen.

Nasrani had heard all the arguments over the years. Quijano's anti-Semitic rants had spewed mere Roman background noise for him. More sophisticated justifications against the Jews were used these days, dressing up the wolf at the door like a sheep.

The Federal Republic is a Nazi country run by state fascists of the Nazi generation. Therefore, the foundation of Israel is a trick to force innocent Arabs to pay the price for Nazi atrocities. Former Nazis are scattered throughout positions of power in West Germany. Older generations refuse to discuss what had happened in the Nazi period; and there is a willingness of the occupying Western powers to overlook Nazi crimes in return for German subservience. Some said the Palestinians had been forced to pay the price for Western crimes against the Jews.

So that is why, near Tel Aviv, in a faceless warehouse in an obscure commercial district, guarded by special operations personnel and monitored with hidden cameras, they study Nasrani's poetry in the black, moleskin notebook provided by the Vatican employee, whose code name is Jericho.

Decoded, the notebook says,

> ***I have successfully planted the unwitting sleeper agent. He possesses explosive files so that should we need their release in the future, it can be done without any trace back to Tel Aviv. It is good for both our enemies and our friends to fear we possess unusual capabilities to protect our interests.***
> ***My assessment is . . .***

And Nasrani's report went on.

CHAPTER 37

God's Betrayal

"Out of the depths I cry to thee, O Lord, O Lord, hear my voice!"
PSALM 129

FATHER GABRIEL GARZA RETURNS TO Washington, D.C. and to his priestly ministry with his newly minted Master's Degree. What has all the research, and discussion, and writing done for him?

Father Garza, so well educated now in the history of Judaism and Christianity, has more questions now—tough questions. He will spend the rest of his life trying to find answers.

From his espresso meetings in Rome with the secret Jew, one question sticks in his mind like an old Motown refrain, but without the Detroit rhythm: *WHY WON'T OUR GOD TAKE BETTER CARE OF HER CHILDREN?*

Maybe he could say, "She's doing the best she can."

Or, if Gabe was being literary for the moment, he might quote Kurt Vonnegut, "Hi-ho."

Why say "her" children? Women did not deserve to be identified with what this god needed to answer for. It was a male god who ordered Abraham to kill his son. And it was a male god who let the Romans torture to death his only begotten son. And it was this same god who stood by while his chosen people were exterminated over and over again.

Bowing his head, as if in prayer, *Only the message of Jesus can undo God's betrayal.*

Over the years, the uniforms of The Watchers down the street from St. Anthony's rectory changed: dark suits—to khaki pants and blazers—to dark windbreakers and hoodies.

The cars changed too, over the years, evolving to the nondescript but utilitarian Chevrolet Suburbans—always black.

SELAH.

About the Author

Ben Leiter found inspiration for this compelling thriller in his own Roman Catholic faith and his experience as a seminarian. He is the author of two other books: *Baby Boomers' Love-Betrayal*, a romance noir, and *City Management Snapshots: On the Run*, a memoir of his eventful career in city management. During this career he was city manager in seven different US cities, and he has represented the profession in delegations to West Germany, Poland, and Japan.

His writing also includes short stories published in two literary anthologies. A member of the California Writer's Club, Leiter holds a master of arts degree in addition to a master of public administration. *God's Betrayal: The Credo* is the third book in a series that examines how the baby boomer generation collides with politics, religion, and romance.

Made in the USA
Middletown, DE
09 December 2018